Acknowledgements

With thanks to:

my husband, Peter Ingham, for his love, encouragement and support throughout everything.

Adam Craig for the beautiful cover design.

And Jan Fortune, not only for being a marvellous editor, but for being a true friend.

To my daughter, Felicity Dawe,
for her love of the moon and the stars.

Even the air I breath feels bruised sometimes
but there is power in pain.
Pain intensifies intention.

ScorpiusLuna, 2017

THE REMAINS
OF THE DEAD

MICHELLE ANGHARAD
PASHLEY

INDEPENDENT INNOVATIVE INTERNATIONAL

Published by Cinnamon Press
Meirion House
Tanygrisiau
Blaenau Ffestiniog
Gwynedd
LL41 3SU
www.cinnamonpress.com

British Library Cataloguing in Publication Data. A CIP record for this book can be obtained from the British Library.

Designed and typeset in Garamond by Cinnamon Press. Cover design by Adam Craig © Adam Craig.

Cinnamon Press is represented by Inpress and by the Welsh Books Council in Wales. Printed in Poland.

The publisher gratefully acknowledges the support of the Welsh Books Council.

THE REMAINS OF THE DEAD

Prologue

At the sight of the still body lying in the cot, she staggered backwards against the wall and slid to the floor. A deep-throated howl filled the air. The newly decorated room danced with star and moon patterns from the night-light and the delicate voile curtains shifted in the breeze. The mobile above the cot swayed gently. She reached forward, picked up a discarded teddy, struggled to her feet and laid the teddy next to the baby.

She went into her room and removed a black holdall from the wardrobe. She walked into the hall, opened the airing cupboard and placed several nappies, a white cot blanket and some clean baby-grows into the bag. She leaned back against the door and heard the click as it closed. She stood for a moment before making her way downstairs to the kitchen. Here, she packed the baby bottles, the steriliser kit and milk formula into the holdall. Trudging back upstairs she packed clothes and toiletries for herself into an overnight bag. She returned to the nursery, pulled the yellow cot blanket aside and lifted the still body into a Moses basket. She went around the house, shutting windows and locking doors. She loaded the bags and the basket into the car. The shovel and boots were already in the back. Her husband liked to be prepared.

She drove along the quiet roads and parked in a lay-by adjacent to the woods. Standing by the car she looked up and down the road, before pulling on her boots and grabbing the shovel. The air smelled fresh. She could hear an owl in the distance. She stumbled onwards. Just off the main track a willow tree stood by the side of the lake. In the moonlight, she dug.

Leaning against the trunk for a moment, holding the baby close to her chest, she looked out over the lake. It was a beautiful spot and it crossed her mind how strange it was that she'd never been there. She looked down at the tiny lifeless body and lowered her into the hole.

It looked like a grave. It mustn't look like a grave. She found stones and twigs and arranged them over the area, but now it looked like a grave heaped with stones and twigs. She dragged her hand across her forehead, smearing mud and tears across her face. Looking around, she noticed the nearby trees were each surrounded by a neat circle of flattened earth. She fell to her knees, snatched up the stones and threw them into the lake. She stood, kicked the twigs away and struck the earth repeatedly with the back of the spade.

Clutching the spade, she opened the boot and stared at the black holdall—a holdall containing her baby's clean clothes and fresh nappies. She swayed, grabbed the tailgate and took several deep breaths. She threw the spade into the boot, retrieved the Moses basket from the back seat and placed it with care next to the black holdall. With one last glance towards the woods she got back into the car.

Chapter 1
London February 2013

Madeline Driscoll took a deep breath and removed the manila envelope from her pigeonhole. She ripped it open as she made her way across the incident room towards her desk. After a cursory glance at the single sheet of A4 she swore, chucked it into the bin and snatched up the phone.

Inspector Reed glanced up from his desk and sighed.

Madeline caught his eye and gave a small shrug. She started at the sound of a clipped female voice in her ear. 'Superintendent Marshall's office.'

'Morning, Joyce, Madeline here. Is he in?'

'He is.'

'I need to speak with him.'

'He is quite busy and…'

'I'll be quick. Tell him I'm on my way.'

Superintendent Marshall sat behind his huge desk, repeatedly glancing at his watch.

'I'm sorry, sir. I'm obviously keeping you from something.'

'What?'

'You keep checking your watch. I wondered if you had to be somewhere else.'

'You asked to see me. Just get on with it.'

'Right, well, I was hoping you could give me some pointers.'

'Pointers?'

'Yes, sir. As you know, this is the third time I've failed to be selected for promotion, even though I gained top marks in the OSPRE.'

'I hardly need remind you, Sergeant, that marks are not the be-all and end-all of what makes a good Inspector.'

'Oh, I quite agree, sir, but I'd like to respectfully remind you that I've been appointed Acting Inspector on two occasions now and, as far as I'm aware, there were no complaints about my performance. In fact, when Inspector Reed returned from his recent leave, I believe he informed you that, in his opinion, I was more than ready for promotion.'

'Inspector Reed may well be biased. Don't you agree?'

'I'm sorry?'

'Oh, come on, let's face it, my dear, you're young and attractive and Joe Reed, well let's just say, he's a certain age and leave it at that.'

Madeline clenched her jaw. 'I *beg* your pardon? My relationship with Inspector Reed is, and always has been, professional.'

'If you say so, my dear...'

'I am not your *dear*, Superintendent, and I...'

'Sergeant Driscoll, you need to accept the fact that the reason you've been unsuccessful in your applications for promotion is down to you and you alone. In my opinion, you are not ready.'

'And when, in your opinion, *sir*, will I be ready?'

Superintendent Marshall again glanced at his watch. 'Who can say? Perhaps you should consider a transfer to somewhere less stressful. After all, London can be a very violent place.'

'Are you suggesting I should devote my time to helping old ladies find their lost kittens, sir?'

'We all have our role to play, Sergeant, and looking after the elderly would be a most suitable role for a young woman, yes, most suitable.'

Madeline's pupils widened. She leaned forward, hands gripping the edge of Marshall's desk. 'That is the most...'

The desk phone trilled loudly.

'Marshall here,' he bellowed, as he waved Madeline away.

Closing the door with sufficient force to produce a satisfying thud that shook the frame, she flounced past Joyce and took the stairs to the roof two at a time. Leaning back against the wall, she reached into her bag to retrieve her cigarettes.

In his office, Joe Reed checked his desk drawer and waited. Madeline stormed in ten minutes later.

'I take it you've heard,' she said.

'I think we all heard Marshall's door slam,' said Joe. 'I really am sorry.'

'It's not your fault, Jesus, don't *you* apologise.'

Joe pulled open his desk drawer and removed a bottle of whisky. 'Drink?'

Madeline nodded. 'Purely medicinal.'

'Of course,' he said, pouring out a couple of measures before striding over to his door, scowling at his colleagues and pulling down the blind.

She collapsed onto a chair and took a sip. 'That's it then. I'll have to apply for a transfer.'

'Any thoughts about where you'll go?'

Madeline shrugged. 'A tiny rural village where the biggest crime is failure to purchase a TV licence?'

'Don't be ridiculous.'

'That's all Marshall thinks I'm fit for.'

'And since when did you value his opinion?'

Madeline gave Joe a wry smile. 'Fair point.'

'So, I repeat, any idea where you want to go?'

'I haven't really thought.'

'I'll ask around,' said Joe. 'Something will turn up. And no matter what that sycophantic, arse-licking Marshall thinks, you are most definitely ready for promotion.' He raised his glass. 'I'd stake my pension on it.'

Madeline knocked back her drink. 'Thanks Joe, I appreciate that.'

Head down, she plodded back towards her desk. Her colleagues fell silent. She chucked her bag into the footwell and grabbed the phone again.

'Maddy, as I live and breathe,' he cried. 'I feared you were dead.'

'Hello, Dad. Full of your usual wit I see.'

'I don't know what you mean, poppet. How the devil are you?'

'Oh, bloody brilliant I am.'

'I take it there's been no change on the promotion front.'

'You take correctly.'

'What happened this time?'

'Same old. I went to see Marshall in the foolhardy belief that he'd have something constructive to say,' she said, as she sat. 'God, he's a prick. How the hell he got to be a Superintendent I'll never know. Spends his life licking the bums of his superiors, I suppose. Anyway, this latest promotion went, surprise, surprise, to the son of the Commander who, it just so happens, Marshall plays golf with every week. I've had ten years of this, Dad, and I swear to you if I have to suffer one more year of kowtowing to that overweight, pompous, brown-nosing Marshall I'll…'

Sergeant Carter thumped Madeline on her shoulder. She let out an involuntary yelp.

'Maddy, are you alright?'

Seeing Marshall striding towards her, she replied, 'Got to go, Dad. Talk later.'

She slammed the phone down and scrambled around her desk for a file. Opening it at random she stared blindly at the page.

Marshall's huge bulk cast a shadow over Madeline as he reached out for the file and flipped it shut. To Madeline's dismay she saw it was a report on bicycle thefts. 'That's the ticket,' said Marshall. 'Much more your sort of thing although, to be honest, given the talent you say you have, I'm somewhat surprised to find the case remains unsolved. Still, there we are.'

'I was, well, I was…'

'Not interested. We need to close as many cases as we can in order to meet our target this month. I don't want a repeat of last month's lamentable figures.'

Madeline stuck her tongue out as Marshall swept past her desk.

Arriving home to her spotless flat, Madeline was greeted by the plaintive miaows of her cat. She sighed. 'Oh, Zelda, my life's fucked. One more day of dealing with that patronising pig-headed man will send me over the edge.'

She shucked her jacket and flung it across the back of the sofa bed, took two strides over to the fridge and grabbed some wine. The cat twirled through her legs. The miaowing became more intense.

'Alright, alright, Zelda, give me a bloody minute.'

She filled a glass, took a huge swig and retrieved the cat's bowl. Ripping open a sachet of cat food succeeded in sending splashes of cold, fishy jelly over her hand. 'Shit and double shit to hell and back,' she cried, as she shook the sachet's contents into the cat's bowl and slammed it onto the floor. Giving her hands a desultory rinse under the tap, she kicked off her shoes and threw her mobile onto the coffee table, before collapsing onto the sofa. She switched on the TV, muted it and lay back in the dark, watching the flickering light play against the walls and ceiling.

The sound of her phone vibrating across the table startled her awake.

'Maddy, are you alright? You hung up rather abruptly this afternoon.'

'Dad, yes hi, fine, sorry about that. Marshall was lumbering towards me.'

'Right, OK, good. Now look, I wasn't going to say anything, but your mother insists and as you know…'

'No one ignores Mum when she insists.'

'Quite.'

'So?'

'So, we had a visit from old Harry Spencer this evening.'

'Who?'

'Harry Spencer.'

'Yes, Dad. The question I'm asking is, who is Harry Spencer?'

'Oh, right, yes. He and I both started off as PCs in Northallerton. Anyway, he's been persuaded out of retirement by Avery, the new Superintendent, to clear a backlog of unsolved cases left behind by the recent retirement of the incompetent Inspector Curtis.'

'As in a Cold Case unit?'

'Exactly.'

'And this has what to do with me exactly?'

'Didn't you hear what I said?'

'Yes, Dad, I heard perfectly clearly what you said. Visit from Harry. Retirement of some bloke called Curtis, crap at his job and…'

'That's the relevant bit, Maddy. The retirement. It's a…'

'Oh, no, you know how I feel about nepotism.'

'Jesus, Maddy, how the hell can it be nepotism? I haven't worked in Northallerton since the bloody 70s. I should imagine Avery was still in nappies at the time. The point is, there's a vacancy.'

'And this Harry bloke just happened to pop over to tell you this on the very same day I heard I'd failed another promotion interview, did he?'

'Yes.'

'Give over, Dad.'

'OK, fine, your mother might have suggested I should do some ringing round.'

'Hah!'

'Look, are you interested or not?'

Madeline closed her eyes and clutched the phone to her chest.

'Maddy?'

'Oh, Dad, yes I'm interested, of course I'm interested, but I'll need a recommendation from Marshall. He'll block it, I know he will.'

'True, but the Commander isn't the only one who plays golf, Maddy. So does the Assistant Commissioner. And it may interest you to know he's been keeping an eye on Marshall. A quiet word in his ear will do wonders. Leave it with me. Your transfer application to Northallerton will be a shoo-in. Your application to become the new Inspector, however, will be entirely down to you.'

Chapter 2
Thursday May 9th / Friday 10th May

In the sleepy village of Binton-on-Wiske, Barbara Driscoll sat in Browsers café, reading *The Yorkshire Herald*.

'Shall I bring your coffee over now?' said Carla. 'Or do you want to wait for Jack?'

'He shouldn't be long. I'll wait.'

Carla pulled up a chair. 'Are you alright?'

'Me? Yes, fine. Why?'

'Barbara, you and I have been friends for more years than I care to dwell on, so don't give me that guff.' She laid her hand on Barbara's arm. 'What is it?'

'It's Madeline.'

'Madeline,' exclaimed Carla. 'But I thought her transfer to Northallerton was going ahead.'

'It is.'

'Sorry, you've lost me. Isn't that what you all wanted—and don't just say 'it is' again or I'll thump you.'

'It's brilliant, of course it is and I'm thrilled…'

'Is that a fact?'

'Carla, it's her interview tomorrow. What if she doesn't get it?'

'Oh, don't be ridiculous, of course she will. Jack said she'll walk it,' said Carla, glancing out the window. 'And look, there he is, bless him, striding along attempting to put his jacket on while simultaneously talking on his phone; net result, complete entanglement and loss of phone in the hedge.'

'I despair, I really do,' said Barbara.

'Fear not, dear friend, I'll go and rescue him.'

Barbara watched as Carla rummaged around in the hedge while her husband disentangled himself from the twisted mess of his jacket.

'Here we are, all sorted,' said Carla, pulling a chair out for Jack. 'So, two lattes?'

'Smashing thanks,' said Jack, plonking himself down opposite his wife. 'Sorry I'm late, love, I got tied up.'

'So I saw,' said Barbara. 'Who was on the phone?'

Carla waved across towards the counter. 'Hannah, two lattes over here. Thanks.'

'Christopher Baker. Do you remember him?'

Barbara's eyes flashed. Her lip twitched. 'Dear lord. Do I remember him? Of course I remember him. I've tried to forget, God knows I have.'

'Sounds intriguing,' said Carla.

'Barbara, come on, don't be mean,' said Jack.

Blinking feigned innocence, Barbara said, 'Christopher Baker, a retired officer of the law, used to dress up as a woman, Carla. It was a terrifying sight. A hulking six-foot man, with a beard I might add, flouncing about in a pink nylon wig dressed in some ghastly low-cut floral dress with chest hair poking out.'

'He only did it for police fundraising functions, Barbara, it's not as if he made a habit of it.'

'Oh, he'd get on well with Olivia's husband then,' sniggered Carla. 'He also has a penchant for that sort of thing.'

'He's in the army, isn't he?' said Jack.

'Yes, he's away somewhere abroad at the moment, all very hush-hush.'

'They're renowned for it, or so I hear,' said Jack. 'I know Christopher carried on the tradition when he transferred to the RMP, said the chaps couldn't get enough of it.'

'Here we are,' said Hannah, placing the coffees on the table.

'Thanks, love,' said Carla, turning to follow Hannah.

Barbara reached out and tapped Carla's arm. 'Talking of Olivia, have you heard from her since she dashed off on Sunday?'

'I have, yes,' said Carla, 'but she wasn't very forthcoming. To be honest, I'm rather worried about her.'

Jack patted the chair next to his. 'Come on, why don't you join us for a bit, I'm sure the lovely Hannah can cope.'

Carla glanced around the café. Apart from Barbara and Jack, there were only two other customers. 'Yes, you're right. I could do with a break. Back in a tick.'

Over at the counter, Carla went through the ritual of making herself a cup of mocha. Listening to the gentle hissing sound as the milk frothed, Carla thought back to Olivia's phone call on Monday.

'Carla, I...'

'Olivia, thank God. Are you alright? Is the baby alright? I've been out of my mind with worry. Where the hell are you?'

'I'm fine. Amelia's fine. I had a phone call yesterday morning, can't remember exactly when, but it was still dark outside. I had no choice, Carla, so, here I am.'

'Here you are where, exactly?'

'Didn't I say?'

'No, Olivia, you didn't.'

'I'm in London.'

'London! What the hell are you doing there? According to Peter, you left in a tearing hurry.'

'Peter?'

'The Reverend Peter, he was wandering around the graveyard, mithering about his sermon, when he saw you leave.'

Silence hummed down the line.

'Olivia? Are you still there?'

'Yes, yes, I'm here. It's just, well, I didn't see anyone. Anyway, as I say, here I am.'

'So you've said, but why? And when are you coming back? I mean, apart from anything else, isn't Lawrence due back soon?'

'He's back on the 19th. Anyway,' continued Olivia brightly, 'apologies for my dramatic exit from the village but I'll see you soon, bye.'

'But you haven't…' Carla realised the line was dead. She replaced the receiver. 'But you haven't answered any of my questions,' she'd said to herself.

'Carla, watch out, the milk,' cried Hannah.

'Oh, hell,' said Carla, as milk frothed over the edge of the jug, 'I was miles away.'

'Give it here, I'll do it,' said Hannah. 'You go and sit down.'

'So, did Olivia say when she's coming back?' said Barbara.

'No, not really. Oh, I don't know, it just seems to be a hell of a time to be taking a trip all the way down to London.'

'I'm sure she knows what she's doing, I really wouldn't worry,' said Barbara, tapping Carla's arm. 'Are we still on for tomorrow?'

'Oh God, what are you two planning?' exclaimed Jack.

'Nothing. Carla simply suggested another day out visiting old haunts. We thought we'd pop over to York and…'

'And then move onto Thirsk. That's not a problem, is it?' said Carla.

'It'll take my mind off Madeline and her interview,' said Barbara.

'Madeline will be fine, you worry too much,' said Jack. 'Now then, am I to assume this day out will involve yet *another* trip to the Reclamation Centre?'

Barbara sipped her latte.

Carla grinned.

'Anyway, Jack,' said Barbara, setting her coffee down, 'what did he want?'

'Who?'

'Christopher Baker.'

Jack frowned.

'The phone call,' exclaimed Barbara.

'Here we are, boss, one *carefully* prepared mocha,' said Hannah, giving a little curtsey before retreating back to the counter.

'Thin ice, my girl, thin ice,' said Carla with a smile.

'Oh, yes, Christopher—actually, do you know what; I'm not really sure,' said Jack.

'Well, what did he say?'

'He burbled on about finding it all a bit much this year. Said this might be the last time he'd do it and…'

'Do what, Jack?'

'The Pennine walk. He goes every year with some old mate from university.'

'And that's why he rang?'

'Haven't a clue, love of my life, haven't a clue.'

Barbara raised her eyes heavenwards. 'For goodness sake.'

'Oh, he did mention fishing.'

'Fishing?'

'Yes, you know that thing we men do with rods and…' he ducked to avoid the swish of a napkin directed towards his head. 'Watch it, Barbara, you'll have my eye out.'

'Think yourself lucky it was just a napkin—so, why did he mention fishing?' She glanced across at Carla. 'Honestly, it's like extracting blood from a stone.'

'He's thinking of taking it up again and wondered whether I'd be game to join him.'

'And would you?'

'It's a thought, isn't it?'

'It's a thought, Jack, yes. The question is, has the thought resolved itself into any sort of conclusion?'

Jack shrugged. 'He said he'd ring again once he was home. But he mentioned something about having to be around for his wife for a while, before he could swan off and do his own thing again.'

In Thirsk, the following day, Carla and Barbara sat in The Bliss Café sipping coffees. 'Jack's going to have a fit when that delivery van turns up next week.'

'Nonsense, he'll love it all,' said Barbara.

'Are you sure? You did buy quite a lot.'

Barbara's eyes took on a misty appearance as she stared off into the distance. 'Do you remember when we used to sneak out of school on Wednesday afternoons to come here? How we never got caught I'll—good grief,' she cried, reaching out and grabbing Carla's arm with such urgency that most of Carla's coffee left its cup and cascaded down onto the pristine white linen tablecloth.

'Bloody hell, Barbara, watch out!'

'Sorry, but isn't that your friend Olivia?' said Barbara, frantically dabbing at the pool of coffee.

Looking around the café, Carla asked, 'What? Where?'

Barbara pointed across Carla's head towards the street. 'Not in here. Look, there,' she exclaimed.

Carla jumped up from her seat. 'Olivia, Olivia,' she yelled, as she snatched open the café door.

Olivia turned. Her face paled. She lifted her arm and gave a hesitant wave.

Striding across the road, Carla said, 'What the, I thought you said you were in London—and where's Amelia?'

'I, I…'

'Carla, Olivia,' called Barbara from across the street. 'I've ordered more coffee. Are you both coming?'

'On our way, Barbara,' said Carla, as she took hold of Olivia's arm. 'What's going on, Olivia?'

'Nothing's *going on*, Carla, honestly. No, it's perfectly simple. I've been dashing hither and thither recently and today, well today I thought I could do with a bit of me-time.'

Still holding onto her arm, Carla dragged Olivia across towards the café. 'If I'd known you were going to be in the area, rather than down in London, you could have joined us,' said Carla, pulling open the café door.

'Carla I...'

'I thought it was you,' declared Barbara. 'Oh, where's Amelia?'

'Oh, yes, good question. Olivia was just about to tell me.'

'Come and sit down,' said Barbara. 'The coffee won't be a moment. I ordered you a latte, I hope that's alright.'

Olivia nodded as she took a seat.

'So,' said Carla. 'Amelia?'

'Yes, right, Amelia. She's um, she's with, Penny.'

'And who's Penny when she's at home?'

'A friend of mine.'

'And she lives here in Thirsk, does she?'

'No, she lives in London and...'

'You've left Amelia in London?' exclaimed Carla.

'No, of course not,' snapped Olivia. 'If you'd just let me explain.'

Barbara cleared her throat. She moved the salt and pepper pots from one side of the table to the other. 'Goodness, those coffees seem to be taking an age,' she said, straining her head round. 'Where's that waitress got to?'

'Penny's been through a traumatic time and so I thought the best thing would be for her to come and stay with her parents. They live in Scarborough, just up the road from here really.'

'I know where Scarborough is, Olivia.'

'Yes, of course you do. Anyway, they live in a lovely cottage. Beautiful sea views. Restful. Ideal for Penny, especially at this time. So, there we are. They, Penny's parents, have been most kind and thought I could do with a break.'

'Three lattes,' called out a waitress.

Barbara's hand shot up. 'Yes, over here. Thank you.'

Olivia reached out and grabbed a coffee as soon as the waitress placed them on the table. She bent her head down and took a sip.

'Olivia, why don't you start from the beginning?' said Carla.

'Sorry?'

Carla took a deep breath. 'You vanished, Olivia. I tried to ring you. Your phone went to voicemail…'

'I didn't exactly *vanish*.'

'Alright, you failed to materialise for your usual coffee at the café. The point is…'

'I rang you as soon as I got your message.'

'Yes, from *London,* but you never actually explained *why* you were in London.'

Carla and Barbara picked up their own coffees and peered at Olivia over their rims.

Olivia stared back.

'So, come on, why did you slink off to London without a word to anyone?' said Carla.

'I did not, as you put it, *slink off,* I simply left in a hurry.'

Carla's eyebrows shot skywards. 'Let's, for a moment, accept that you didn't slink anywhere. The point is, you left under cover of darkness and…'

'Nor did I leave *under cover* of darkness, for goodness sake,' protested Olivia. 'It was getting light.'

Barbara patted and fussed with her perfectly neat hair. 'Carla, I don't want to interfere, but perhaps Olivia doesn't want to discuss her whereabouts with us. It may be, well it may be delicate and personal.'

Carla threw an incredulous glance towards Olivia. 'Is it?'

'No, of course not,' said Olivia with a nervous laugh. 'No, it was, well, it was such a shock. I mean they'd always seemed so happy, the perfect couple and then, when she eventually got pregnant, she told me how happy they were. But well, obviously that wasn't the case.'

'Jesus, Olivia, are you trying to be deliberately obtuse or what?'

Olivia's eyes widened.

'Who are *they,* and *what* obviously wasn't the case?' demanded Carla.

'Penny and Marcus. I was at university with Penny,' said Olivia, with another nervous laugh. 'She's the one who persuaded me to go to the party where I met Lawrence.'

'Really? You've never mentioned her before.'

'Have I not?'

'No, you haven't.'

'I thought I had,' said Olivia. 'Anyway, Penny was a good friend of mine, well she still is. She met this Marcus bloke when she was in her final year, I never took to him; he was married for one thing. Anyway, he divorced his wife and married Penny. Naturally, she was thrilled. I tried to be too, but I don't know, there was just something about him.' Olivia took a sip of coffee. 'Sadly, it seems I was right because now, with this baby, it's all come crashing down and Marcus has moved in with Nancy, some girl who he claims makes him feel young again. Bloody fool.'

'So, you've been looking after her?' said Barbara. 'That's kind of you.'

'Trying to, yes, but with Lawrence due back soon I was beginning to panic. I couldn't just abandon her. And then I remembered her parents lived up in Scarborough.'

'So, you drove her up here?' said Carla.

Olivia sipped her coffee and nodded.

'When?'

'Yesterday.'

'Why didn't you ring me to let me know?'

'I just didn't think,' said Olivia in a quiet voice. 'Sorry.'

Carla put her coffee cup down. 'Am I missing something here? Penny's with her parents now, correct?'

'Yes.'

'So, how come you're still with her? Why aren't you back at home?'

'The thing is, well you can imagine. It was a shock for her parents too. They're not in the best of health so I thought I'd better stay for the weekend, just to make sure everyone's alright. Hopefully, I'll be back at Honeysuckle Cottage sometime next week.'

'Next week?'

'Yes.'

'Lawrence is due back next week.'

'I'm perfectly aware of that, Carla,' said Olivia in an exasperated tone.

Barbara fiddled with her napkin and asked brightly. 'Carla tells me Lawrence is away on some mysterious mission. Sounds most exciting.'

'What?'

'Your husband, dear, away…'

'Oh, yes, it's his last mission, thank goodness.'

'I do hope he copes with being retired. Jack was impossible at first. He rattled around the place, never settling to anything. Drove me insane.'

'Oh, Lawrence will be fine. He plans to write a book about his life in the army,' said Olivia.

'Yes, he was telling me,' said Carla, spreading her arms wide. 'I can see it now, 'My Life in Barracks,' by Major L. Hamilton. People will be beating down your door for the film rights.'

Olivia bit her lower lip. 'You never know,' she said, 'it might not be that bad.'

Barbara cleared her throat. 'How did you find life being married to an officer?'

Carla snorted. 'Remind me, Olivia. How did you describe the officers wives?'

'I believe I may have described them as a load of pretentious, self-satisfied toffee-nosed, fox-hunting twits,' said Olivia, a smile lighting up her face.

'Ah, yes, that was it.'

'Oh, dear me. Not your sort of people then?' said Barbara.

'Not really, no.' She glanced at her watch. 'Oh God, look at the time. I must be getting back.' Pushing back her chair, she downed the last of her coffee. 'Lovely to see you both. I'll ring you next week, Carla. Bye.'

Olivia stepped out onto Millgate, looked back at the café, gave a final wave and dashed off down the street. She took a sharp left onto Marage Road and stumbled on towards the footpath down to Cod Beck. Sitting on a bench, with the sound of water tumbling over stones, she closed her eyes and thought back to that day, last April, when Lawrence had dropped his delightful bombshell. A smile danced at the corners of her mouth as she recalled the sight of Lawrence sitting on their front doorstep.

'What have you been you been up to?' she'd asked.

He'd taken hold of her hand, led her through to the kitchen, sat her down at the table and handed her a thick manila envelope. 'I know how much you *love* being an officer's wife and how you adore living in these wonderful quarters,' said Lawrence, as he swept his arm around to encompass the dreary kitchen in which they sat. 'But I am also mindful of the fact that you'd rather have a home of your own. Open the envelope.'

Unlike Lawrence, who would savour the moment and open the envelope with care, she ripped the top section off, plunged her hand down and removed the thick bundle of papers. The top sheet was a letter from Frinton, Chatsworth and Rowe: Solicitors, relating to the sale of Honeysuckle Cottage. Olivia frowned and looked up at Lawrence.

'Read it,' he said.

She read it.

Setting the papers onto the kitchen table, she looked up again. 'Is this for real?'

Lawrence nodded.

'I don't understand,' said Olivia. 'I thought you loved life in the army.'

'I used to.'

'But not anymore?'

Lawrence shook his head. 'No, not anymore. The army isn't what it used to be, Olivia. That's why I've decided to retire. There are things that need to be said.'

Olivia frowned again.

'I'm going to write a book…'

'But…'

'Look, that's not important, not at the moment,' he said, sitting down and taking hold of Olivia's hands. 'You remember Honeysuckle Cottage, don't you?'

'Oh, Lawrence, of course I remember. We spent so many happy summers there. It's, it's…' she burst into tears.

Lawrence enveloped her in a hug, 'I thought you'd be pleased. There would be no problem with your job. You do all your editing from home and…'

She pulled herself away and roughly wiped at her tears. 'I'm happy, Lawrence, really happy.'

'Shit, Olivia, I thought I'd made a major cock-up on the accommodation front.' Picking up the bundle of papers from the table, he quickly flicked through them. 'Here we are,' he said, handing her a handwritten note. 'We can collect the keys from Martin next week and move in whenever we're ready.'

After glancing at the note, Olivia placed it on the table and flattened it with the heel of her hand. She smiled up at Lawrence, stood and brushed down her skirt. 'Right, time for a change of clothes, I think.'

'Sorry?'

'Well, I can't start packing dressed like this, can I?'

Lawrence stood to attention. 'I can collect packing-cases from stores.'

At the kitchen door, Olivia turned. 'Off you go then, Lawrence, collect away.'

'There's just one thing…'

'What?'

'I've got one last assignment before I retire.'

'Where?'

Lawrence remained silent.

'You mean you can't tell me?' cried Olivia. 'Oh, Lawrence.'

'I'll be perfectly fine. It's a multinational force and I'll be overseeing, well, I'll be overseeing stuff. I'm not due to leave until November,' he said. 'There'll be loads of tedious briefings beforehand as per, but…'

'How long will you be away?'

'Just for six months, Olivia, and then that's it. I'll be home, for good, next May.'

They'd moved into Honeysuckle cottage in June, during an intense thunderstorm. On that first evening, stood in the kitchen doorway as the rain splashed onto their legs, they'd laughed and peered out across their garden to the fields beyond, where they could just make out the blurred shapes of sheep huddled beneath the hedges.

A clank of stone on stone, followed by a soaking, dragged Olivia back to the present. She snapped open her eyes and was confronted by a little boy standing, head bowed, clutching a small rock.

'God, I'm so sorry. Billy, look what you've done. I've told him again and again not to throw stones into the beck. Say sorry to this poor lady.'

'It's just water, I'm fine, please don't worry,' said Olivia, glancing at her watch again. 'In fact, you've done me a favour. I was miles away and, if Billy here hadn't startled me, I'd have been late for my appointment.'

Barbara had watched the retreating figure of Olivia, before turning towards Carla. 'Well, that was a surprise,' she said. 'Fancy that.'

'Yes, fancy that,' said Carla.

'Are you alright?'

'I'm not sure, Barbara. Didn't you think she was acting rather strangely?'

'She did seem to be on edge.'

'She's hiding something, Barbara.'

'Oh, for goodness sake, whatever could she be hiding?'

Carla raised her eyes towards the ceiling. 'Well, I don't know, do I?'

'She's probably just tired. I mean, if she's been looking after a new-born and Penny and then driven all the way up here from London…'

'Yes, I suppose,' mumbled Carla, picking up her coffee. She took a sip and screwed her face up. 'Cold.'

'Mine too,' said Barbara. 'Do you want a fresh one?'

Carla nodded.

'I'll get them. Try not to worry about Olivia, I'm sure everything's fine.'

A wave of concern passed across Carla's face. 'Let's hope so.'

Chapter 3
Monday 13th May

Madeline sat opposite Superintendent Avery in her glass-walled office, from which they could see the large, bustling incident room. Phones were ringing and officers were communicating using the tried and tested method of shouting across their desks.

Avery, glancing across Madeline's shoulder, gave an indulgent smile. 'Don't look so worried, you'll soon get used to it.'

Madeline smiled.

'Have you managed to find suitable accommodation?'

'Not as such. I moved in with my parents over the weekend. Not ideal, but it'll do for the moment,' said Madeline. 'They've got a rambling old place in Binton-on-Wiske, so there's plenty of room.'

'Oh, so not too far away then.'

'No, but I'm keeping my eyes open for a flat to rent here or in Thirsk.'

'Good luck with that,' said Avery. 'There don't seem to be too many about.'

'No, so I've noticed.'

Avery glanced down at the desk diary before checking her watch. 'Are there any questions before I take you downstairs to see our new facilities?'

'I understand you've recently set up a Cold Case unit. Will I be involved in that at all?'

'I shouldn't think so, no. It's a small two-person unit with a limited remit.'

'Right.'

'I believe your father's an old friend of the officer in charge, Harry Spencer.'

Madeline cleared her throat. 'Yes, I think my father may have mentioned him.'

'Indeed,' said Avery, with a smile. 'I understood it was he who informed your father of Inspector Curtis's retirement.'

Madeline blushed. 'Well, I... Yes, he did.'

'It seems I have a lot to thank him for then,' said Avery. 'Now, just to be clear, your appointment here was based on your OSPRE grades and your performance in the interview alone. Frankly, I was astonished you hadn't been promoted to Inspector at your old station.'

'Um, yes, but I think it best if I refrain from commenting on that.'

Avery's lip twitched as she inclined her head. 'I understand you worked under Superintendent Marshall.'

Madeline nodded.

'Then I know all I need to know,' said Avery. 'Now, was there anything else?'

'You said the Cold Case unit consisted of two people.'

'The other team member is Justin Waverly-Hawkins.' Avery waved her arm towards the far corner of the incident room. 'You can't see him, he's holed up behind that bank of filing cabinets; he likes his privacy. No doubt you'll meet him sometime, but don't expect scintillating conversation. His skills lie elsewhere.' Avery pushed her chair back and again glanced at her watch. 'Is that it, because I really need to get on?'

Down in the new forensics laboratory, Madeline was introduced to Dr Jeremy Lawson, the chief pathologist, and Dr Donald Richards, the chief forensic scientist.

'We're proud of our new facilities,' said Avery. 'Your father will be extremely jealous. In his day specimens had to be sent to the central forensic lab. Getting results back could take weeks.' She looked over Jeremy's shoulder. 'Is Hopkins about?' Turning towards Madeline, she added, 'He's our Forensic Anthropologist.'

'Looking at some tired and dusty bones dug up over near Nether Silton,' said Jeremy, as he shook Madeline's hand. 'It's always a pleasure to see a pretty face about the place.'

'*Dr* Lawson,' exclaimed Avery.

Jeremy bowed deeply. 'I jest, I jest.'

Donald extended his hand and smiled. 'Welcome to the team. Looking forward to working with you.'

'Oh, as am I,' said Jeremy, eyes twinkling.

'I despair. Come along, Madeline, I'll introduce you to your sergeant.'

Pushing open the double doors into the incident room, Avery lowered her voice. 'Just to give you the heads up; Sergeant Scott has been working as Acting Inspector since Curtis left. She's performed well, a few more years and she'll be ready for full promotion.'

They made their way past desks positioned at crazy angles, interspersed with grey industrial-looking filing cabinets, towards a small office at the back of the room where Rose Scott was waiting. The noise of phones ringing, filing drawers clanging and officers shouting across desks still filled the air.

'I'll leave you in Sergeant Scott's capable hands. Good to have you on board. I'll be in my office for the next couple of hours if either of you needs me.'

'Welcome to the madhouse,' said Rose. 'We've heard a lot about you.'

'That sounds ominous,' said Madeline.

'Oh, don't worry. We all know what Superintendent Marshall's like. Apart from the fact that some of the lads have worked with him in the past, Inspector Soames, he's in the office next door, is a good friend of your Inspector Reed and he's told us Marshall's a complete dickhead.'

Madeline snorted loudly as she removed her jacket. She was about to reply when Avery marched in. 'Don't get comfortable, we've just had a report of a baby-snatching. She's just two months old. In Thirsk. 50 Front Street. It happened an hour ago,' she said, handing Madeline a slim folder.

Slipping her jacket back on, Madeline took the folder and quickly ran her eyes over the single form. 'Right you are, come on, Scott.' At the door she turned back to Avery. 'Is anybody with Mrs Green at the moment?'

'Two constables, Brian Jones and Steve Walsh; they're expecting you.'

The two constables had managed to take a brief statement from Mrs Green before she broke down. The cup of tea Constable Jones had made earlier sat untouched on a small glass coffee table. Madeline went directly over to Mrs Green and sat down beside her.

'My name is Madeline,' she said. 'Inspector Madeline Driscoll and this is my colleague, Sergeant Rose Scott.'

Sally Green looked up from the damp and mangled handkerchief in her hands and managed a weak smile.

'I won't bore you with platitudes,' said Madeline. 'We're here to try and find out what happened. *Anything* you can tell us, no matter how banal, may well prove to be useful. I know you've already spoken to the constables here, but if you could manage to talk to me and tell me everything you can remember, we will do our utmost to get your baby back.'

'I, I… Jesus, this isn't happening, it can't be. We were… we were supposed to be meeting Beth in the park. We were going for a coffee.' Her voice cracked.

'Take your time, Mrs Green,' said Madeline. 'Is there anyone we can contact to come and be with you?'

'I've rung her husband, Mr Stephen Green,' said Constable Jones. 'He should be here shortly.'

'Good, good. Now then, Mrs Green, the sooner we can start looking the better, so, from the beginning.'

Taking a deep breath, Sally Green balled the handkerchief tightly in her hands. 'She said she was a university research associate or something, she had a plastic card thingy hung around her neck.'

'Did she mention which university?'

'I, I don't think so, no, she just said she was conducting a survey for some Department of—oh, I can't remember.'

'Don't worry about that for the moment. What about her name, did she tell you that?'

Mrs Green nodded. 'Yes, yes, she said it was Yvette Young.'

'And she had an identity card you say?'

Mrs Green nodded again.

Rose interjected. 'And you examined this card?'

Mrs Green dragged her eyes away from Madeline. Her eyes flashed. 'Of course I did! I'm not a bloody idiot.'

Madeline reached out to rest her hand gently on Mrs Green's arm. 'No one is trying to infer anything of the sort. It's easy these days to produce very realistic-looking identity cards. They can even fool police officers,' she said, throwing Rose a cautionary glance.

'She said it was a follow-up study, checking on babies born in the last few months. Comparing how breast-fed babies developed compared with bottle-fed babies. She said it was just a few questions and a quick weight check.' She looked up at the sound of the front door crashing shut.

'Sally, Sally, I'm here,' cried Stephen. Pushing past Constables Jones and Walsh, he rushed to his wife's side. 'What the hell's going on? The police said something about Lilly, someone taking her. How the hell...?'

'She said she was doing research and she, she took Lilly, Stephen, oh, God, she just took her.'

'How the fuck...?'

'Your wife has just been taking us through what happened, sir. As soon as we have some information about this woman we can start a search.'

'Right, right, yes of course, sorry,' said Stephen, collapsing onto the settee and throwing his arms around his wife.

Sally buried her head in his arms and broke down again.

'Perhaps you could make Mr and Mrs Green some fresh tea,' said Madeline, handing Constable Jones the cold cup of tea from the coffee table.

'Right you are.'

'Mr Green?'

Stephen looked up, his face pale and full of anguish. 'Yes,' he croaked.

'Your wife was just telling us what happened. I know this must be difficult, but the sooner we know the facts, the sooner we can start searching for your baby.'

Stephen cleared his throat. 'Yes, right, of course.' He eased Sally into an upright position and gazed into her eyes. 'Sally, the police need to know what happened. They need to know soon so they can start looking for Lilly.'

Sally let out a heart-rending howl.

Stephen threw Madeline a look of fear.

'It's alright, Mr Green. When's she's ready.'

The sound of Sally's sobbing filled the room. As her fit of despair subsided she began taking small gasps of air.

'Sally,' said Stephen, 'there's some tea here. Constable um…?'

'Constable Jones, sir,' said Brian.

'Constable Jones has made it for us, love,' said Stephen, as he handed Sally the tea.

Sally looked up and gave Brian a weak smile. 'Thank you.'

'So, Mrs Green,' continued Madeline. 'Can you tell us what happened next?'

Sally's hands shook as she raised the tea to her lips. Stephen steadied the cup as she took a small sip. 'I, I invited her in,' said Sally. 'I even offered the woman a bloody coffee, but she said she had more appointments and she didn't want to be on a caffeine overload. She was quite bloody jolly, now I come to think about it, the bitch.'

'So, where was Lilly?'

'In my, in my arms,' gulped Sally.

'You're doing very well,' said Madeline. 'Carry on.'

'Stephen, can you take this?' said Sally, handing him the cup.

'So, you offered the woman a drink, which she declined,' said Madeline.

Sally gave a small nod. 'Yes. I'd just finished feeding Lilly and was about to change her nappy before making myself a coffee.' She looked up at Stephen. 'That's why I offered her one; it seemed the polite thing to do. Oh, God.'

Stephen brushed Sally's damp fringe clear of her eyes. 'It's alright, love.'

'What happened after she declined your offer of a coffee?' said Madeline.

'We um, we came in here. She sat over there,' said Sally, nodding towards the settee where Rose was sitting. 'She said it was excellent timing because she could weigh Lilly before I replaced her nappy and she got, she got these scales out and…'

'Sorry, where were these scales?' asked Madeline.

'In her black holdall thing.'

'Excuse me, Inspector.'

Tutting, Madeline looked up. 'What is it, Jones?'

'I'm sorry to interrupt, ma'am, but when Mrs Green kindly allowed me use of her downstairs toilet I happened to notice a set of scales in the corner, behind the door.'

'We don't have a set of scales,' barked Stephen.

'Nevertheless, sir, I saw them.'

'Could you show Mr Green, Constable Jones?'

A moment later they returned with the scales.

'Those are the scales the woman used,' cried Sally. 'But I don't understand. I saw her put them back in the holdall.'

'Bag them up, Jones,' said Madeline, throwing him her car keys. 'There are some large evidence bags in the boot.'

'What the hell are they doing in our downstairs toilet?' asked Stephen.

'Did the woman use your downstairs toilet at any point?' said Madeline.

Sally pulled and tugged at her handkerchief. 'Oh dear, oh, yes, yes, she did. It was after she put the scales back into her bag. She said she'd leave them by the front door, out of the way. Then, when she got into the hall, she called out and asked if she could use the loo.' She took a gulp of air. 'Yes, that's right. And then, when she came back, she asked me if the offer of a coffee was still open and of course I said yes.'

'And so you left her alone, with Lilly, while you made the coffee?'

'Yes!' screamed Sally. 'But I didn't expect her to run off with her, did I?'

'No, no, of course not,' Madeline said. 'Nobody would expect that to happen, no one is blaming you. It is *not* your fault.'

Stephen mouthed a silent *thank you* to Madeline as his wife continued. 'When I came back into the living room, she was gone. I couldn't take it in at first. It didn't make sense, she'd been sitting on that settee with Lilly, she'd said we could fill in the questionnaire over a coffee and then she'd told me she'd have to dash.'

'And you didn't hear her leave?' asked Rose.

Again Sally impaled Rose with a look of distain. 'No, Sergeant, I didn't hear her leave. If I had, don't you think I might have rushed out to check on Lilly?'

'Yes, yes, of course you would.'

'So what did you do next?' asked Madeline.

'I'm not sure,' said Sally, gripping Stephen's hand. 'I think I just stood in the middle of the room and looked around,' she gave a hysterical giggle, 'as if they were going to magically appear from somewhere. I mean, how stupid. Then, I think I rushed to the front door. Yes, I must have, because the next thing I remember is standing in the driveway. I think I was screaming. I couldn't see them anywhere.' She took several gulps of air before continuing. 'Mrs Harper came out and, and she, she told me to go back inside. She said she'd ring the police. I screamed at her, I definitely remember that. I pushed past her and I ran out onto the street. I called out Lilly's name but, but oh, God, they were nowhere to be seen. They'd vanished.'

'And Mrs Harper is?'

'Our next-door neighbour, number 52, a nosey old biddy but she means well,' said Stephen, as he held tightly onto his sobbing wife. 'You will find this, this person, won't you?'

'We'll certainly do our best,' said Madeline. 'Do you think your wife would be able to give us a description? I know this is difficult, but the more…'

'A description, yes, of course,' said Stephen. He eased his wife away from him again and gently wiped her eyes. 'Darling, can you tell the Inspector here what this woman looked like?'

'Woman?'

'The woman who came to the house, Sally, the woman who took Lilly.'

Biting her lower lip, Sally nodded. 'She had blonde hair, in a sort of bob, it came to her shoulders and um, she was, oh, I don't know, just sort of average.'

'Was she tall or short? Young or old?' asked Madeline.

'I *can't* remember.'

'Just give it a moment. Try and think back to when you opened the door to her. Did you look up at her, down or…?'

Sally gasped. 'Oh, that's right. I looked down at her and that's unusual. Most people tend to be taller than me.'

'So that would make her about five foot then,' remarked Madeline, quickly estimating Sally's height.

'I suppose so, yes,' replied Sally.

'And her age?'

'I'm really not sure, somewhere between thirty and fifty. Sorry.'

'You're doing fine,' said Madeline. 'Just a few more questions. Is that alright?'

Sally gave a small nod.

'Can you remember what the woman was wearing?'

Sally glanced at the ceiling and closed her eyes. 'It was a rather dull, grey suit, I think. Yes, a knee length pencil skirt, a bit old fashioned now I come to think about it.'

'And was she thin, fat?'

'Oh, not fat, no,' said Sally. 'No, she was well, normal I suppose.'

'I wonder, would you be prepared to talk to our police artist…?'

Sally grabbed Stephen's hand and shook her head.

'I'm not expecting you to go to the station,' said Madeline. 'He would come to you. A picture, albeit a photofit, in the local paper, could jog someone's memory.'

'Sally?' said Stephen.

'I'll try.'

'Thank you, Mrs Green. Now, can you remember if she wore medical gloves when she weighed Lilly?'

'Do you mean those latex things?'

'Yes, that's right.'

Sally nodded.

'And a car, did you see a car?'

'I don't remember seeing one in the driveway.'

'If the woman parked on the street,' interjected Stephen, 'Sally wouldn't have seen it. Our hedge blocks the view.'

'You've been very helpful, Mrs Green, and very brave. We'll leave you in peace now. I'll organise for a family liaison officer to contact you this afternoon. He or she will keep you informed of our progress.' At the living room door, Madeline turned. 'By the way, do you breast or bottle-feed, Mrs Green?'

'I don't see what that's got to do with anything,' said Stephen.

'Probably nothing,' said Madeline, 'but you never know. Mrs Green?'

'I bottle-feed,' she said, 'and she'll need another feed soon, oh, Stephen, our baby, our poor baby.'

'Just one more thing,' said Madeline.

Stephen glared at her. 'What?'

'Sorry, but it's important,' she said. 'Please don't mention the name the woman used to anyone else. Especially not the press.'

Once outside, Madeline instructed Jones and Walsh to carry out house-to-house enquiries. 'Mrs Green may not have noticed a car,' she said, 'but it's possible that one of the neighbours did.' She looked up and down the street. 'Make some enquiries in those two side streets as well. Maybe she parked her car there, out of sight of the house, and then walked. Scott and I will see you back at the station.'

Thirty minutes after Madeline and Rose had driven away, Jones and Walsh were about to start interviewing the occupants of the two side streets. 'You take Green Lane, Brian,' said Constable Walsh. 'I'll do Silver Street. OK?'

'Makes no difference to me, Steve,' said Brian. 'They'll all give the same answer; *'Sorry, Officer I didn't hear or see anything'*.' He glanced at his watch. 'See you back here in what, half an hour?'

Steve turned into Silver Street and sauntered towards a battered old mini parked on the side of the road. Glancing over his shoulder, Steve gave the roof of the mini a sharp slap with the palm of his hand. The occupant of the mini uncurled himself from the vehicle, stepped out and without acknowledging Steve, jogged up Silver Street and turned left into Front Street.

'What now,' screamed Mr Green, 'my wife has answered…' he stopped as he took in the appearance of the wiry, longed-haired man standing on his front door step. 'Who the fuck are you?'

The long-haired man held up his press badge, 'My name is Guy Richards, from the…'

The door was slammed in his face.

Replacing his press badge into his top pocket, Guy turned on his heel and went next door to number 52.

'Goodness, I do seem to be popular today. I'm Mrs Harper,' she said. 'How can I help you?'

Again Guy held up his press badge. He went through his usual introduction speech, explaining he was an investigative reporter from the *Yorkshire Herald,* preparing himself for the inevitable, when he realised that the door was still open and Mrs Harper was inviting him in for a cup of tea.

'Such a terrible thing to happen to such a lovely couple,' she said, as she handed Guy a bone china cup of Earl Grey tea. 'Do you take sugar?'

'No, thank you,' said Guy, as he took a tentative sip of the fragrant liquid before placing it on the coffee table and taking out his notebook.

'I was wondering,' he said. 'Did you by chance see the woman?'

Putting her cup down too, Mrs Harper smiled, 'Oh, yes, young man, yes, I most certainly did. She arrived at Mrs Green's door at precisely 9.15am. She looked very business-like with her large black bag and she was very neat, yes, very neat.'

'You seem very certain about the woman's time of arrival,' remarked Guy.

'Oh, yes, I have a most particular routine. Every morning I collect my milk from the doorstep at precisely 9:15, never earlier, never later and that's when I saw her.'

Guy nodded as Mrs Harper took him through the events of that morning. 'Poor Sally, she was in such a terrible state, inconsolable she was. Such an awful thing to have happened. I mean, whatever could drive a woman to do such a wicked thing? To take another woman's baby,' she clutched at her neck. 'It makes me feel ill, it really does.'

'Was it you who rang the police?'

'Yes it was. Sally was in no fit state, as I say, she was hysterical. Well, you would be, wouldn't you? Anyway, the police were very quick in their response, yes indeed, very quick. No one could fault them on that, no, not at all.'

Guy smiled and pushed himself up from the settee.

'You're not going, are you?'

'You've been very helpful, but...'

'Won't you stay and have another cup of tea?' said Mrs Harper, picking up his cup. 'Oh, you haven't drunk this yet.'

'No, sorry, but I really must dash.'

'I expect you'll be writing an article about all this, won't you?' She cleared her throat. 'Did I mention my name?'

'You did, yes,' replied Guy.

'So, just to be sure then, it's Harper, Mrs Harper, widow, number 52, Front Street and good friend of the Greens.'

During the drive back to Northallerton, Madeline had a gentle word with Rose. 'Avery tells me you performed your duties as acting Inspector extremely well,' she said, 'and I do appreciate how galling it must be to have me come in and take charge. Trust me, I know how that feels.'

Rose opened her mouth to respond but Madeline continued. 'I just want you to know, you don't need to prove yourself. Questioning victims is, as you know, a delicate process. It's very easy to alienate them and although both your questions were pertinent, you could perhaps have worded them slightly differently.'

Rose kept her eyes forward and remained silent.

Madeline went on. 'Now, how long, on average, would you say it takes to make a cup of coffee?'

Rose glanced at Madeline.

Madeline flicked her eyes towards Rose and smiled.

'Well, assuming the water's straight from the tap, I'd say, about two to three minutes, tops.'

'Yes, that's what I reckoned too. So, this Yvette Young only had a narrow window of opportunity to abscond with the baby. The fact that the scales were found in the downstairs loo suggests to me that the baby was placed in the holdall, as if it were a carrycot, thus allowing her to walk away from the house with her holdall looking no different than when she'd approached the house.'

'She must have had a car,' said Rose.

Madeline nodded. 'I agree.'

'So, she could be anywhere by now.'

'I know. Let's hope the constables come up with something, otherwise we're buggered.' She pulled up at the Bridge Street traffic lights and turned towards Rose. 'The thing that really worries me is the fact that she had the foresight to have an identity badge, scales in a holdall and latex gloves. This wasn't a sudden spontaneous action. This was planned.'

Madeline dashed down to forensics to deliver the scales to Donald. 'The woman wore latex gloves,' she said. 'But see what you can find.'

'Baptism of fire, I see,' said Donald.

'The baby's just two months old, it's awful.'

'I'll see what I can do. But if gloves were worn, then I fear there won't be much.'

Back at her desk, Madeline reviewed her notes before calling Rose into the office.

'Any news from Jones and Walsh?'

Rose shook her head as she slumped into a chair.

'OK, let's think. Mrs Green said the woman was involved in medical research.'

'But that would have been a ruse, wouldn't it?'

'Almost certainly. It's also extremely unlikely that the woman used her real name.'

'But, hang on,' she exclaimed, 'isn't it possible that Yvette Young *does* exist?'

Madeline frowned.

'I'm not saying that she, this Yvette Young, if she does exist, was the woman who snatched Lilly. No, I'm suggesting that the woman who did snatch Lilly used that name as an alias. It would make sense if a woman called Yvette Young really *was* involved in such research, for this woman to use that name, wouldn't it?' Rose paused to take a deep breath. 'Do you see what I'm saying?'

'I think so,' said Madeline, 'and, if you are right, it would give us a lead of sorts.'

'I could check the medical research database now,' exclaimed Rose, jumping up from the chair.

'Excellent, and could you also check for recent baby deaths in the area,' said Madeline, returning her attention to her notes.

'What about miscarriages?'

Madeline rubbed her temples and looked up. 'On the basis that a woman who'd suffered one would, what, pop out and immediately steal a baby?

'No, I'm not suggesting that,' said Rose. 'I was thinking more along the lines of a woman who may have suffered multiple miscarriages. Carrying babies for up to twenty-four weeks and then losing them…'

'Sorry, yes, you're right.'

'And then there are stillbirths. They can happen any time from twenty-four weeks onwards. Imagine how awful it would be to carry a baby for six or seven months, only for it to die in the womb.' Rose shuddered. 'I mean, can you imagine?'

'Especially if it'd happened before.'

Rose nodded.

A couple of hours later Rose knocked on Madeline's office door. 'There's no record of anyone called Yvette Young listed on the medical research database, either now, or in the past ten years.'

'I suppose that would have been too much to hope for —what about baby deaths?'

Rose handed Madeline a slim folder. 'I checked the registry and I also spoke to Gillian Johnson, the regional head of Yorkshire and Humber Royal College of Midwives, an extremely efficient woman. She supplied me with the names in that folder. The top sheet contains the names of the women who've suffered multiple miscarriages over the last five years. The most recent ones occurred in March of this year. The other sheet shows the women who've suffered stillbirths; the names at the top of the list are the ones that occurred two months ago.'

'Oh, this is brilliant,' said Madeline as she glanced down at the lists. 'Not for the women concerned, obviously,' she added.

'Before I rang her I checked with the coroner's office to see if there were any baby deaths under investigation; there weren't. I then checked if there were any baby deaths awaiting registration; again, nothing.'

'Worth a try,' said Madeline, turning her attention back to the lists. 'There are lots of names here, Rose.'

'I know, but if you look in the margins you'll see a BMI figure—they record it because it's a risk factor—and you'll notice that the majority are over 27.'

'Meaning?'

'They're overweight.'

'And Yvette Young wasn't.'

'Quite. So, we can ignore those women and concentrate on the rest.'

'And that leaves us with how many?'

'Fifteen.'

'We need to talk to these women as soon as possible. Three teams of two should do it,' said Madeline, scanning the incident room. 'Any suggestions?'

'Sergeants Stuart Bennett and John Ross over there, the desks behind mine,' said Rose, 'they look like they're free.'

Madeline strode across. She extended her hand. 'Inspector Madeline Driscoll. No time for any social niceties, I'm afraid, we've got an abducted baby to find.'

Ross and Bennett stood. 'What do you need?'

'Help with some interviewing, we've got fifteen possibles. Take a constable of your choice—Sergeant Scott will give you the names of five women to visit. Meet back here as soon as possible. OK?'

'As good as done.'

Making their way to the car, Rose said, 'One of the reports I read said that stillbirths are a third more likely in the North than in the South West, and nearly a quarter of them occur between January and March. Isn't that weird?'

'Fascinating,' mumbled Madeline, slamming the car door. 'However, we've got five suspects to interview and time is of the essence. I assume you've worked out the quickest and most logical route.'

'Right, yes, sorry, hold on,' said Rose. 'I wrote it down somewhere.'

Tapping the steering wheel, Madeline waited while Rose rooted around in her bag. 'Here it is.' Pulling the seat belt across her ample chest, she read out the route.

'Let's hope they're all home,' said Madeline.

'It did cross my mind, given the time it was going to take to check, but...'

Madeline let out a scream.

'...don't panic,' continued Rose. 'I didn't.'

Constable Jones appeared at the driver's window, gesticulating wildly. 'Inspector Driscoll, wait, we may have something.'

Winding the window down, Madeline said, 'Oh, tell me you've identified the car used and we have a solid suspect.'

'Not exactly,' said Jones. 'But one neighbour across the road from Mrs Green's house,' he glanced at his notebook, 'Mrs Granville, saw a car parked outside her house this morning that she didn't recognise.'

'And?'

'Well, she *thinks* it was black, or maybe dark green.'

'Is *that* it?'

'And it was big.'

Constable Walsh, who as far as Madeline could recall had not yet spoken, nodded wildly, causing his helmet to adopt a rakish angle.

Madeline sighed. 'And did she see the woman?'

'No.'

'What about Mrs Green's immediate neighbour, the one who rang the police, did she see the woman?'

'Mrs Harper, oh yes, she was very chatty, told us the woman arrived at precisely 9.15 and gave a description matching that given by Mrs Green, including the black holdall,' he said. 'She also saw her leave just thirty minutes later.'

'Alright, thank you Jones. Leave your report on my desk and I'll look through it later.'

'Yes, ma'am.'

'It shouldn't take me long,' she muttered, as she closed the window.

The town clock struck 3 o'clock as Madeline and Rose trudged upstairs to the incident room. A quick scan of the room showed that Bennett and Ross were still out. 'Right, I need a fag.'

Clutching two mugs of coffee, Rose joined Madeline at the back of the station. 'Well, that was a royal waste of time.'

'We'll need to check their alibis, but I agree, I don't feel it here,' said Madeline, tapping her sternum.

Rose took a sip of coffee. 'Stuart turned up when I was doing the coffee. He's on his way down.'

'Stuart?'

'Sergeant Bennett.'

'Right, good—any sign of Sergeant Ross?'

Rose shook her head.

'Ah, there you are,' boomed Stuart. 'Don't suppose you can spare a fag, can you?'

Madeline chucked her packet across.

'Supposed to be giving up but, well, say no more,' he said, taking a huge drag and blowing an impressive smoke ring that encircled Rose's head.

'Any joy?' said Madeline.

'I've left my notes on Rose's desk, but don't hold your breath. You?'

Madeline shook her head.

'To add to your misery, John just called in.'

'Not good?'

'Not in his opinion, no—obviously you'll need to check, but…'

'None of them will turn out to be our perp?'

'I don't think so, no.'

Rose gulped down her coffee. 'I'll go and make a start on those alibis.'

Madeline and Stuart leaned back against the wall and finished their cigarettes in silence.

Superintendent Avery gave a brief press release, stating that Baby Green had been abducted from 50, Front Street that morning, by a woman approximately five feet tall, with blonde hair, who claimed to be carrying out research into the effects of breast and bottle milk on growth and development. She did not mention the name, Yvette Young.

An overweight, greasy-haired reporter stood up. 'David Mason, *Thirsk Post*, have you got any leads?'

'We are currently following several lines of enquiry,' replied Avery.

'So, you have a suspect?'

'If they have,' retorted a voice from the back of the room, 'they're hardly going to tell you, are they? Think about it. They don't want the press broadcasting any names before they've had a chance to interview them.'

Superintendent Avery peered out into the crowd. 'Well, I think your question's been answered by...?'

'Guy Richards, the *Yorkshire Herald*.'

'By your colleague, Guy Richards,' said Avery. 'Thank you all for your time. You'll find copies of a photofit compiled with the help of Mrs Green on the table by the exit. That's the end of the press release.'

Three hours later, Madeline leaned back in her chair, bent her head back, closed her eyes and stretched her arms towards the ceiling. Bringing her head forward she caught sight of Rose in a pool of yellow light, hunched over her desk. Sighing, she pushed herself up and made her way over towards her. 'I think we should call it day.'

Rose rubbed the heels of her palms into her eye sockets. 'I've double checked every statement, Inspector. There's no way any of those woman could be our Yvette Young.'

'I thought not.'

'So, what now?'

'We need to rethink,' said Madeline, 'but not now. Get on home. We'll make a start in the morning.'

Closing the front door, Madeline tiptoed down the hall.

'You look done in, poppet,' said Jack.

Madeline jumped. 'Dad,' she exclaimed, 'I thought you'd be in bed.'

'On your first day as an Inspector, don't be silly. So, how was it?'

'A baby-snatching took place this morning, in Thirsk. No leads, apart from a vague description of the woman concerned. She used the name Yvette Young, probably false. And there's a possible sighting of a big, black or dark green car. We've interviewed fifteen women but so far, nothing. Our only hope is that *someone* saw *something* and that they'll ring the incident room when they read the report in tomorrow morning's paper.'

'Keeping the name out of the press, I hope.'

Madeline screwed her face up. 'Yes, Dad, obviously.'

Chapter 4
Tuesday May 14th/Wednesday May 15th

THE ABDUCTION OF BABY LILLY GREEN
BY GUY RICHARDS

...shocking event occurred on Monday, 13th May. Mrs Harper, the Green's next-door neighbour and close friend, is devastated. 'Such a terrible thing to happen to such a lovely couple,' she said. According to Mrs Harper, the woman arrived at 9.15am looking business-like, carrying a large black bag.

The woman was described as small, approximately five foot tall, with blonde hair styled in a bob (see photofit).

This is an atypical case. My research shows that it's more usual for children to be abducted from a public place. Often it is an opportunistic and desperate action carried out by a distraught woman. It seems to me that the abduction of Lilly Green, from her own home, was a carefully planned operation. If so, I think it is highly likely that she would have approached other women in their homes, before finally selecting Lilly Green. I use the word 'selecting' purposely, because this whole scenario suggests to me that this woman was searching for a particular baby and...

'Who the hell does he think he is,' yelled Madeline, brandishing the newspaper. 'He's going to start a panic, with women thinking we've got a serial child abductor nicking babies to order.'

'But you thought it was a carefully planned operation too,' said Rose.

'That's not the point.'

'Anyway, I wouldn't be too harsh on him,' said Rose.

'Oh, I think I...'

'The thing is, Inspector, we've had calls from a dozen women who recognised the photofit and they all say they had a visit from her last week.'

'A dozen?' exclaimed Madeline.

'Yes.'

'Bloody hell.'

'And their babies were all born in March, just like Lilly Green.'

'So they were all two months old.'

Rose nodded.

'But their babies weren't taken,' remarked Madeline.

Rose shook her head.

Madeline frowned.

'What?' said Rose.

'The babies were all two months old.'

'I know, I just said that.'

'Not new-born.'

'No! They were born in—oh, right I see.'

Grabbing her jacket, Madeline said, 'Right then, we'd better have a word with them.' Walking through the incident room, she called out, 'Constable Walsh with me, Jones with Sergeant Scott. Come on, snap to it.'

Later, the officers convened in The Bliss Café, in Thirsk, for a coffee and a review of the findings. 'This woman's behaviour was identical on each occasion,' said Madeline. 'She arrives, flashes her identity card, gives the spiel about carrying out research into growth and development, refuses any offer of a drink, weighs the baby and then buggers off.'

'Except in the case of Mrs Green, when she buggers off with Mrs Green's baby while a coffee is being made, dumping the scales in the downstairs loo,' added Rose.

'Exactly,' said Madeline. 'It's as if she was searching for some sort of ideal baby.'

'What, like that reporter, Guy Richards, was postulating?' suggested Rose.

Madeline skewered her with an intense look. 'Yes, thank you for that.'

'So, we have twelve babies, all female and all born in March but only one is taken,' said Rose. 'So, what was it about Lilly Green that ticked the boxes for Yvette, or whatever her name is?'

Madeline slammed her cup down, splashing coffee onto the white linen cloth. 'Shit,' she exclaimed. 'We should have asked for photographs.' She flipped her notebook open. 'Mrs Parker's just over the way, number 16, Sutton Road, you call in on her, Rose and then go onto Mrs Poole and Mrs Green.' She scrawled a couple of hurried lists. 'Jones, you do the three over in Bagby, Walsh, the three in Sowerby. I'll do the rest.'

At the door, Madeline added, 'And while you're at it, find out their baby's weight, double-check whether they breast or bottle-fed and ask if they put an announcement in the local paper announcing the happy event.'

Later, having dismissed the two constables, Madeline and Rose were back in the café looking at the baby photos.

'What do you reckon?' asked Madeline.

Rose picked up the photographs and examined them closely before spreading them back out on the table. 'Obviously, she was looking for a female baby.'

'Obviously,' said Madeline, 'the question is, why Lilly?'

'Well, I don't wish to be rude, but Mrs Parker's baby seems a tad chunky compared to the others.'

In an effort to maintain professionalism, Madeline nodded gravely. She cleared her throat. 'Yes, Sergeant Scott, I would concur with that observation. Anything else?'

Rose glanced at the photos again. She pointed to the picture of Lilly Green and Grace Sinclair. 'They're the only ones without much hair, but apart from that, no. I mean, a baby's a baby; hardly bursting with distinctive characteristics at such an early age.'

'What about the feeding issue?' asked Madeline.

Rose picked up Jones and Walsh's lists. 'They've got four who bottle-fed, two who breast-fed.' She glanced down at her own notebook. 'I've got one bottle, two breasts.'

Madeline grinned. 'Glad to hear it.'

Rose grimaced.

Madeline checked her own notes. 'I've got the same.'

'So, what's the significance?'

'I've no idea. Probably nothing,' said Madeline. 'What about announcements in the local paper?'

Rose nodded. 'All mine did and,' she scanned the other lists, 'so did these. What about yours?'

'Yes, mine did too.'

'Some of them put announcements in both the *Thirsk Post* and the *Yorkshire Herald*,' said Rose.

Madeline nodded. 'Same with my lot.'

Rose sipped her coffee and waited.

Madeline picked up her coffee and peered at Rose over the rim. 'Where's the nearest library?'

'The library?'

'Yes, Rose, the library.'

'On Finkle Street.'

Madeline gulped down what was left of her drink, gathered up the photos and stood. 'Come on.'

Once outside, she lit a cigarette and asked, 'Which way?'

'Down this road and right at the bottom.'

Flicking her cigarette butt into a conveniently positioned bin outside the library, Madeline made her way to the front desk, showed her badge to the women there and asked her if she could recall a small, blonde-haired woman visiting the library in the past week, to view recent back editions of the local papers. 'I was on holiday last week,' she said. 'But the senior librarian, Miss Webb, might be able to help. I'll fetch her.'

'Ah,' said Rose, as they waited for Miss Webb, 'You think our suspect scanned the local papers to get the names and addresses of women who'd given birth in March.'

'Precisely.'

'That's inspired.'

'Why, thank you,' said Madeline, giving a little bow.

'I meant, it was an inspired idea of our perp.'

Madeline stuck her tongue out.

The sound of someone clearing her throat alerted Madeline to the arrival of the formidable-looking Miss Webb. Instinctively lowering her voice, Madeline repeated her question.

'As it happens,' replied Miss Webb in clipped tones, 'I do. We have excellent resources here, but unfortunately the good people of Thirsk rarely make use of them. The woman you are referring to is, I assume, the same woman who stole poor Mrs Green's baby; such a terrible thing, tragic.'

'I'm afraid I am not at lib…'

Miss Webb held up her hand. 'Say no more, Inspector, say no more. I *quite* understand. Now then, give me a moment.' She cocked her head to one side and stared off into the distance. 'Yes, that's right, she came in on the Tuesday I think. Yes, last Tuesday. I remember because it was like a mausoleum in here.' She surveyed the library briefly. 'Not unlike today, and not unlike any other day as it happens, and so, *any* visit is a noteworthy event.'

'Could you show us where you keep these back copies?'

'Of course, follow me,' she said, as she strode off. 'I can even show you exactly which back issues she looked at. Our new system registers which papers are selected. We find this most helpful. Sadly, we've had instances of vandalism, moustaches drawn on…'

'Miss Webb, the back copies viewed by the woman in question.'

'Yes, of course. Here we are. On Tuesday May the seventh, Anne Smith,' Miss Webb looked up from the computer, 'not her real name, I assume?'

'If you could just…'

'Right, sorry, you can't comment,' said Miss Webb, turning her attention back to the computer. 'So, on Tuesday

May the seventh, Anne Smith accessed back copies of the *Thirsk Post*. The fifteenth and twenty-second of March editions to be precise.'

'And that was all?'

'Yes.'

'She didn't access back copies of the *Yorkshire Herald*?'

Miss Webb sighed. 'If she had it would have registered on the system. It didn't register, therefore she didn't access back copies of the *Yorkshire Herald*.'

'Thank you,' said Madeline.

Miss Webb stood to one side. Holding herself erect with her hands clasped loosely over her abdomen, she glanced left and right, much like a meerkat on guard.

'Thank you, Miss Webb,' said Madeline. 'You can return to the front desk now, we can take it from here.'

Brushing invisible dust from her skirt and patting down her tightly-permed hair, Miss Webb harrumphed and left.

Close inspection of the Births, Deaths and Marriage section of the newspapers showed clear indentations, indicating that a piece of paper had been placed on top and information copied out.

Madeline scanned the lists. 'There are almost fifty announcements here, including the dozen who were visited by Yvette Young.'

'So why did she only visit a dozen?' said Rose.

'Because she found what she wanted before she'd finished going through the list.'

'Oh, yes, right.'

Madeline peered at the papers again. 'Look at this, Rose.'

'What am I looking at?'

'Here, in the March fifteenth edition—how many announcements are there?'

Rose ran her finger down the list. 'Twenty.'

'And how many indentations do you reckon there are?'

Rose held the paper up towards the light. 'Difficult to say, there could be overlap, but—ah, I see what you're getting at—it's certainly less than twenty—but presumably that's because she was only interested in the female births.'

'OK, what about this one?' Madeline pushed the March 22nd edition towards Rose.

'Twenty-five announcements, but again, not all copied out.'

'We need to know which ones she copied out,' said Madeline, scooping up the newspapers. 'Evidence bag, Rose.'

'But wouldn't she, as I've just said, only be interested in the women who gave birth to girls?' said Rose, running her finger down the names in the March 15th edition. 'And that would mean, just a moment—that's eight names from this one and,' she picked up the other paper. 'And nine names from this one.'

Madeline nodded. 'Yes, I agree, but we need to check. Did she make a note of all the women who'd given birth to girls?'

'Presumably, yes,' said Rose, handing Madeline a large plastic evidence bag.

'Presumably? I don't deal in 'presumably' Rose,' said Madeline, dropping the papers into the bag.

Miss Webb marched towards them. 'Excuse *me*,' she spluttered through pursed lips. 'Those are for reference only and not to be taken out of the library.'

'My sergeant will give you a receipt, Miss Webb,' said Madeline. 'These newspapers are needed for evidence. They will be returned to the library once the investigation is concluded.'

'I, I well, I…'

Rose tore a receipt from her pad and handed it to Miss Webb. 'Thank you for your help.'

Walking back to the car, Madeline lit a cigarette. 'So, it seems she only looked at the March birth announcements.'

'And those babies are now two months old,' said Rose.

'Quite. If she'd had a miscarriage, or given birth to a dead baby, then her 'ideal' substitute would be a new-born not a two month old baby.'

'But I checked. There haven't been any baby deaths recorded this month, not locally anyway.'

'I know, that's what's worrying me,' said Madeline. 'Two disturbing thoughts spring to mind; one, the woman isn't local and, or, two, she didn't report the death of her baby.'

'We're stymied then.'

'Let's hope Donald can determine which names the woman copied out and then, well then, hopefully that will tell us *something*.' Madeline took a drag on her cigarette, exhaled and sighed. 'Although, God knows what.'

'We do have one small lead,' said Rose.

'Really? Pray, enlighten me.'

'We know she used a car…'

'Oh, yes, that's right. We know she used a large black or dark green car. Bloody brilliant.'

'Yes, but when I arrived at Mrs Parker's house, to ask for a photo of her baby, she had a visitor with her. I meant to say earlier but we got tied up. Anyway, this visitor, Mrs Sharp, lives in Byland Avenue, a street just across the road from Mrs Parker's house and she mentioned seeing a strange car parked opposite her house on Friday the tenth of May.'

Madeline took a final drag of her cigarette. 'And?'

'And she confirmed what we already know…'

'That it was black or green and large? How frightfully helpful.'

'Actually, she's convinced it was green,' said Rose. 'She also said it was a boxy-looking car. And that made me wonder if it might be an older car, you know, like a vintage model.'

Madeline flung her cigarette butt to the ground as she opened the car door. 'Still doesn't help much though, does it?'

Madeline and Rose were back in Thirsk the following morning to talk to Mr Shaw, the Manager of the Poplars Hotel near the train-station where a woman, matching the description of Yvette Young, had registered under the name of Anne Smith.

'It was certainly a shock, seeing that photofit. Hard to believe we were harbouring a bloody criminal,' he said, brandishing the Tuesday edition of the *Yorkshire Herald*.

'We had no idea, no idea at all,' said the woman behind the desk. 'She seemed, well, she seemed so ordinary.'

'When did she arrive?' said Madeline.

'First thing, about 7.30 in the morning,' said the woman, checking the registration book. 'Yes, here we are, Anne Smith. She signed in on the fifth of May.'

'And when did she depart?'

'She left on the thirteenth, before lunch.'

'All very sudden, in retrospect,' added Mr Shaw.

'She asked for a quiet room and helped herself to one of these,' said the woman, picking up a Thirsk to York train timetable from a plastic holder on the reception desk. 'We didn't see much of her after that, did we, Malcolm?'

'Nope, she kept very much to herself. Had her evening meals in her room and she was up and out every morning before breakfast.'

'When she arrived, how did she seem to you?'

'How do you mean?' asked Malcolm.

'Was she relaxed or stressed, for example?'

Malcolm shrugged. 'Difficult to say, given I'd never met the woman before. What do you reckon Norma?'

'She seemed dejected and worn down to me,' said Norma.

'Her dress certainly looked worn down,' said Malcolm.

'Worn down?' said Madeline.

'Like she'd been enjoying some outside recreational fun, if you get my meaning.'

'Malcolm,' exclaimed Norma.

'Could you describe the dress?'

'Mid-length, floral,' said Norma. 'It had red poppies on a cream background. Very pretty it was.'

'What you could see of it through the mud.'

'That's enough, Malcolm,' exclaimed Norma.

He gave an exaggerated wink as his gaze shifted towards Madeline. 'I'm just saying.'

'And she had that hat on,' said Norma.

'Bloody ridiculous thing that was too,' said Malcolm. 'It hid most of her face.'

'Sorry, am I missing something here?' said Madeline. 'How exactly were you able to identify her from the photofit if you couldn't see her face?'

'Because we both got a good look at her on the Monday, Inspector,' said Malcolm.

'That's right,' said Norma. 'It was when she got back from York and...'

'She went to York?' said Madeline.

'Yes, I told you, she picked up the train timetable. Anyway, she'd obviously been shopping, laden down with bags she was and that seemed to have cheered her up. I remember saying to her how well she was looking, and she said it was amazing what a trip to the hairdressers can achieve. And we laughed at that, because whenever I'm feeling down I get my hair done too, don't I, Malcolm?'

'You do, love. Costs a bloody fortune too.'

'So, no hat?'

'No, no hat.'

'Did she give a home address when she registered?'

Norma pushed the registration book across and pointed to the entry. 'Here we are, 215 Warwick Road, Kensington, London W14.'

'No doubt that'll be a false address. Happens all the time in this business,' said Malcolm.

'Nevertheless, we need to check.'

'So, is that it, my loves?' said Malcolm, 'only we need to get on.'

'Just one more question,' said Madeline. 'Did you notice what car she was driving?'

'Nope,' said Malcolm. 'Our car park was being resurfaced. We issued customers with passes so they could use the station car park across the road. I issued her with a pass, so she definitely had a car, but I never actually saw it, sorry.'

'You've both been very helpful, thank you.'

Malcolm watched as Madeline and Rose made their way across the road towards the railway station, before picking up the phone.

'Who are you ringing?' asked Norma.

'*The Yorkshire Herald.*'

'Whatever for?'

'Publicity, Norma, publicity'— 'Ah, good day to you, my name is Mr Shaw, manager of the Poplars Hotel. I'd like to speak to Guy Richards'— 'It's about the Lilly Green abduction'— 'Yes, thank you, I'll hold.'

Walking back to the car, Madeline rang the desk sergeant and asked for a check on the London address. The answer came back within moments. The address was a pub that had closed in 1990. 'No surprise there,' said Madeline. 'Right, come on, let's see if the train station car park has CCTV.'

Ten minutes later Madeline slammed her hand down onto the roof of her car. 'What a wimp,' she exclaimed, then, parroting the whinging voice of the stationmaster, she continued, '*I'm so sorry, officer, but the cameras are constantly being vandalised. We inform the police but nothing's ever done and we simply can't afford to keep replacing them,*' as if it's my bloody fault.'

Rose flopped onto the passenger seat and battled with the seatbelt. 'So, she arrives here on Sunday morning, lies low all day and ventures out on Monday to York.'

'Where she goes shopping.'

'And visits the hairdressers.'

'Then, on Tuesday, she visits the library.'

'Because she's come up with a plan?'

'Possibly—Rose, what *are* you doing?'

'This bloody thing's stuck,' she cried, yanking the belt.

'Let it go and then pull on it *gently.*'

'Her visits start on the Thursday,' continued Rose, as she clicked the seatbelt into place. 'So, what was she doing on Wednesday? Checking out babies in York?'

'It's a possibility, Rose, a definite possibility,' said Madeline, turning the ignition and pulling out onto the main road. 'We'll contact the York police and get them to put out a television and radio appeal, requesting mothers to contact us if they'd been visited by this woman.'

There was a note from Donald on Madeline's desk, asking her to ring the lab.

'Hi, Donald, it's me, Madeline.'

'Ah, thanks for ringing,' he said. 'I'm afraid I've had no luck with those scales. Not a trace of evidence to be found. Whoever used them was very careful.'

Madeline sighed. 'I thought that would be the case. Is there anything about the scales that might help us trace this woman?'

'I'm afraid not. They're made by Mebby; a very popular make. You can buy them in all branches of Mothercare across the country,' said Donald. 'Hundreds are sold every week.'

'And what about the newspapers, any luck there?'

'Give me a chance. You only gave them to me yesterday. I'll let you know as soon as I have anything.'

Chapter 5
Friday 17th May - 20th May

Amelia spent most of the journey home on Friday screaming. Olivia's nerves were in tatters. Holding the distraught child tightly in her arms, she pushed the front door open with her hip and shut it with a backward flick of her foot. The screaming reached new levels of intensity.

'Bloody hell, Amelia, give Mummy a break.'

The silence that descended the moment the milk flowed into Amelia's mouth was painful. Olivia closed her eyes, leaned back on the settee and sighed.

Pulling the nursery door shut, Olivia tiptoed downstairs, made a coffee and settled back onto the settee. Cradling the mug in both hands she raised it to her lips, but before taking a sip, her eyes caught sight of the previous day's newspaper lying on top of the pile of mail that had been pushed aside by the front door. She put the mug on the table and retrieved the paper.

BABY-SNATCHER IN LOCAL HOTEL
BY GUY RICHARDS

'Of course, the more I thought about it, the more suspicious I became,' said Mr Shaw, the Manager of the Poplars Hotel, in Thirsk, where the woman who abducted Lilly Green stayed for eight nights.

Mr Shaw told this paper that the woman arrived on the morning of the 5th July in a dishevelled state, wearing a large brimmed hat that obscured most of her face.

The following day she travelled to York where, it seems, she visited the hairdressers. Mr Shaw stated that the woman was most insistent that he and his wife admired her new hairdo. But after that, nothing.'

THE ANGUISH OF CHILD ABDUCTORS

DR Philip Norman, head of the Farrah Trust, a support charity for women who kidnap children, said most child abductions are carried out by women who have lost a child or were unable to have children. In situations where a child has died, Dr Norman commented, 'They cannot accept this and may spend days, weeks or even years looking for a child of the same age who resembles the one they lost. Sometimes, they believe that the child they take is a reincarnation of their own. In these situations the kidnapped child is never at risk.'

It is known that other women were approached in the week prior to Lilly Green's abduction. This implies that a particular baby was being sought. Could it be that the woman who took Lilly Green had recently lost her own baby in tragic circumstances?

If anyone knows of a woman who has suffered such a loss, our only hope is that they will have the courage to come forward. I urge you to contact this paper or ring the Northallerton Police Incident Room.

'There we are, Mavis, one cappuccino—oh, sorry, excuse me,' said Carla, picking up the phone as she slid the coffee across the counter. 'Browsers Café, Carla Marchese speaking.'

'Honeysuckle Cottage, Olivia Hamilton speaking.'

Carla squealed. 'Olivia, at last! When did you get back?'

'A few hours ago.'

'Are you coming over to the café, or shall I…?'

'Actually, would you mind if we left it for today? I'm exhausted. Amelia's zonked out and I'm just about to get in the bath.'

'Oh, OK. So, when will…?'

'I'll bring Amelia over to the café tomorrow sometime, but I can't stay long. I've got so much to do, you know, with Lawrence due back the day after tomorrow and everything. You do understand, don't you?'

'Yes, of course I do. I'll look forward to your brief visit tomorrow then. Bye.'

Mavis Fitch, the obdurate local village gossip, pursed her lips. 'I take it the wanderer has returned.'

'Assuming you're referring to Olivia, then yes, she's back.'

'Didn't say what she'd been up to then,' said Mavis. 'Probably off with some fancy man.'

'For God's sake, Mavis, I've never heard anything so preposterous. If you must know, she's been in London helping…'

'London! Well, there you are, a well-known hot-spot of scandal, intrigue and extramarital affairs, you mark my words,' she said, taking her coffee and marching across to a nearby table.

Turning towards Hannah, Carla raised her eyebrows and mumbled, 'Bloody woman.'

'I reckon she needs a good seeing to,' remarked Hannah.

'What was that, Hannah?' snapped Mavis.

'She was just saying it will be good seeing Olivia again,' said Carla.

Hannah clamped her lips together and concentrated on wiping the counter.

Mavis harrumphed. 'When you've finished wiping that perfectly clean counter, I'll have one of those fairy cakes.'

'Certainly, Mrs Fitch.'

As promised, Olivia called in at the café the following day. Amelia was snuggled up in her papoose, fast asleep.

Mavis, sat at her usual corner table, looked up as the door-bells jangled. 'And here she is, at long last.'

Olivia managed a weak smile. 'Yes, hello, Mavis, here I am.'

'It's so good to see you,' said Carla.

'I can't stay long.'

'Well, I assume you're going to have a coffee.'

'Yes, of course I am, don't be silly. It's just that Amelia's still tuckered out after all the upheaval.'

'And whose fault is that?'

'Yes, thank you, Mavis—now then, Olivia, what will you have?'

'A cappuccino, please.'

'To be honest, I was expecting you home earlier in the week.'

'Yes, that was the intention, but you'll never guess who I bumped into in Scarborough?'

'Given your recent escapades, I wouldn't be surprised to hear you'd met Count Dracula.'

'That's Whitby, Carla. No, it was Ian and Miranda Frazer.'

'Who?'

'My old Prof and his wife from York.'

'Oh, right, and?'

'They invited me over to theirs. I couldn't really say no.'

'They would have understood, surely?'

'It was only for a few days.' She spread her hands wide and declared, 'And look, here I am, back safe and sound.'

'More than can be said for that poor baby,' muttered Mavis from the corner table.

Olivia whirled round. 'Mavis, Amelia's fine, she's just…'

'Yes, yes, I'm sure,' said Mavis. 'I'm not referring to your poor exhausted baby, but to Lilly Green.'

'Such an awful thing,' said Carla. 'The report was in Tuesday's paper. Did you see it?'

'We only take the Thursday edition. It has the science section,' said Olivia. 'But I did see something about it on the front page, when I got back yesterday.'

'Fancy stealing someone else's baby,' exclaimed Mavis. 'Obviously some deranged mental case. Needs locking up if you ask me.'

'Yes, well, thankfully no one's asking you,' said Carla, retrieving Tuesday's copy of the *Yorkshire Herald* from under the counter. 'It happened last Monday. There's a photofit of the woman, but so far, nothing. She just seems to have vanished.'

'And nobody knows who she is?'

Clara shook her head as she slapped the paper onto the counter and pointed at the article on the front page.

Olivia glanced down. The photofit was set next to a picture of a distraught-looking Mrs Green.

'Do *you* recognise her?'

'Who?'

'The woman in the photofit, Olivia.'

'No. But photofits are not that reliable.'

'Well, that's all the police have got,' said Carla. 'Poor Madeline, talk about being thrown in at the deep end.'

Olivia frowned.

Carla raised her eyes heavenwards. 'Madeline, Madeline Driscoll, Barbara and Jack's daughter. She applied for a transfer to Jack's old station in Northallerton.'

'Oh, that's right, yes, I remember you telling me about her. She had an interview for promotion, didn't she?'

Carla nodded. 'She's *Detective Inspector* Driscoll now. Of course you'd have known that if you hadn't swanned off to London.'

'Oh, Carla, please let's not go over that again.'

'Sorry. Anyway, according to the report, it was a carefully planned abduction,' said Carla, throwing a withering glance in Mavis's direction, 'the work of a distraught woman, not a deranged one.'

'May I see?'

'Help yourself. The report continues on page three— take it, I'll bring your coffee over.'

Olivia settled herself down at a table and read the article. Deep in thought, she closed the paper and stared again at the photofit.

'The fact that the woman went to the house to take the baby gives me the creeps,' said Carla, setting Olivia's coffee down. 'It's so cold, so calculated.'

Olivia stroked Amelia's head. 'I can't imagine what those poor parents must be going through.'

'It doesn't bear thinking about.'

Mavis glanced down at the paper as she swept past them on her way to the door. 'It could be you, that could.'

Carla raised her eyebrows. 'Oh, do give it a rest, Mavis. Even you would bear a passing resemblance to that photofit if you wore a blonde wig.'

Muttering to herself, Mavis gave a dismissive wave and left.

'Stupid old cow,' muttered Carla.

Olivia gulped down her coffee and stood. 'Anyway, lovely to see you, but I'd better get going too.'

'Already?'

'Sorry, I did say I couldn't stay long.'

'Jesus, Olivia, you've only just sat down,' exclaimed Carla. 'I assumed we'd have time to chat, at least.'

'I know and I really am sorry, but I've still got so much to do. We'll catch up when Lawrence and I get back from Spain.'

'When are you off?'

'Our flight leaves at 2am on Tuesday.'

'Poor Lawrence. He'll be exhausted.'

'Madness I know. It would have been fine if he'd got back on the first but, well, there we are, nothing we could do about it. At least he's finished with all that soldiering now.'

'And of course, I shall wait with bated breath for his book to be published.'

Olivia turned at the door and stuck her tongue out.

'Bye, darling,' said Carla, with a smile.

Over in Northallerton, Madeline snatched up the phone in her office.

'Donald, hi—tell me you've got something useful.'

'I've managed to decipher the names copied out from the newspapers,' he said. 'As to whether this will prove useful, I'm afraid I can't say. Do you want me to bring the list up to you?'

'Please.'

Madeline looked up from her desk at the sound of the door opening. 'That was quick.'

'I aim to please,' said Donald, handing her the list. 'As you can see, she copied out all seventeen names of the women who had female babies.'

'So, no names left out. Are you sure?'

'Positive.'

Madeline opened the Lilly Green file and removed the photocopies of the newspapers. 'Can you call out the names on your list?'

'With pleasure.'

Madeline hunched over her desk as she ticked off each name.

'That's it,' said Donald.

Madeline looked up. 'OK, I agree. She's copied out all the names.'

Up went Donald's brows.

'I know, just checking.'

Rose popped her head round the door. 'Any joy?'

'Ah, Rose. Well, you were right. She did copy out all seventeen names.'

'OK, and?'

Madeline extracted the list of Yvette Young's visits. She scanned the names as she ran her fingers down Donald's list. 'Interesting.'

'What is?' said Rose.

'She organised her visits by place, rather than by the order of announcements,' said Madeline, as she continued to cross-reference the names. 'She visited the three women in Bagby on Thursday morning, the three in Sowerby on Thursday afternoon. Friday, she concentrated on the women in Thirsk.'

'You certainly can't dispute her organisational skills,' said Donald.

Madeline continued to run her finger down the interview list. 'Look at this, it's methodical. She started with

Watson, Wright and Sinclair in the morning and then Poole, Lee and Parker in the afternoon.'

'Leaving her with three more in Thirsk, one in Binton-on-Wiske and one in Dalton to interview,' said Donald.

Madeline nodded. 'But she spoke to Mrs Green at 9:15 on Monday morning and walked out with Lilly Green some thirty minutes later.'

'Meaning she wouldn't need to visit Taylor and Davies, in Thirsk, Philips, in Binton or Jones, in Dalton,' said Rose.

'No, it seems not.'

'You don't sound convinced,' said Rose.

'We're simply *assuming* she didn't visit these four women,' said Madeline.

'They didn't report being visited,' said Rose.

'Nevertheless…'

Rose stood. 'You don't like assumptions,' said Rose. 'I'll ring them now.'

'It certainly seems like she was looking for a particular baby. One to replace a dead baby, perhaps?' said Donald.

Madeline ran her hand through her hair. 'I know, but we've interviewed the local women we know who lost their babies recently.'

'*Local* and *know* are the two key words there,' said Donald.

Madeline lowered her head into her hands. 'That thought has already crossed my mind, Donald. And if that *is* the case then we don't stand a chance. It's been five days now, there have been no sightings, nothing, zilch. Where the hell are they?'

Rose returned to Madeline's office where Madeline and Donald were sat, deep in thought. 'We were right.'

'Sorry?' said Madeline.

'Yvette Young didn't visit Taylor, Davies, Philips or Jones,' said Rose.

'Because she'd already found what she wanted at Mrs Green's house,' said Donald. 'Her ideal replacement.'

On Monday morning, Barbara was enjoying a cup of coffee in Browsers, when Lawrence and Olivia popped in to say farewell before they set off for the airport. Amelia was in her papoose, strapped firmly to her father's chest; only her legs and the top of her head were visible.

'Carla,' called Barbara. 'Olivia's here.'

The back office door flew open and Carla dashed out.

'We're leaving in about an hour,' said Olivia.

'Already?'

'We're calling in on Lawrence's parents on the way.'

'You've hardly been back and now you're off again. I'll miss you,' she said. Turning to Lawrence, she reached out to fondle Amelia's little foot.

Lawrence gave Olivia a quizzical look. 'Hardly been…?'

'We'll be back on the twelfth of July,' said Olivia in a bright voice. 'Not long really.'

'Your parents are so lucky. I fear Madeline's years away from producing a grandchild,' said Barbara, fondling Amelia's other foot.

'The twelfth of July,' exclaimed Carla. 'That's almost two months. Amelia will have *doubled* in age.'

There was a moment of silence as all eyes fixed on the top of the tiny head jutting out from the papoose.

'Have you heard how Penny and her baby are doing?' asked Carla.

Lawrence gave a small frown. 'Penny?'

'Yes, hasn't Olivia mentioned…' began Carla.

'Actually, Lawrence,' said Olivia, glancing at her watch. 'We'd better get a move on. No doubt Amelia will need a nappy change before we set off and we don't want to be late. You know what your father's like. He'll go on and on about what route we should have taken and…'

'We've got plenty of time, Olivia. I thought you wanted a coffee.'

'I did, but time marches on and all that, sorry,' she said, as she grabbed Lawrence's hand and marched him towards the door.

'It looks like we're off. Bye,' said Lawrence.

'Have a safe trip. And don't forget to send us all a postcard once you get to Spain,' yelled Carla, as the pair of them made a hasty exit onto the street.

Chapter 6
June

The television and radio appeals issued in May had failed to bring any new information. There had been no more sightings of the small, neatly dressed woman with blonde hair. Guy Richards wrote regular articles for the *Yorkshire Herald*, keeping the case in the public eye over the following weeks, but other events soon caught the headlines. Madeline and Rose became swept up in other cases and Lilly Green remained missing.

Guy worked from home most days, emailing his copy to the paper. His third floor flat in Northallerton consisted of three rooms; an open-plan living, dining and kitchen area, a bedroom and a bathroom. The most important thing, as far as Guy was concerned, was the fact that he had access to a private garage for his beloved old mini.

Sat at his desk under the window in the living room, with his hands folded behind his head, he leaned back and contemplated the Artex ceiling. Allowing his chair to right itself with a thump, he rested his elbows on the desk. His cat was sat on the windowsill, staring out of the window, chittering at the birds perched in the top branches of the trees.

'OK, Merlin, let's think about this. A baby died, how is not important at the moment. Well, it is obviously, but well, anyway, a baby dies. The mother, distraught, does what?' He screwed his eyes shut and rubbed his forehead. 'Rings for an ambulance? The police? You'd have thought so, wouldn't you? But I can't recall there being any instances of unexplained baby deaths in the last few months. So, she buries the baby in secret?'

Merlin's chittering took on a birdlike quality as the objects of his desire flitted from branch to branch, twittering in alarm and tantalisingly close.

'The good Dr Norman asserts that she wouldn't be able to accept being childless and would go in search of someone else's baby. One that looked like her own and born around the same time.'

Merlin's pupils widened as he continued to watch the birds.

'So, somehow she's got to get rid of her dead baby, find a replacement and get it back into her home before anyone notices there's a problem. How the hell is she going to do that?'

Merlin gave a plaintive miaow.

'It was a rhetorical question, Merlin. OK, let's concentrate on how she'd go about finding a two-month-old baby.' Guy leaned back in his chair again. 'God, I hate Artex,' he muttered.

Merlin jumped onto the desk, walked over the computer keys and settled down on yesterday's copy of the *Yorkshire Herald*, purring with enthusiasm.

The frantic twittering of the birds ceased and in the silence Guy absentmindedly stroked the cat. 'Births, Deaths and Marriages,' he cried. 'It's obvious.' He righted his chair and began typing. 'She stayed at the Poplars Hotel in Thirsk. Lilly Green was taken from Thirsk, so it stands to reason she'd check the local papers.'

Within minutes he was staring at the Births, Deaths and Marriages section of the *Thirsk Post* for Friday the 15th of March, where he saw the same twenty announcements seen by Madeline and Rose. He then loaded the 22nd of March edition and saw the twenty-five announcements listed there. One of those was for Lilly Green.

'Bingo,' he said, as he pressed print. 'OK, now for my rag.'

He loaded the relevant editions of the *Yorkshire Herald* and printed out the fifty-one announcements. Scanning through them, he noted that several names appeared in both papers. 'You lot were obviously very keen for the world to know you'd given birth. OK, I need to think—coffee time.'

Sat back at his desk, coffee in hand, Guy looked through the lists again. He took a sip of coffee and rubbed his forehead. 'Right, Lilly's a girl, so I think it's safe to assume that the dead baby, if there is one, was also a girl—agree, Merlin?'

Merlin, who was now curled up on one of Guy's old jumpers, made no response.

'I'll take that as a yes. So, she'd only be interested in the women who gave birth to girls.'

He went through the lists and eliminated those who'd given birth to boys, leaving him with twenty-six names. Fourteen had announcements in both the *Post* and the *Herald*, three in the *Post* only and nine in the *Herald* only.

'Surely she didn't have time to visit twenty-six bloody women,' exclaimed Guy, patting the piles of papers on his desk. 'Where the hell is it?—ah, got you,' he said, as he located his mobile.

'Hi there, Steve, do you fancy a drink tonight?'—'No, reason, I…'—'OK, fine, I just want to run something past you, I'm not expecting you to reveal any confidential police information.'—'Hah, hah, most amusing.'—'It's just an idea I'm working on.'—'About the Lilly Green case.'—'I know that Steve, that's why I'm working on it. She's got to be *somewhere*, for God's sake.' He glanced at his watch. 'About 7ish?'—'Great, see you in The Fox; you're a star.'

Guy was at the bar, ordering his drink from Frank, when he felt a tap on his shoulder. 'You're nicked.'

Frank raised his eyebrows. 'Change the bloody record, Steve.'

'He can't help it, Frank,' said Guy, 'he's a child at heart.'

'Just remember who asked for help,' said Steve.

Guy flashed him a disarming smile. 'Duly remembered. Your usual?'

Steve nodded.

'You go and sit down,' said Frank. 'I'll send Susan over with the drinks.'

'We'll be in the snug,' said Guy, putting his arm round Steve's shoulder. 'Busy day?'

Steve nodded.

'Me too, I've been racking my brain about this Lilly Green case.'

'So you said.'

'So, no more news at your end then?'

Steve shook his head.

'Here we are gentleman, two pints of our finest.'

'Thanks, Susan,' said Guy, picking up his beer and taking a huge swig. 'I'll get straight to the point, Steve. When we spoke back in May, you told me several women rang the station after reading my article.'

'Yes, and?'

'Can you tell me how many rang in?'

Steve thought for a moment. 'I don't see why not,' said Steve, taking a sip of his pint. 'It was twelve.'

Guy frowned. 'Are you sure it was only twelve?'

Steve nodded. 'Certain. Why?'

'If I showed you a list of names,' said Guy, pushing his list over towards Steve, 'would you be able to say if the names on that list corresponded in any way with the names of the women who rang the station?'

Steve took another swig of beer as he glanced at the list. 'I could.'

'And does it?'

Steve nodded.

76

'So, to be clear,' said Guy. 'The names of the twelve women who contacted the police are on my list?'

Steve nodded again. 'As well as Mrs Green, of course.'

'Obviously, Steve, and I assume all twelve were interviewed?'

'Yes.'

'Anything interesting materialise?'

'You spoke to Mrs Harper, didn't you?'

'Yes.'

'You know about as much as I do then.'

'Ah, but that's it, Steve, *about as much* isn't the same as *as much* so, what do you know that I don't?'

'Is that meant to be a serious question?'

'You know what I mean.'

'*If* I knew something you didn't, then that's probably because it's sensitive information *not* to be revealed to the press, mate. I'm not that bloody gullible.'

'Fair enough, so, are we…'

'We?'

'Alright, so, are the police working on the theory that this woman was looking for some ideal baby?'

'Something like that, yes.'

'And have they any idea why that may be the case?'

Steve shrugged. 'Who knows? I thought you knew more about that side of things,' he said, staring down at the remains of his pint. 'You're the one constantly quoting that Trust bloke.'

'Alright, let me put it another way,' said Guy. 'Are the police looking for a woman who's recently lost a baby?'

'Not now, no,' said Steve.

'Oh, why's that?'

Steve levelled Guy with a hard stare.

'Bloody hell, Steve, got a sudden attack of conscience?'

Steve lowered his voice. 'For God's sake, Guy. We followed that lead but didn't find a likely suspect. OK?'

'Thank you. So, I take it the police are now working on the theory that there's a woman out there who didn't report the death of her baby,' said Guy, 'because that's what I reckon.'

Steve concentrated on drinking the remainder of his beer.

'Well?'

'Are you ready for another?' said Steve.

Guy emptied his glass. 'If you're offering.'

Steve held up his glass. 'Susan, when you're ready, love.'

'So, am I right, or what?'

'It's a thought, I suppose,' said Steve.

'OK, I get it, you're not going to answer that one. How about the other names on my list then?'

'What about them?'

'Well, they gave birth to babies in March too. Why weren't they visited?'

'I'd have thought that was bloody obvious. Call yourself an investigative reporter.'

'Here we are, gentleman.'

'Cheers, Susan,' said Steve, taking a sip.

'Well?'

'Bloody hell, Guy, she obviously didn't need to visit any more women once she'd nicked Lilly Green, what would have been the point?'

'So, what now? Case closed?'

'Case unsolved,' said Steve, taking a swig of beer. 'And unless we get some further information, that's how it will stay.'

Guy lifted his glass towards his mouth.

'What?' said Steve.

'I didn't say a word.'

'You've got that look in your eye.'

'I just thought I might have a word with these women— see if I can pick up on anything.'

'You'll be wasting your time, Guy. Inspector Driscoll isn't like Curtis—she's thorough.'

'Even so, it would be useful to know which twelve women from my list rang the police,' said Guy, pushing the list closer towards Steve. 'What harm could it do? Just a little pencil mark.'

'If you're going to write another report you'd better not use any of their names.'

'Come on, Steve, I'm not an idiot.'

Steve snatched up the pencil. 'And you'd better not mention my name.'

'I never grassed you up at school, did I?'

Steve blushed.

'And that was bloody good weed that was.'

'Oh, say it a bit louder, why don't you?'

Guy snorted. 'Don't panic officer, no one heard.'

Back at his flat, Guy wrote each of the names onto cards, along with the town where they lived. He also made a note of the birth dates of each baby. He then stuck them onto the wall.

He placed Mrs Green's card at the top, with the twelve cards containing the names of the women who'd contacted the police, arranged in a block of three by four beneath it. The remaining thirteen cards he placed in a single column on the far right.

He stood back and stared at the column. 'So, is Steve right? Were you lot ignored simply because the woman found her ideal baby at Mrs Green's house?'

He poured himself a whisky and took a sip. 'Or is there another reason?'

Guy drove over to Thirsk the following morning.

'Oh, yes, she came here at 3pm on Friday, the tenth of May,' Mrs Parker gabbled. 'I've already spoken to the police. They said I was *most* helpful. It was your article in the

Yorkshire Herald that prompted me to ring actually. Anyway, this woman, Yvette Young, oh shit,' she exclaimed, 'me and my big mouth. I um, well I wasn't meant to mention that name to anyone.' She gave Guy an apologetic look. 'Especially not the press, oh, God, please don't print that name, the police will…'

Guy held up his hand. 'Don't worry, I won't. This is 'off the record', alright?'

She nodded. 'Anyway, I shouldn't think it's her real name. I mean, she's hardly going to be that stupid, is she?'

'So, can you tell me what happened?'

Mrs Parker told Guy what she'd told the police. 'It was all over in a matter of minutes.'

'And you'd never seen the woman before?'

'No, never.'

'And did you see the car?'

'No, but my friend Joyce saw it. It was parked opposite her house in Byland Avenue. She told the police but, as far as I know, they never found it—mind you, all she was able to say was that it was green, large and boxy looking.'

'Ah, so not much to go on then.'

'No, not really,' said Mrs Parker, sniggering. 'Oh, I shouldn't laugh, she was only trying to help.'

'And this Yvette made no attempt to take your baby?'

Mrs Parker shook her head.

'Right, well, thank you very much for your time.'

'Are you going to speak to Angela and Lisa? The police spoke to them as well, you know.'

Angela and Lisa?'

'Mrs Wright and Mrs Sinclair. They had visits from the woman too.'

'Oh, yes, do you know them?'

'I do, we all attend the clinic together, as did Sally Green before, well before…'

'Yes, quite.'

'It's just that I know they'll tell you exactly the same as I've told you. The woman followed the same routine, except with Sally. You see, when Sally offered the woman a drink she accepted. And then, while Sally was making it, she made off with the baby. Awful.'

'I see. So, do *you* think the woman was looking for a particular baby?'

'Who knows,' said Mrs Parker. 'I suppose I was lucky because, for some reason, my Alice wasn't the chosen one.'

Guy removed one of his cards from his inside jacket pocket and handed it to Mrs Parker. 'If you think of anything else, *anything*, please don't hesitate to call me.'

'And you won't say anything about that name?'

'Don't worry. I promise.'

Immediately after speaking to Mrs Parker, Guy visited Mrs Wright and Mrs Sinclair and, as predicted, they told him the same story.

Between other assignments over the following weeks, Guy managed to talk to all twelve women who'd contacted the police. Nothing jumped out at him. He still had no idea why this woman had done what she'd done, where she'd come from or where she'd gone to. He feared Steve had been right. It had been a waste of time. He stared at the thirteen names on the cards arranged into the single column. 'So, if Yvette hadn't found Lilly on Monday morning, you lot could have been next. Think yourselves bloody lucky.'

He sat himself down at the computer and began typing out what would probably be his last report on the Lilly Green case. He titled it, *The Lucky Thirteen*. It was due to be published on Monday, the fifteenth of July, nine weeks after Lilly Green's abduction.

Chapter 7
Friday July 12th

On Thursday night, July the eleventh, a violent thunderstorm raged over Vicar's Moor Wood, uprooting several trees. The following morning, the air was crisp and the lush greens of the wood sparkled in the sunlight. Fat water droplets hung from leaves like fruit until, finally, their weight wrenched them free and they plummeted towards the ground.

A solitary man and his dog were taking their regular walk along the path by the lake. 'Will you look at this,' the man said to his dog, as he passed each fallen tree, 'It looks like a war zone.'

The dog wagged his tail and continued, head down, sniffing the ground until he arrived at a damaged willow tree. Here he stopped. The wind had managed to split the old trunk, partially uprooting it. The rain had washed away soil from its base. The dog gave a single bark and began to dig.

'What is it, boy?'

The dog gave another excited bark.

The man wandered across.

The dog wagged his tail, dived towards a gaping hole and retrieved a bone.

Driving down the A167 from the station, the sun once again beating down, it took Madeline a little while to realise she was driving along the road she drove along every morning to get to work. 'Where are we going to again?' she asked.

'Vicar's Moor Wood,' said Rose.

'Uh huh, and where exactly is this wood?'

Rose furrowed her brow. 'It's not far from where you live,' said Rose. 'Haven't you ever been there?'

'No.'

'But it's only about a mile out of your village, on the road towards Thirsk,' said Rose. 'It's an important wildlife area. The lake's a haven for water fowl.'

'Is that a fact? How absolutely fascinating.'

They parked in a small lay-by on the Newsham Road, donned their wellies and trudged across the sopping ground towards a tented area that had been erected by the side of the lake.

Jeremy Lawson looked up as Madeline and Rose entered the tent. 'Ah, ladies, good of you to pop along.'

Holding her breath, Madeline knelt beside Jeremy.

'Rose, I warn you, it isn't a pretty sight.'

Rose nodded and remained by the tent entrance.

A tiny skeleton, held together by strings of yellowing connective tissue, lay exposed in the mud. There were small patches of leathery skin attached to the ribcage. Weaving their way through the eye sockets were dozens of small beetles. Madeline closed her eyes momentarily. 'The left leg seems to be missing,' she said in a small voice.

'There's no fooling you is there, my dear?'

Madeline gave him a cold, hard stare. 'And do we know where the leg has gone?'

'Sealed in an evidence bag. It was snapped off very recently, as indicted by the freshness of the damage, by a small terrier who's very pleased with himself. He's currently sitting with his appropriately named owner, Mr Graves, near the lake behind us.'

'It always seems to be dog walkers who discover dead bodies,' remarked Madeline to no one in particular. 'Note to self; don't get a dog.'

The sound of retching filled the air.

Jeremy sighed. 'Oh dear, I did try to warn her.'

'The size of these remains, so tiny, I assume they belong to a baby,' said Madeline.

'Either that, or we've stumbled across an entirely new miniature human species.'

Madeline clenched her jaw. 'So, any thoughts on how long the body's been here?'

'Months rather than weeks,' he replied.

'Two months?'

'At least.'

'Oh, God.'

'You're thinking it could be Baby Lilly?'

'Well, I don't know, do I, Jeremy?' snapped Madeline. 'It could be her, or it could be our perp's dead baby, or another bloody baby entirely. Look at it, for God's sake.' She shifted her angry glare towards Jeremy. 'Even you haven't got a clue, have you?'

Jeremy said nothing as he continued his examination.

Madeline took a deep breath. 'How long will the postmortem take?'

'Once I get the remains back to the lab, it shouldn't take me too long. Initial examination hasn't revealed any obvious cause of death. No head trauma, for example. I'll know more once I start the full examination.'

'What sort of thing will you be looking for?'

'If I knew that, my dear, then I wouldn't really need to look, would I?'

Madeline nodded. 'And you'll start the postmortem when?'

'Tomorrow, first thing.'

Rose was making her way back to the tent as Madeline emerged, lit a cigarette and took a satisfying drag.

'I've spoken to Mr Graves, the dog-owner,' said Rose. 'Not much to add really. He saw his dog digging around in the loosened earth and came across to investigate. His dog proudly dropped the leg bone at his feet. When he peered into the hole, he could see that the remains were human. He rang the police immediately.'

'How is he?'

'Oh, he's fine, says it's all been very exciting. I've taken his details and sent him on his way, I hope that's alright.'

'Absolutely fine, Rose, well done.'

Rose looked over her shoulder and shuffled her feet.

'Is there something else?' asked Madeline.

'That reporter, Guy Richards, he was here just before we arrived,' explained Rose.

'How the hell did he manage to get here so fast?'

Rose shrugged.

'Did Mr Graves speak to him?'

'Yes he did, but there wasn't much he could tell him, except that the remains were human.'

'Shit! Well, he's going to put two and two together and come up with five. I can see the bloody headline now; *Remains of Baby Lilly found by Dog.*'

'Not necessarily,' said Rose. 'His other reports struck me as being well researched. I don't think he's going to jump to the conclusion that these remains are those of Lilly Green, even though they probably are.'

'They can't be,' said Madeline, a hint of desperation in her voice. 'I mean why would someone go to all that trouble to select a particular baby and then kill it?'

'An accident?'

'A psychopath on the loose?'

'Oh, God, you don't think that, do you?'

'No, not really. Actually, I think they're more likely to be the remains of Yvette Young's baby. Either way, we need to get over to Thirsk pronto. Mr and Mrs Green need to be aware that remains have been found,' said Madeline.

From inside the tent, Jeremy Lawson called out, 'Don't forget to collect DNA samples from them so we can compare them with the results from these remains.'

'Yes, thank you for that, Dr Lawson,' she called back, flicking her cigarette aside. 'I'm hardly likely to forget.'

Stephen opened the door to them. 'Inspector Driscoll,' he cried. 'Have you found Lilly?'

'May we come inside for a moment, Mr Green?'

Stephen stood to one side. 'Yes, yes, of course, sorry, come in, come in. Sally's in the living room. She's, well she's not coping, Inspector. She hasn't left the house since you were here last.'

The curtains were drawn, the atmosphere thick and oppressed. Sally, her eyes red and swollen, looked up. 'Have you found her?'

Madeline sat on the settee beside her. 'Not as yet, no.' She looked up at Stephen. 'I'm very sorry to have to tell you this, but the remains of a baby…'

Sally let out a heart-rending sob. 'Tell me it's not Lilly. It can't be Lilly.'

'We don't yet know,' said Madeline. 'We need to do tests.'

'Tests? What tests?' asked Stephen.

'DNA,' replied Madeline.

Sally began to shake uncontrollably. 'Oh, God, Stephen, I can't bear it.'

'It won't be her. It can't be her,' said Stephen, rushing to his wife's side.

Madeline cleared her throat. 'Are you both happy to give us a sample of your own DNA, for comparison? It's a simple swab of your cheek cells.'

Stephen swallowed. 'Sally?'

Sally looked up at Madeline. Her eyes bulged with fright.

'I'm so sorry, but we really need the DNA to be, well, to be sure.'

'How long will it be before we…' Stephen cleared his throat. 'Before we know?'

'This case is top priority, Mr Green. We should know in a few days. I can only imagine how hard this is for you both, but rest assured, we're working as fast as the science allows us.'

'Thank you,' said Stephen.

'I can arrange for the Family Liaison Officer to…'

Sally grabbed Stephen's hand and shook her head.

'No, Inspector, we'll be fine. Sally's mum is staying with us. She's just popped out to the shops.'

Madeline nodded. 'We'll let you know as soon as we can.'

Superintendent Avery burst into Madeline's office after lunch. 'The vultures are gathering outside. I've got a meeting with the Chief Constable who, surprise, surprise, wants these remains identified ASAP and the culprit apprehended yesterday. So, I'm afraid you'll have to talk to them.'

'But what am I supposed to say? We only…'

Avery held up her hand. 'You don't need to tell me, I know. Just keep it brief. The usual stuff, time remains were found, cannot comment on cause of death, autopsy to be carried out first thing tomorrow morning, we're following lines of enquiry etc, etc. OK?'

Madeline stood on the main steps of the police station. A motley group of reporters peered up at her. 'Good afternoon,' she cleared her throat. 'We're sorry to report that the remains of a baby were discovered in Vicar's Moor Wood this morning by a dog walker and…'

The greasy-haired, overweight reporter, who'd been at Avery's initial press briefing back in March, stood up. 'David Mason, *Thirsk Post*. Is it Lilly Green?'

'You never learn, do you?' yelled someone from behind him. 'What an inane question. They only found the remains a few hours ago.'

'Why don't you just shut the fuck up,' retorted David.

'And why don't you listen to your colleague,' remarked Madeline, as she gave a small nod in the general direction of where the other voice had come. 'He, at least, seems to be talking some sense.'

'Guy fucking Richards is an arsehole. Thinks he's something special, he does. Just because of his dear daddy. More fool him.'

Ah, the ubiquitous Guy Richards, thought Madeline. 'We have spoken to Mr and Mrs Green, but,' she said, staring out towards David Mason, 'we are not yet in a position to say who the remains belong to. The autopsy is due to start tomorrow morning. The findings will be reported to the Greens and the press will be informed later. Until then, perhaps you could all show some respect for the Greens and leave them in peace at this difficult time.'

'Is that it?' demanded David.

'We're currently following several lines of enquiry. That's the end of the statement. Thank you.'

'But…'

'The *end*, Mr Mason.'

Over in Binton-on-Wiske, Olivia and Lawrence walked through the gate at Honeysuckle Cottage. 'This weather's unbelievable,' exclaimed Olivia. 'It's hotter than Spain.'

'I could murder a cup of tea,' said Lawrence, as he lifted Amelia above his head and wrinkled his nose. 'However, I rather think a nappy change is urgently called for. I'll unload the car in a bit.'

'Oh, I've missed this place,' said Olivia, pushing open their rickety gate. She stepped onto the haphazard stone pathway and stopped for a moment, listening to the sound of bleating sheep in the fields beyond. 'I'll put the kettle on.'

'Excellent,' said Lawrence

After lunch, they walked over to Browsers. The usual suspects were present at the café and they crowded around to admire Amelia. She'd been cooing and giggling all the way to the café, slapping at the bells and rattles strung from the hood of her buggy, each time looking mildly alarmed at the sounds they made. The transformation, as everyone crowded around, was sudden and spectacular. Her smile was replaced by a scrunched-up face as she let rip an ear-piercing howl.

Carla emerged from the storeroom. 'What the hell, it sounds like someone's being—Olivia!' She dashed across the café and threw her arms around her friend. 'Welcome home,' she said, before yelling at everyone to give Amelia some space. 'Poor thing, look at her, she's terrified. Imagine what it must look like to her, all your ugly mugs bearing down on her.'

Everyone muttered apologies and backed off.

'That's better,' said Carla, folding her arms across her chest. 'Ooh, I could hug her to bits. How's she been? She's certainly caught the sun and she's grown. Still, I suppose it would be somewhat odd if she hadn't. I don't know why people always say that really, I mean obviously she's grown, she'd hardly shrink. That *would* merit some comment, still, gosh, she *has* grown.'

Lawrence unstrapped Amelia and held onto her tightly as he muttered soothing sounds.

'Oh, she's adorable,' said Carla, leaning towards the baby.

Amelia instantly grabbed hold of Carla's silver pendant and tugged at it.

'Oh, God, sorry. It's her new trick,' exclaimed Olivia. 'I should have warned you.'

'Nonsense, it's my own fault.'

Amelia was not letting go. Her eyes danced with delight as the sunlight reflected off the pendant. 'Help,' cried Carla.

Olivia handed Amelia her favourite rattle and she immediately released the pendant to grab hold of it, shaking it enthusiastically and giggling.

Carla straightened up and rubbed her neck. 'Oh, well done you.'

'Did you both want a latte?' Hannah called out from behind the counter. 'Or would you prefer a cold drink?'

'Oh, a cold drink please,' said Olivia. 'Some of your fresh apple juice would be great.'

'I'll get Amelia settled at that table over by the window,' said Lawrence, as Olivia and Carla made their way towards the counter.

'Have we missed any exciting events in the village?'

Carla nodded her head towards Mavis and lowered her voice. 'She cracked a smile the other week, but apart from that no, not really.'

'Don't be mean. I feel sorry for her.'

'You'd be the only one—so, come on, how was Spain?'

'Hot.'

'Apart from that.'

'It was fine. Lawrence took loads of photos.'

'Oh, God, really?'

'Yes, loads and so we wondered if you and your friend Barbara, and her family of course, would like to come for drinks next Saturday evening. He's very proud of his photographic skills and he'd love to show them to you.'

Carla grimaced. 'Gosh, that would be lovely.'

'Shall I ask Barbara or…?'

'No, it's OK, I'll give her a ring now and see if they're free.' Moments later Carla returned with the news that Barbara and Jack would love to come. 'She couldn't speak for Madeline though. It all depends on her workload.'

Chapter 8
Saturday July 13th

After a short walk around the village, Olivia called into Browsers with Amelia. Mavis Fitch was standing centre stage, clutching the Saturday edition of the *Yorkshire Herald* to her chest. 'Such terrible news. I mean who could *do* such a thing?' she was saying. 'What must her poor parents be going through?'

'The remains haven't been identified yet, Mavis,' said Carla. 'The article clearly states that a post-mortem has to be carried out first. You can't just jump to conclusions like that.'

Waving the *Yorkshire Herald* in front of her, she cried, 'Well it's obvious, isn't it? I mean, look at the facts,' she announced, gesticulating with her hand as she counted. 'One, a two-month-old baby is snatched from her mother by some mysterious woman, two, there's been no sighting of this woman *or* the baby since and three, the remains of a two-month-old baby are discovered buried a few miles from where the baby was snatched. I mean, for heaven's sake, it has to be the same baby. It stands to reason.'

Olivia gripped the handles of the buggy.

'Nevertheless, Mavis, with all due respect,' said Carla, 'we simply don't know and all this spec…'

There was a dull thud as Olivia crumpled to the floor.

'Jesus, Olivia,' gasped Carla. 'Hannah, call your granddad, quick!'

Twenty minutes later, Olivia was reclined on one of the café's leather settees, sipping a cup of sugary tea. Hannah's grandfather was packing his stethoscope back into his medical bag and patting Olivia's arm.

Carla stood by their side, cuddling Amelia. 'Is she alright, Edward?'

'All tickety-boo now. Someone needs to make sure she eats a proper breakfast in future.'

'Yes, I'm so sorry. How embarrassing,' remarked Olivia. 'I should know better.' She started to sit up.

Gently pushing her back down, Edward said, 'I'd rather you remained reclined for a little bit longer.'

'Dr Prior's right,' said Carla. 'Take your time.'

'And when you're feeling better, I recommend you *eat* something. You, of all people, should know how important breakfast is.'

'Yes, doctor, sorry,' mumbled Olivia.

'I despair sometimes, I really do,' said Carla.

The walls and floor of the autopsy room were fully tiled, spotlessly clean and smelt surprisingly fresh. Bright early morning light filtered in through the high narrow windows and, with the addition of four large halogen lights suspended over each of the autopsy tables, it looked almost cheerful. On the right were two large sinks and up above, to the left, was an observation balcony where Rose was standing. She gave a tentative wave.

Taking a deep breath, Madeline entered. The man working at the first table glanced up as she passed and gave a brusque nod. 'Quite a challenge, this,' he said, indicating a mass of bone fragments laid out on the table, 'better than a 1000 piece puzzle any day.'

Madeline gave him a weak smile.

'Hopkins, Bryan Hopkins, Forensic Anthropologist,' he said, 'and you must be our new Inspector. Lawson's been telling me all about you.'

'Ah, right, yes, said Madeline, averting her eyes from the array of bones. 'Good to meet you,'

'Skull fragments,' said Hopkins, 'from a farm over Nether Silton way.'

'Looks complicated.'

'The complicated bit was sifting through all the silt to recover the fragments in the first place,' said Hopkins. 'It's taken us nearly two months. The new owners are rather put out. It's certainly put a halt to their plans for converting the place into a glamping site which, if you ask me, is no bad...'

'Driscoll, are you going to join me over here, or has Hopkins overwhelmed you with his charm?' said Jeremy.

'On my way—good luck with your puzzle,' said Madeline, making her way across to the far table.

The sight of the tiny skeletal remains on the massive stainless-steel table nearly sent Madeline over the edge. Even Jeremy looked drawn. 'No matter how many of these I do,' he said, 'it's never easy.'

Madeline nodded, swallowed and remained silent.

'Right,' said Jeremy. 'To summarise. These are the remains of a female baby, aged approximately two months. She was found lying, exposed, in a shallow grave, close to the lake in Vicar's Moor Wood. Various factors, including the location and weather, allow me to estimate that the burial took place eight to nine weeks ago.'

Madeline screwed her eyes shut. 'That takes us back to May, doesn't it?'

'It does.'

'Lilly Green was abducted in May.'

'Indeed she was.'

'Any idea how the baby died?'

'Not really. Apart from the leg the dog ripped from the remains, there's no evidence of any trauma, pre or post-mortem to the skeleton. The fingers of both hands were tightly clenched. I extracted some yellow fibres. These are currently being analysed in the lab. I've also sent a bone sample across to Donald for DNA analysis.'

'And how long will that take?'

'Avery has prioritised the work, so days rather than weeks.'

'Are the clenched hands significant?'

'An excellent question and, as it happens, yes, they do have significance.'

Madeline waited. Jeremy busied himself with the remains.

'Well?'

'Well, what?'

'The *significance*?'

'Ah, yes. Clenched hands are often found when an individual has been fighting for breath. This could be due to suffocation, intentional or unintentional, or, in the case of babies of this age, it could be due to SIDS.'

Madeline frowned.

'Sudden infant death syndrome, more commonly referred to as cot death.'

'So, you're saying we don't know if this baby's death was due to murder or natural causes.'

'Exactly. All I will say is there's no blunt force trauma to the skull and this leads me to doubt a violent murder. Babies who are killed are usually shaken violently first, then either struck with a weapon of some sort, or banged into a wall,' he said, as he moved over to one of the sinks to wash his hands.

'But the death could have been an intentional suffocation?'

'Possibly.'

'Or, the baby could have died from cot death.'

'Again, possibly,' said Jeremy, scrubbing his hands, 'but we're entering a minefield here, my dear. I have no lungs to examine, no heart and no brain for a start. I'd also need to know *where* the baby died and I'd need to review the baby's medical records, and even then I couldn't be sure. Often, in such cases, we're left with concluding that we know what *didn't* cause the death, but as to whether it was cot death, frankly it's just another way of saying we don't know.' He ripped a paper towel from the dispenser and turned to face Madeline. 'There are about three-hundred babies a year whose deaths are put down to cot death.'

'Three-hundred?' exclaimed Madeline.

Jeremy nodded. 'Yes, ninety percent of them are under six months old, with the peak occurring at two months.' He tossed the towel into the bin.

'The same age as the remains.'

Jeremy nodded again. 'It might also interest you to know that some research suggests that premature babies are more at risk of dying from cot death than full term babies, although, as in all medical research, not everyone agrees with that.'

'OK, well that's something at least, thanks,' said Madeline. She looked up towards the observation balcony and gave Rose a brief nod as she made her way towards the door.

She was about to reach for the handle when the door was thrown open and she was confronted by the expansive chest of an imposing figure. 'Hello there. I've just been chatting to Rose. It seems you've been thrown in at the deep end. I'm just sorry I haven't been able to help. Still, Joe assures me that you're more than capable,' he said, extending his arm towards Madeline. 'Inspector Richard Soames, Joe Reed's friend. He may have mentioned me.'

Madeline tilted her head so that her eyes no longer focused on Richard's chest and smiled up at him as she shook his hand. 'Ah, yes, he most certainly did. Good to meet you.'

Richard inclined his head towards Jeremy. 'Remains of a two-month-old baby, I hear.'

Madeline nodded.

'Coping alright with that?'

'As well as can be expected, I suppose.'

'That's the ticket,' said Richard.

'Soames, when you've finished chatting,' said Hopkins, 'you might be interested to see this skull. It seems to have an interesting hole in the temporal bone.'

Richard's eyes blazed. 'A gun-shot wound?'

'Highly likely, I'd say.'

'Interesting,' said Richard. Turning his attention back to Madeline, he added, 'When we're both free of human remains, we must go for a drink. Good luck with finding Lilly Green. Let's hope she's not currently lying on Jeremy's table.'

Chapter 9
Tuesday 16th July

Madeline's mobile woke her at 7am. In a voice thick with sleep, she mumbled, 'Madeline Driscoll.'

'Jeremy Lawson here. Sorry to wake you, but I thought you'd like to know. Donald's just sent me the DNA results.'

She sat bolt upright. 'And?'

'Well, as you no doubt know, when comparing DNA samples we're looking for common mark…'

'Get to the bloody point. Are the remains those of Lilly Green or not?'

Jeremy cleared his throat with thunderous force.

'Jesus, Jeremy,' exclaimed Madeline, moving the phone away.

Bringing the phone back towards her ear, she heard Jeremy saying, '…so, there we are, good and bad news I suppose.'

'What?'

'The *results*. They're good in some ways but…'

'I didn't hear the results,' exclaimed Madeline.

Jeremy tut-tutted. 'The DNA of Mr and Mrs Green do not match the DNA of the remains. This means the remains are…'

'Jeremy, I'm perfectly aware of what that means,' she said through gritted teeth. 'It means the remains in the woods are *not* those of Lilly Green.'

'Quite right my dear, so, good news for the Greens at least. I'll talk to you later, no doubt.'

Madeline ended the call and let the phone drop onto the bed. She leaned back against the headboard and closed her eyes. *So, where are you Lilly? Who took you? And whose are the remains?*

She threw the bedclothes back, scrabbled into her clothes, stumbled down to the kitchen, flicked the kettle on and lit a cigarette. She scrolled through her contacts and hit the call button.

'The shit's well and truly hit the fan,' she said. 'I need you at the station pronto. Get your butt in gear and…'

'Dear lady, may I make two small requests? One, would you be kind enough to moderate your language and two, please inform me of your identity.'

'I, you what? Sorry, who the hell are you?'

'I believe I asked first. I await your response.'

'Look, I haven't got time for all this, put Rose on.'

A sharp intake of breath winged its way down the line.

'Fine, this is Inspector Madeline Driscoll speaking and…'

'There we are, that didn't hurt, did it? I am Dorothy Scott, Rose's mother. Hold the line, I shall fetch her.'

Madeline's brows knitted into a frown as she stared at the phone. In the background, she heard Rose's irate voice demanding the return of her phone. There was a clunk and then, 'Inspector, sorry about that. Is there a problem?'

Madeline explained.

'Bloody…'

'Rose, please!' cried Mrs Scott from the background.

A tiny smile flickered at the corner of Madeline's mouth.

'Mother,' exclaimed Rose. 'I'm on my way, Inspector. See you at the station.'

Rose rushed into Madeline's office. 'Mother insists on sticking her nose in.' She swallowed. 'I hope she wasn't too blunt.'

Madeline held up her hand. 'Don't worry about it.'

'Anyway, the case—I suppose it's good news for Mr and Mrs Green,' said Rose.

'Yes, I *know* that,' snapped Madeline. 'Doesn't get us any closer to knowing where the bloody hell their baby is though, does it?'

'Well no, but…'

'And now we've got an unidentified dead baby to deal with as well.'

'Yes, I realise that, I was just saying…'

'Oh, shit, Rose, sorry. It's just…'

'You hoped we would have located Lilly Green by now.' Madeline nodded.

'At the risk of having my head bitten off, I repeat, we can at least give Mr and Mrs Green the good news that the remains aren't those of their baby.'

There were several reporters hanging around outside the Green's house when Madeline and Rose arrived, including the obnoxious David Mason who lumbered up to Madeline and thrust a microphone under her nose. 'David Mason, *Thirsk Post*. So, have you identified the remains? Is it Lilly Green? Have you got any suspects?'

Guy Richards muttered under his breath. 'For the love of God.'

Madeline bent towards the microphone.

David salivated.

'No comment, no comment and no comment,' she said. 'And if you don't extract that thing from my face and move out of my way instantly, I'll arrest you for obstruction. Do I make myself clear?'

Muttering obscenities under his breath, David Mason slunk away.

Guy moved forward. 'Guy Richards, *Yorkshire Herald*. I…'

'No bloody comment,' she exclaimed.

'I was just going to ask if there's going to be a police statement later on today.'

'Ah, right, sorry,' she said, 'yes, a press statement will be made later today, but I'm afraid I don't know when exactly.'

'No reason why you should,' he responded with a warm smile. 'Good luck with the Greens. It can't be easy.'

Madeline flashed him a smile. 'Thanks.' Turning, she nodded towards Rose and they made their way up the drive towards the front door.

'Was there any evidence of foul play?' David yelled, as Mr Green opened the front door.

Stephen grabbed Madeline's arm. 'Just get inside,' he growled. 'They've been there since Friday. Fucking vultures. Can't you order them to leave us alone?'

'As long as they remain outside the boundary of your property, I'm afraid there's nothing I can do, sorry.'

Stephen slammed the door shut and ushered them into the kitchen.

'Sally,' he said quietly. 'The police are here.'

Her eyes darted towards Stephen, who gave a small shrug.

'I won't keep you in suspense,' said Madeline. 'The remains found in Vicar's Moor Wood on Friday are not, I repeat *not*, those of your daughter.'

'I *knew* it! Didn't I say, Stephen? I said it couldn't be her. I felt it here,' she cried, as she clutched at her chest. 'Thank you, oh, thank you.'

Stephen closed his eyes for a moment and asked, 'So, what happens now?'

'We have two issues now. One is to identify the remains that were found in the wood, which of course isn't your problem. The other is to locate Lilly.'

'Oh, Stephen, where's our poor baby?'

Stephen gazed at his wife as tears began to form in his eyes. 'I don't know, Sally. I simply don't know.'

'If it's any help,' interjected Rose, 'I can tell you that in almost all cases of child abduction by women who have suffered a traumatic loss, you know, like the death of their baby, the child they take is well cared for and loved.'

Stephen's eyes lit up. 'Are you saying the remains in the woods are those of that Yvette woman's baby? Does that mean you've found out who she is?'

Madeline threw Rose a stern look. 'As I said, Mr Green, we haven't been able to identify the remains as yet. All we know for certain is that they're not Lilly,' she said. 'As soon as we have any news, we'll be in touch.'

At the front door, Madeline turned as Stephen came rushing down the corridor.

'Inspector, about what,' Stephen nodded towards Rose.

'Sergeant Scott.'

'Yes, sorry. About what Sergeant Scott just said, you know, about the woman looking after our baby,' he gabbled. 'Sally said the woman asked her what milk powder Lilly was used to, how often she had a bottle and what volume she normally drank. And she was thinking that this implied, you know, that Lilly's being looked after and everything. That's right, isn't it? I mean, we can at least take some comfort in that, can't we?'

Madeline rested her hand on Stephen's arm. 'Let's hope so, yes.'

Back at the station, Madeline made her way towards the incident boards while Rose collected a couple of coffees. 'OK you lot, gather round. We've now got two investigations. The abduction of Lilly Green, she tapped the first incident board with a marker pen, 'And,' tapping the second incident board, 'the unidentified remains of a two-month-old baby found buried in Vicar's Moor Wood.'

All eyes were on her.

'Let's review the Lilly Green case. We've got a description of a car that's so vague it's useless. We've got two names, Yvette Young and Anne Smith, both used by the perpetrator and almost certainly fictitious. We have evidence that a woman fitting the description of Yvette Young stayed at the Poplars Hotel, travelled to York and visited the library in Thirsk. We have statements from twelve women who were visited by Yvette Young in the days preceding Lilly Green's abduction.' She took a sip of coffee. 'The question we asked was, why Lilly Green?' She peered at her audience.

All eyes remained fixed on her. No one spoke.

'In other words, why had the perpetrator rejected the first twelve babies? What was it about Lilly Green? At first it seemed likely that she was looking for a replacement, one that was similar to a baby she may have lost recently.'

A hand shot up. 'But we dismissed that idea,' said Constable Walsh. He looked around as a wave of doubt crossed his face. 'Didn't we?'

'Yes, we did, lad,' said Sergeant Bennett.

Madeline moved across to the second incident board. 'We know these remains are not the remains of Lilly Green,' she said, taking another sip of coffee.

Rose nodded. 'We also know that they are the remains of a two-month-old baby that have been in the ground for about two months.'

'So, are you saying the remains are those of Yvette Young's baby?' said Sergeant Bennett.

'I think they could be, yes, Stuart,' said Madeline.

'It certainly correlates with the time Lilly Green was abducted,' said Rose.

'But we won't know for sure until we find Yvette Young.'

'Has Jeremy determined cause of death?' asked Sergeant Bennett.

'Not really, no. There was no evidence of blunt force trauma to the skull. The current theory is the baby died from suffocation,' said Madeline, uncapping the marker pen and writing 'no blunt force trauma', 'clenched hands' and 'SIDS' onto the board.

'SIDS?' said Constable Jones.

'That's cot death to you and me,' said Madeline, as she recapped the pen. 'It's more common in babies aged two months, and also more likely to affect premature babies.'

'So, shouldn't we be looking into recent cases of premature births?' asked Jones.

Madeline levelled a glowering look over the assembled officers. 'Sorry, are Sergeant Bennett and Constables Jones and Walsh the only ones awake here?'

Sounds of foot-shuffling and paper-riffling filled the air.

Madeline's eyes rolled skyward. 'To answer your question, Jones, Jeremy's reluctant to put too much weight on the premature baby issue, but it's all we've got.' Madeline took a huge gulp of coffee. 'Jesus, Rose, I don't know how you can drink this shit,' she moaned, as she chucked the grey liquid into the soil of a fig plant, donated to the station by her mother.

'You'll kill it,' said Rose.

'Rather it than me,' said Madeline, staring at the two boards. 'We're stuck. I can't see how we can move forward on either case.' She threw the pen at the board. It bounced off and rolled to the floor. 'It's bloody hopeless.'

'Excuse me.'

'Yes, Jones?' snapped Madeline.

'Did anyone check garages about that car?'

'Check what? I've just explained the description was less than useless.'

'But we know it was green, large and boxy, don't we?'

'Yes, Jones,' said Madeline, full of exasperation, 'but we don't know the model and we haven't got a single digit or letter from the registration number.'

'I know,' said Jones, 'but large and boxy implies vintage to me.'

'That's what I said,' said Rose.

'What's your point, Jones?'

'My brother owns a garage in York, ma'am. He specialises in vintage cars. He does alright, vintage cars need a lot of maintenance, you see. I'd be happy to check.'

Madeline ran her hand through her hair. 'We don't even know if this woman is local, Jones. She could have come from anywhere.'

Sergeant Bennett broke in. 'It might be worth letting the lad speak to his brother though, Inspector.'

'Oh, fine, what the hell,' said Madeline. 'Go ahead. It can't do any harm.'

Rose stepped forward and retrieved the marker pen from the floor. She placed a cross over Vicar's Moor Wood. 'We're looking for a woman who buried her baby here,' she said, tapping the position of the wood. 'So, we need to find where this woman might live; I reckon we should concentrate on places within what, a twenty-mile radius?' She drew a circle on the map.

'That's a bloody big area,' said Sergeant Bennett.

Rose looked. 'Too big?'

'Make it a ten-mile radius. What does that give us?'

'We're guessing either way,' said Rose, redrawing the circle.

Madeline cocked her head to one side as she examined the area. 'So, we're working on the theory that Yvette's premature baby dies of cot death at two months. In shock, she drives her dead baby from one of these villages to Vicar's Moor Wood. Once there, she buries the baby.'

'Yes,' asserted Rose, 'and, having completed this gruesome task, she sets off in search of a lookalike as a replacement.'

'So one; she didn't report the death of her baby and two; she was in shock and so wouldn't be able to drive far?' said Sergeant Bennett.

'Exactly,' said Rose, turning to Madeline. 'It makes sense, doesn't it?'

'It's all we've got,' said Madeline.

Rose recapped the marker pen with a flourish. 'In other words, there's a woman out there who has a baby that looks like her baby, but it isn't her baby because her baby has died and she's nicked Sally Green's baby.'

'Exactly, couldn't have put it better myself,' said Madeline with a trace of a smile. 'Right, we need to concentrate on women who gave birth to premature babies in March. So, Rose, can you get onto that?'

Rose set her virtually full cup of coffee on the nearest desk and dashed over to her computer.

'And, Jones, follow up on your idea with your brother.'

Jones looked around the room and nodded.

'Today would be good.'

'Oh, yes right, sorry.'

'Anything Sergeant Ross and I can do?' said Bennett.

'Go over the statements from the Lilly Green case, see if we missed anything.'

'No problem.'

'The rest of you, try to get your brains into gear. We need a lead, and we need it soon.'

Half an hour later, Rose knocked on Madeline's door and stepped inside. 'This is hopeless,' she said.'

'What is?'

'The numbers. I had no idea there were so many babies born around here. There were four thousand babies born in Northallerton alone last year, four thousand in Middlesbrough and two and a half thousand in Harrogate. That's over eight hundred babies born each month. About five percent were premature, which means we've got at least forty premature babies.' She retreated back towards the door. 'If I include all the NHS and Private maternity units in the ten-mile radius, we'll end up with hundreds.'

Taking a deep breath, Madeline said, 'Right, so we need to get you some help.'

'I could get Justin onto it.'

'Justin?'

'Haven't you been introduced to our living, breathing search engine?'

'I beg your pardon?'

'Justin Waverly-Hawkins, our resident computer whiz; brain the size of the Large Hadron Collider and an ego to match.'

'Oh, yes, Avery did mention him. Are you saying he can collate data quickly?'

'I am.'

'So, what are you waiting for?'

'I'll get him onto it straight away,' said Rose.

Madeline picked up the autopsy report on the Vicar's Moor baby. She read it through and sighed. Scanning the first page again, she shot out of her chair. 'That's it,' she exclaimed.

Clutching the page to her chest, she dashed over towards Rose. 'Hold everything. I'm an idiot. It's so obvious. I mean I can't believe I didn't think of it before.'

'Didn't think of what?'

'It's in the report, Rose, it's been staring at me all this time. Jeremy took extensive measurements of the remains.'

'Yes, and?'

'So, we know the length of the dead baby *and* we also know the head circumference.'

Rose frowned. 'I'm obviously missing something.'

Madeline flopped onto the chair next to Rose. 'My mum has detailed records of my growth from birth to one year. She has them in a red book issued by her postnatal clinic. Head circumference, length, weight.' Madeline took a deep breath. 'Don't you see? She has measurements from the day of my birth until I reached one year of age. Your mother will have one too, *all* mothers have them and all clinics will have records of those measurements.'

Rose's eyes widened. 'Oh, I see,' she exclaimed.

'Babies usually have reviews at regular intervals and one of those reviews is carried out at about eight weeks. And, if we're on the right track, this Yvette wouldn't have attended this review because that's when her baby died.'

'And, if she didn't turn up with her baby for that review, she would have been contacted,' said Rose.

'Exactly.'

'I'll let Justin know.'

Madeline looked over towards the bank of filing cabinets. 'He has a little nest area over there doesn't he?'

'A nest area yes, absolutely, an excellent description,' said Rose with a smirk.

'Well, come on, I'd like to meet this genius.'

'He's not particularly sociable.'

'I'm not about to invite him to a party, Rose.'

'Fine, follow me.'

Justin looked up when Madeline, arm held in front of her, appeared from behind his filing cabinet wall. 'I'm Inspec…'

'I know who you are. I've been thinking,' he said. 'At first, I thought we should concentrate on the premature babies whose measurements at two months matched those of the remains…'

'But, that's just it, I was…'

'But of course, if your theory is correct, there won't be a measurement because the baby would have died. She would have missed her review appointment.'

'And the clinic would have…'

'Rung her or sent a letter, yes, Inspector, thank you. I have the relevant information here and I've made a start, but I need to get on.' He gave a curt nod and resumed tapping at his keyboard.

Holding her head high, Madeline did an about turn and negotiated her way around the filing cabinets. Rose followed.

Chapter 10
Thursday 18ᵗʰ July

Guy's report, 'The Lucky Thirteen', had been shelved the moment the remains had been discovered. His new report appeared in the Thursday edition of the *Yorkshire Herald*.

```
             BABE IN THE WOODS
             BY GUY RICHARDS

… it has been established that the baby isn't Lilly
Green, it's my belief that the baby belonged to the
woman who took Lilly Green. If this is true, then it's
highly likely that she lives near that wood.
     One can only imagine the pain and torture this woman
was suffering; pain that drove her to commit such a
heinous crime, a crime that has caused terrible anguish
and grief to Sally and Stephen Green.
     It is difficult to know how the police can proceed.
They will have DNA from the baby's remains, but without
any DNA to compare it with, the mother will remain a
mystery. It seems that somewhere, probably somewhere
not too far away, a woman is raising a child who is not
her own; a child named Lilly Green.'
```

Madeline threw the paper onto Rose's desk. 'Have you seen this,' she yelled.

'Uh huh.'

'Has he got a bloody microphone in the police station?'

'I assume that's a rhetorical question,' mumbled Rose.

'Or, has someone been talking to him?'

'I hope you're not suggesting that I would talk to a reporter about an ongoing case, I mean, really?'

'No, no, of course not, sorry,' said Madeline, perusing the sea of faces now glaring up at her from their desks. 'Was it one of you lot then?'

Rose blanched. 'I honestly wouldn't have thought so, no,' she said, as she began to ease Madeline back towards her office.

Sergeant Bennett catapulted himself from his chair and blocked their progress. 'I realise you must be frustrated, Inspector, but I'd advise you to be very careful about throwing accusations like that about.'

A voice boomed out across the room. 'Ah, Inspector Driscoll, I was going to leave this file on your desk.'

'Ah, Donald, excellent timing,' said Madeline, as she manoeuvred her way around Bennett. 'Please tell me you've got me a decent lead.'

'Not exactly,' he said. 'It's about those yellow fibres.'

'And?'

'I fear the results will not help much with identification.' He flipped the file open. 'I've summarised my findings here,' he said, indicating the relevant section. 'The fibres are 8 ply wool, colour-code Yellow-065. The brand is Ashford Tekapo DK, from New Zealand, available from most decent wool shops. It's sold in Leeds, York, Manchester, Liverpool and London, I could go on. I'm told it's very popular, especially for items such as cot blankets,' he said, handing her the file.

Madeline's shoulders dropped. 'Right, fine. Well, thanks for taking the time to bring the results directly up to me.'

'No problem. I like to pop up on occasions, to see how the other half lives,' he said, as he examined the room.

Madeline followed his gaze. 'Not exactly like your pristine shiny lab,' she said, as she glanced over her shoulder towards Sergeant Bennett. 'Still, they do say it's not the environment you work in, but the people you work with that matter, isn't that right?'

Bennett bowed his head.

'Quite right, Inspector,' said Donald, 'indeed, some of the most important scientific discoveries have been made in the humblest of establishments. For example, I remember…'

Avery's hand landed on his shoulder.

'Donald, do give it a rest, we're already late. The committee meeting started ten minutes ago.'

'It seems duty calls. Sorry the results couldn't have been more helpful.'

In the gardens of the *Duck Inn,* Binton-on-Wiske, the Thursday edition of the *Yorkshire Herald* lay open on the table, amidst the detritus of lunch.

'Oh, Olivia, it's terrible, isn't it?' remarked Barbara, as she scanned the report.

Jack and Lawrence, deep in conversation, gave cursory nods.

Olivia raised her eyebrows. 'They look like little school boys discussing their past pranks.'

'I know,' said Barbara. 'Fancy your Lawrence knowing Jack's old friend Christopher. It's a small world.'

'As dear Carla would say,' said Olivia, 'old drag queens tend to stick together.'

Still deep in their own conversation, Jack burst into raucous laughter and thumped Lawrence's shoulder. 'Now that I would have liked to have seen,' he said.

'It was alarmingly good fun,' said Lawrence.

'I just can't imagine, well, you know,' said Barbara, inclining her head towards Lawrence.

'Lawrence sashaying about in high heels and a frock,' said Olivia. 'No, I know. I wish you could have seen Carla's face when she discovered his little box of lurid costumes.'

'Carla did mention something about it,' said Barbara, a smile playing at the corner of her mouth. 'It was soon after you moved to the village last year, wasn't it?'

Olivia nodded. 'Yes, it was during the last week of June. Lawrence had to attend a briefing, one of many in Aldershot, before his last assignment. Carla and Martin were brilliant. They helped with the decorating and, at one point, Carla was on a ladder waving a loaded paintbrush around her head. I swear she was putting more paint into her hair than onto the wall,' exclaimed Olivia with a smile.

'Typical, Carla,' remarked Barbara, as she returned her attention to the report in the newspaper.

Olivia smiled and stared off into the distance as she thought back to that time, just over a year ago, when she had watched the drips of white paint land in Carla's wild tangle of thick black hair.

'I could hardly believe my ears when Martin told me who was buying his parents' old cottage,' Carla had said, oblivious to the smirks on the faces of Olivia and Martin as drips of white paint continued to land in her hair.

'And I could hardly believe my ears when Lawrence told me he'd bought it. As you know, I was devastated to be leaving our army quarters.'

'Oh, I quite understand,' said Carla. 'A terrible wrench to leave such tastefully-decorated accommodation.'

'And goodness knows how I'll cope without all those exciting activities.'

'Oh, my dear Olivia, you poor, poor thing. What *will* you do with yourself stuck out here in this idyllic spot?'

'And of course, I shall especially miss those charming officer's wives.'

'Yes, yes, I quite understand. Such a frightful shame.'

'Now, now ladies,' said Martin. 'I'm sure they couldn't have been that bad.'

'They bloody were, Martin. A more stuck up, pretentious load of self-satisfied twits would be hard to find,' said Olivia. '*And* they all supported fox-hunting.'

'Yes, I hear there's such a problem with foxes worrying the sheep in Aldershot, don't you know,' declared Carla.

'I give up,' said Martin.

'A wise decision,' said Carla, returning her attention to the wall she was painting for a brief moment. 'Oh, by the way, Olivia, do you fancy a trip over to Thirsk next week?

There's a marvellous little reclamation centre there. Barbara and I go there often. We thought you might be able to find some interesting pieces for the cottage, what do you think?'

'Sounds great,' said Olivia. 'What day are you going?'

'Friday, my day off, is that OK for you?'

'That would be great—oh, hang on—it's July next week, isn't it?'

'It is.'

'So, next Friday must be the sixth.'

'Uh, hah,' she muttered, as she concentrated on a particularly tricky corner section.

'Then, sorry, no can do,' replied Olivia. 'A colleague of mine, Dr Philip Sutcliffe, is coming over. We've got the final details to sort out for the symposium, which starts on the thirteenth. I can't believe it. Time's just melted away.'

'No problem, we can go another time.' Carla stepped down from the ladder to admire her handy work. 'Oh, hell,' she cried. 'I've really messed that corner up.'

Martin raised his eyebrows and relieved her of her brush. 'Give it here,' he said. 'I'll sort it out.'

'How about tea?' suggested Olivia.

'Excellent suggestion, but I'd prefer a coffee,' said Carla. 'I'll do it.'

'Did I hear mention of coffee?' said Martin from the top of the ladder.

'You did. I take it you'd like one?'

'I could bloody murder one.'

'I'm afraid the coffee's still in a cardboard box somewhere,' said Olivia.

'OK, no problem,' called Carla. 'I'll find it.'

After ten minutes, Olivia wandered into the kitchen. 'Is everything alright? You seem to have been—what the...?'

Carla was sat cross-legged on the kitchen floor. She was surrounded by a variety of good quality wigs, a selection of brightly coloured feather boas, several large bras, at least half a dozen garish, off-the-shoulder dresses, hats and three pairs of high-heeled shoes.

'These were in a box labelled *L.Hamilton. 1988/91*. Is there something you need to tell me?'

Olivia raised her hand to her forehead. 'Oh, God, how mortifying, I thought Lawrence had put those away. This is *so* embarrassing. Well, there we are, nothing to be done now. You've discovered his secret fetish.'

'Seriously?'

Olivia shrugged.

Carla's mouth dropped open.

'No, Carla, I'm not being serious. God, your face.'

'But, what? Why?'

'Those are the costumes he used for the Army Christmas reviews.'

Olivia's smile broadened, she tapped Barbara's arm. 'Soon after Carla discovered Lawrence's box I remember grabbing hold of a wig and shoving it on my head. So, there I was, dancing around Carla, who'd donned several boas and a massive pink hat, when Martin stuck his head round the door. And then, and then, oh, dear.' Olivia took a deep breath. 'And then, he snatched up a wig, slung a massive lilac bra over his t-shirt and joined in the dancing.'

Barbara snorted. 'Martin, that stick-thin man, adorned in a wig and bra, prancing round your kitchen, now that I would pay to see.'

'He looked surprisingly good actually,' said Olivia, looking at Amelia, who lay sleeping in her lap.

Barbara's attention once again returned to the newspaper report. 'I just can't imagine how terrible it must be for those poor parents, can you?'

'Sorry, what?' said Olivia.

Barbara laid her hand across the paper. 'Lilly Green's parents.'

Olivia cuddled Amelia tightly to her chest. 'Oh, right, yes, it's awful.'

'What do *you* think about what the reporter suggests? I mean, is it plausible that a woman could do such a thing, you know, if her own baby had died. Would that be enough to drive her over the edge?'

'I really don't know, Barbara, I'm a scientist not a psychologist.'

'No, no, of course not. I just wondered, sorry.'

Olivia swallowed. 'It's just not my field of expertise.'

'I appreciate that, I just thought you might have some idea if it could be true.'

'It obviously happens,' said Olivia. 'But research shows that these women are unlikely to harm the baby. It's not as if they're deranged or mentally ill, just desperately sad.'

'You know a bit then?'

'Only what I've read in my editorial role, Barbara.'

'And the DNA thing. Is that right?'

'In what way?'

'He says here...' Barbara searched through the article, 'here: ...*They will have DNA from the baby's remains, but without any DNA to compare it with, the mother will remain a mystery...* Is that right? I mean, if they have the baby's DNA, can't they look it up on a database?'

'The police don't have everyone's DNA on file, thank God, that would be too Orwellian,' said Olivia. 'No, he's quite right. They need a sample of the mother's DNA to compare with the baby's DNA. They look for common markers, the greater the overlap, the greater the likelihood of a relationship existing. So, if...'

'So, if the police don't have a clue about the mother or the father of the dead baby, they can't get DNA samples to confirm or refute their suspicion, is that right?'

'Yes, that's right. Unless either of the parents had a criminal record, in which case their DNA *would* be on file.'

'Madeline was telling me the other day about a case back in 1990 when a five-month-old baby, Ames Glover, was kidnapped and he still hasn't been traced. It's the longest-running child abduction in Britain.'

Olivia stroked the top of Amelia's head.

'Jack,' said Barbara.

He didn't respond. Barbara gave him a thump on his arm. 'Jack!'

'Ow! What?'

'What do you think?'

'About what, dear love of my life?'

'About this case.' She waved the newspaper under his nose.

'It's a tricky one. It's really got to Madeline. But essentially, they've reached a dead end.'

'So, they haven't got any leads?' asked Olivia.

'None whatsoever. And frankly, the longer it goes on, the less likely it is that they'll ever find out what happened. The assertion made by the reporter, that the mother of the dead baby is the same woman who abducted Lilly Green, is entirely plausible, but it doesn't get the police any closer to knowing who that woman is.'

'So it could be another Ames Glover,' said Olivia.

'Oh, you know about that case?'

'Barbara was just telling me. Still, terrible though it is, I suppose the parents of both Lilly and Ames can take comfort in the knowledge that their child is being cared for by someone who loves them.'

'Well, that's true, I suppose,' remarked Jack. 'But I'm sure they'd rather have their child back.'

'Well, quite,' said Lawrence.

'Unfortunately, I fear the woman may well be long gone. She may even have left the country,' said Jack.

'I hadn't thought of that,' said Olivia. 'I suppose the police will just have to hope for some sort of breakthrough and, in the meantime, file it away as a, what do they call it?'

'A cold case,' interjected Barbara.

'That's right. Anyway, changing the subject completely,' said Jack. 'Lawrence, do you fancy a day out, fishing?'

'A day out, fishing? Absolutely, yes.'

'Fishing? I didn't know you liked fishing,' remarked Olivia.

'I haven't been for years,' said Lawrence. 'I used to go with my dad when I was a kid.' He smiled. 'I remember this one time, when Dad didn't catch a thing, and…'

'Happens a lot, I fear,' said Jack.

Lawrence nodded. 'Oh, I know, but Mum was expecting him to bring home the supper, so the old fool panicked and bought a couple of fish from the fishmongers,' Lawrence paused, his lip quivering. 'The only thing was…' He snorted and his eyes filled with tears. 'The only thing was, when the fishmonger asked him if he wanted the fish gutted, Dad said yes!' Lawrence dragged the back of his hand across his eyes. 'Mum was a brick. She took the fish and never said a word. To this day, Dad thinks he got away with it.'

'Oh, that's classic, isn't it, Jack?' said Barbara.

Jack averted his gaze.

'Jack?' said Barbara.

'Yes?'

'You're blushing.'

'Am I? Can't think why,' said Jack. 'So, Lawrence, you're definitely up for it?'

'Absolutely.'

'Excellent. It just so happens that our old mate, Christopher Baker, rang me last week. His wife has consented to give him leave of absence and we arranged to spend tomorrow on the river.'

'It'd be good to see the old devil again,' said Lawrence.

'He's a member of the Northallerton and District Angling Club. There's a brilliant spot on the River Swale, just outside Far Fairholme. Have you got a rod and stuff?'

Lawrence's face fell. 'No, not anymore.'

'No problem, we can rent you the necessary from the club,' said Jack.

'You don't mind, do you, Olivia?'

'I shall have potatoes and salad ready to accompany the fish you bring home,' said Olivia.

Chapter 11
Friday 19th July

Guy was at home, perched on his desk chair, elbows resting on his knees, chin cupped in his hands and eyes focused on the single column of thirteen cards; the *Lucky Thirteen*, which were still stuck to his wall.

He stood and wandered over to the wall. Merlin followed him and sat at his feet.

'What do you reckon?' said Guy. 'Were they lucky, or am I missing something?'

He ripped them from the wall, pulling flakes of paint with them, and laid them out on the floor. Merlin walked over the cards, sniffing each one with great care.

'Well, anything strike you?'

The cat wandered off.

'Obviously not,' said Guy, hauling himself upright and following the cat into the kitchen. He flicked on the kettle, yanked open a cupboard, removed a mug and heaped a teaspoon of coffee into it. He stretched his back and rocked his head from side to side as he waited for the kettle to boil. The cat twirled between his legs, miaowing.

'Something's in here,' said Guy, banging his forehead with the back of his hand, 'something significant, I'm sure.' He poured the boiling water over the coffee granules.

The cat continued to miaow.

'Alright, I get the hint. Tuna or chicken?'

The cat miaowed louder.

'I'll decide then,' said Guy, ripping open a pouch of tuna. 'God, Merlin, this stuff stinks.'

Guy went back to the cards. Sitting cross-legged, he took a swig of coffee and arranged the cards by place. 'OK, so that's two in Thirsk, two in Binton-on-Wiske, one in Dalton, two in Topcliffe and the rest in Northallerton.' He sat back on his heels. 'So, does that help?'

Merlin sauntered back into the living room, plonked himself onto the cards and began his ablutions.

'No, it doesn't help at all. OK, let's go back to the beginning.' He struggled to his feet again, tore a sheet of A3 from a folder and grabbed a pen. Sitting back down and thinking out loud, he began to draw up a mind map. 'A woman's baby dies—she buries it in Vicar's Moor Wood— so, it's likely she lives nearby.'

He encouraged Merlin to move with a gentle shove and checked the cards. 'Well, that doesn't help—you're all quite near to the woods—OK, baby buried—she drives over to Thirsk—books into Poplars Hotel—checks local papers, where, library?—I found twenty-six names. Did *she* find those same twenty-six names? That's a lot of names. Was it just luck that she found Lilly after only visiting twelve of these women? Think man, think.'

He stood up and ripped the remaining thirteen cards from the wall and showed them to Merlin. 'OK, these women were visited by Yvette Young. Sally Green was the thirteenth woman to be visited and her baby was the one selected. But why?' He sat back down and glanced at the cards on the floor. 'And those are the women Yvette Young didn't visit.' He leaned back on his haunches again and rubbed his forehead. He stared up at the ceiling. 'Fuck.' He pushed himself up, dashed over to his desk and began rummaging through piles of paperwork. 'Come on, come on, where are—ah, got you!' He waved the sheet of paper above his head in triumph. Merlin, hating the sound of rustling paper, promptly dashed off towards the kitchen.

He laid the sheet of paper, with his original twenty-six names gleaned from the *Thirsk Post* and the *Yorkshire Herald,* next to the cards. 'Yvette Young visited thirteen women who either advertised in both papers, or just in the *Thirsk Post.* What does that tell me?' He scrabbled for his mobile.

'What do you want now?'

'And good day to you too, Constable Walsh.'

'I'm busy, mate.'

'Just one tiny question.'

'What?' exclaimed Steve.

'Remember that list of names I showed you in the pub?'

'Yes.'

'I told you I got them from the birth announcements section in the papers, right?'

'Yes, and?'

'Is that what Lilly Green's abductor did?'

'Yes. Is that the question, because…?'

'No, Steve, that isn't the question. What I want to know is, what papers she looked in. Can you tell me that?'

Steve sighed. 'I suppose. Just a minute, I'll check the incident board.'

A loud clank rang in Guy's ears as Steve dropped the receiver.

'She got the names from the *Thirsk Post*.'

'What editions?'

'One bloody question, you said.'

'Oh, come on, Steve.'

'March the fifteenth and March the twenty-second.'

'And did she copy out all the names of the women who gave birth to girls from those editions?'

'Yes.'

'So, that was—hold on,' Guy checked his list. 'Seventeen names, right?'

'Yes.'

'And she only visited twelve of them before she got to Mrs Green.'

'Yes—look, is there a point to this call?'

'Bear with me,' said Guy. 'Which women weren't visited?'

'For God's sake, Guy, I…'

'I simply want to cross-check my list, nothing more.'

'Fine, hang on.'

Guy stroked Merlin. 'I bet you I know what names he's going to…'

'Taylor, Davies, Jones and Philips, now, is that it?'

'And they were spoken to, were they?'

'Oh, no we don't bother with that sort of detail here, mate—of course we bloody spoke to them.'

'Did she consult the *Yorkshire Herald*?'

'*No*, I've just bloody told you, she only consulted the *Thirsk Post*, now, I've got to go.'

Guy gathered all the cards together and divided them into three piles; those who placed announcements in the *Thirsk Post* only, those who placed announcements in the *Yorkshire Herald* only and those who placed announcements in both.

Sitting cross-legged on the floor again, the significance of the three piles of cards sank in. 'Right, Ms Yvette Young, according to Steve, you only looked in the *Thirsk Post.*' He picked up the *Thirsk Post* pile. 'So, you would have seen these three names and,' he leaned over to pick up the pile with the names of the women who'd placed announcements in both papers, 'and these fourteen names. These ones, the women you didn't bother visiting, Taylor, Davies and Jones, had their announcements in both papers and Philips had her announcement in the *Thirsk Post* only.'

Merlin slunk back into the living room and flopped down on the remaining pile of cards. Guy pushed him off and picked up the cards. 'So, why weren't you interested in the nine women who only placed their announcements in the *Yorkshire Herald*? If you were so desperate to replace your baby, why did you ignore that paper? What am I missing?' He squeezed his eyes shut and clenched his jaw. A tiny tingle crept up his spine. His eyes snapped open. 'Shit!'

With shaking hands, he picked up the nine cards of the women who'd only placed their announcements in the *Yorkshire Herald* and laid them out on the floor. Six lived in Northallerton, two in Topcliffe and one in Binton-on-

Wiske. He yanked open the bottom drawer of his desk and grabbed the map.

He sat staring at it for a few minutes. 'Look at that, Merlin. Northallerton's about ten miles from the woods, Topcliffe about seven and Binton's only a mile away.' He clenched his fists. 'Am I right? Has the answer been staring me in the face all this time?' He grabbed his jacket from the back of his chair, bent down, stroked the cat again, gathered up the nine cards and stuffed them into his jacket pocket. 'See you later.'

Olivia was in the kitchen, preparing the evening meal for Lawrence's return from his fishing trip with Jack, when there was a loud knocking at the front door.

'Mrs Hamilton?'

'Yes.'

'I'm sorry to bother you,' said Guy, holding up his press badge. 'My name is Guy Richards. I'm an investigative reporter on the *Yorkshire Herald* and I wonder if I could ask you a few questions.'

'About what?' she asked.

'I'm looking into the case of the missing baby, Lilly Green, I assume you've read about it,' he said. 'I was convinced the remains found in Vicar's Moor Wood were going to turn out to be Lilly, but I was wrong and...'

'I'm sorry,' said Olivia. 'But I fail to see how I can help.'

'I got your name from my paper's birth announcements.'

'Right, and?'

'Well, I don't know if you realise this, but your baby was born around the same time as Lilly Green.'

'So were lots of babies, Mr...?'

'Richards. Yes, I know. But I'm concentrating on local births. Anyway, I wrote an article about the latest case in yesterday's *Herald*, where I put forward the theory that Lilly Green may have been selected because...'

'Yes, I read it,' said Olivia, 'and it's an entirely plausible theory. Losing a baby could, in certain circumstances, lead a woman to commit such a crime.'

'Yes, quite. Anyway, as I was saying, given that your baby was born on March the twelfth, just a few days before Lilly Green's…'

Olivia gripped hold of the doorframe and leaned forward. 'What exactly are you implying?'

'Implying? I'm not implying anything. No, yes right, I see, no I'm sorry, we seem to be at cross purposes here.'

'Is that a fact, Mr Richards? Well, let me uncross our purposes. Firstly, my baby is currently sleeping peacefully in her cot upstairs, so any thoughts you may be harbouring that I am the mystery woman are completely erroneous…'

'I…'

'I haven't finished speaking,' said Olivia. 'Secondly, as I've already pointed out to you, large numbers of babies are born every month. For example, last year, on March the twelfth, I believe it was in the order of fifty, and that's just in Northallerton, Middlesbrough and Harrogate. You can easily check this figure.' Olivia held up her hand as Guy began to speak again. 'And finally, if it's any business of yours, I wasn't even in the village at the time—now, I don't wish to be rude, but I really must get on. I fear you've had a wasted journey.'

'Right, that's me told,' said Guy with a nervous laugh. 'Anyway, I was simply wondering if this mystery woman visited you sometime between May the fifth and the thirteenth, but obviously not. So, that's that cleared up.'

'Indeed,' said Olivia, shutting the door.

'Thank you for your time,' muttered Guy to the closed door. He posted his card through the letterbox and wandered back to his car. With music blaring from his radio, he continued along the A167 towards Topcliffe and parked his Mini on the driveway of the Bakers' house.

'Hello, can I help you?'

'Mr Baker?'

'Yes, and you are?'

Holding up his press card, Guy introduced himself and explained his business again. 'You might have seen my reports in the paper,' he said.

'I have, but, sorry, why are you here?'

'Is your wife at home?'

'She is, but I ask again, why are you here?'

'It's nothing sinister.'

'Duly noted—so, what is it?'

'I just wondered if the woman happened to visit your wife.'

'When?'

'Between May the fifth and May the thirteenth.'

'Sorry, old chap, Mary was over in Whitby in May, and I was walking the Pennine Way with an old university friend. We do the Pennines every year, regular as clockwork.'

A voice called out from the back of the house. 'Who is it, Christopher?'

Christopher called back. 'Nobody dear, just some reporter from the *Yorkshire Herald*.'

Guy gave a small flinch.

'Nothing personal, old chap.'

Wiping her hands on her apron, Mary joined Christopher at the front door. He bent down and kissed the top of his young wife's head. 'Is Emma sleeping now?'

'Yes, finally. She's in her pram on the patio,' replied Mary. 'And don't panic, I put the cat net up and the baby alarm is in my apron pocket.' She turned to Guy. 'I think she might be getting her first tooth. It's very exciting, so it is.'

'Her first tooth, gosh,' said Guy, taking a step backwards. 'Anyway, sorry to have bothered you both. It seems I've had another wasted journey.'

'Another?' remarked Christopher.

'Yes, I've just come from Binton-on-Wiske. I was speaking to a Dr Hamilton and…'

'*Olivia* Hamilton,' cried Christopher.

'Yes, why, do you know her?'

'Yes, well, no, not really, well, not at all actually, but I know her husband, Lawrence Hamilton. We were in the army together. I've just been with him, as it happens. Yes, strangest thing, I'd arranged to go fishing on the River Swale with a mate of mine and he brought Lawrence along. Haven't seen him in years. Couldn't believe it when he said he'd retired. Tells me he's writing a book about his life in the army. I said to him, I said, I jolly well hope you're going to include photos of our fun, but risqué, performances in it, otherwise it'll be a bloody boring tome.'

'Sounds intriguing.'

Christopher's barking laugh rang out. 'Yes,' he said, giving a twirl. 'Believe it or not, he and I used to dress up in drag. To entertain the troops, you understand, nothing weird or anything.'

Mary interjected. 'I'm sure Mr, um, Mr…'

'Richards,' said Guy.

'I'm sure Mr Richards isn't in the least bit interested in your infantile antics from all those years ago.' She threw Guy a forced smile.

'All men are the same, I fear,' said Guy. 'My father has also been known to indulge…'

'I'm sorry to interrupt again,' said Mary. 'But we are quite busy.'

Christopher put his arm around Mary and pulled her towards him. 'Oh, come on, love, don't begrudge an old man his memories,' he said. 'We had tremendous fun, Lawrence and I. We made quite a pair, I can tell you. I've just been looking back through my old photo albums as it happens and…'

Mary disentangled herself from Christopher's arms. 'Oh, for goodness sake, Christopher. Mr Richards doesn't want to look at your stupid photos, I...'

'I wasn't going to suggest that at all, no,' said Christopher, giving Guy a wink. 'It's just that meeting up with Lawrence got me thinking back, and for the life of me I couldn't remember what names we used.' He tapped his head. 'Brain failure I'm afraid. In my defence it was twenty-three years ago—anyway, the photos brought it all back.'

'Yes, so you said, dear,' said Mary. 'But now Emma's asleep, we can actually get some housework done.' She smiled at Guy. 'It's impossible while she's awake. She's a demanding little thing, so she is.'

Christopher was staring up towards the sky. A broad grin spread across his face. 'I chose a red wig and a gold-coloured, sequinned dress from Lawrence's box of costumes and adopted the moniker Lucy Lupin and...'

'Oh, Christopher, give it a rest,' said Mary. 'I do apologise, Mr Richards.'

'Not at all,' said Guy.

Christopher's grin broke into another barking laugh. 'Of course, Lawrence, being that much younger, looked marvellous in his garb. I actually quite fancied him when he donned his blonde wig.'

'Christopher!' exclaimed Mary.

'I jest, I jest. Mind you, he used to get love letters from the lads, all in fun of course—well, I assume they were,' he added, thumping Guy's shoulder. 'Each letter began, *I long for your touch, darling Yvette, I can't...*' He ducked to avoid a swipe from Mary. 'Sadly, Mary's not too impressed with my past career as a drag artist.'

'It was hardly a career, Christopher, honestly.'

'No, my love, I realise that. It was just a bit of fun.'

'Anyway, if there's nothing else.' Mary made to close the door.

Guy handed Christopher his card. 'Just in case,' he said. 'I can see your wife's anxious to get on. I'll be on my way. Have a …' The door was firmly shut in his face. He stood for a moment listening to the raised voice of Mary Baker berating her husband.

Guy dug his notebook from his jacket pocket and with shaking hands scribbled, *Two mothers of babies born in March, neither at home during the time of the Lilly Green abduction. Both with husbands who'd performed in drag, significantly, one used the name Yvette. Mrs Parker let slip the name Yvette Young. Can't be a coincidence. Can it?*

With a final look at the house he returned to his car. Hand still shaking, he took out his phone.

'Northallerton Police, Sergeant Bailey speaking, how can we help?'

'I'd like to speak to the officer in charge of the Lilly Green case,' said Guy.

'Who's calling?'

'My name is Guy Richards,' said Guy. 'I'm a reporter on the *Yorkshire Herald* and…'

'Inspector Driscoll doesn't speak with reporters, sir.'

'Nevertheless, I think she'll want to talk to me, you see I have some information and…'

'You can tell me, sir,' said the desk sergeant.

'I'd prefer to speak with Inspector Driscoll.'

'I'm sure you would, sir, but, as I have just explained, Inspec…'

'Inspector Driscoll doesn't speak with reporters, yes I heard,' said Guy. 'Would you be good enough to let her know I called?'

'Certainly sir, is there anything else?'

'No, thank you *so* much for your help.' Muttering under his breath, he redialled.

'Steve, hi. Listen, I think I may have stumbled onto something important concerning the Lilly Green case. I need to speak to Inspector Driscoll.'

'She doesn't...'

'Speak to reporters, yes I know, the desk sergeant said. That's why I'm ringing; could *you* persuade her to speak to me?'

'I doubt it,' said Steve. 'Just tell me, I'll pass it on.'

'I'd rather speak to the Inspector.'

'Oh, right I see, a lowly constable not good enough for you now.'

'Bloody hell, Steve, grow up—Steve, Steve, are you still there?'

Lawrence returned home a few minutes after Guy Richard's departure, to find Olivia bent over the chopping board, wielding a large knife and muttering obscenities.

'A particularly recalcitrant cucumber?' he asked.

'Oh, hi there, I didn't hear the door. How was the fishing trip?' she said, as she put down the knife and tried to peer behind Lawrence's back.

In one smooth movement, Lawrence raised his right hand above his head. Two fish, of uncertain pedigree, were swinging from this hand. 'I bring my woman food.'

'Oh, well done,' she exclaimed. 'I take it you're going to do the necessary? Everything else is ready, the salad's done, well, nearly. The potatoes are peeled and the wine's cooling.'

'Fear not,' replied Lawrence, striding towards the sink. 'Amelia OK?'

'She's fast asleep,' said Olivia. 'Oh, and, to answer your earlier question...'

'Question?'

'About the cucumber.'

'Oh, right, the cucumber.'

'A perfectly innocent cucumber,' said Olivia. 'I was angry because I had a visit from Guy Richards, that reporter from the *Yorkshire Herald*, you just missed him actually.'

Bent over the sink, attempting to look proficient at the job of beheading and gutting two fish, Lawrence muttered, 'Uh, huh.'

'Yes, he was asking about the woman who snatched Lilly Green.'

'Uh, huh.'

'And although he tried to deny it, I got the distinct impression he was accusing me.'

'Uh, huh.'

'Lawrence,' cried Olivia. 'Are you listening?'

He turned to face his wife, his hands dripping with blood and guts. 'Sorry, what did you say?'

'I *said,* I got the distinct impression he was accusing me.'

'Accusing you of what?'

'Of snatching Lilly Green.'

'Why on earth would he accuse you?'

'The stupid man latched on to the fact that Amelia was born a few days before Lilly and jumped to the conclusion that I must, therefore, be the woman who abducted her. Perfectly ridiculous.'

'But, sorry, what?' exclaimed Lawrence. 'Are you telling me he actually accused you of abducting that baby?'

'Well no, not as such, but don't forget his article, Lawrence. In it he puts forward the theory, a perfectly plausible theory, that a woman loses her baby, buries it and then abducts Lilly Green.'

'Yes, but we haven't lost Amelia, have we? She's alive and kicking, as you no doubt pointed out to him,' said Lawrence. 'He's probably just trying to keep the story alive, and that's no bad thing, is it? After all, the baby's still missing.'

'I know that, Lawrence, but...'

Lawrence groaned.

'What's the matter?'

Lawrence shifted his gaze from the sink. 'I'm afraid I've made a complete mess of this.'

Olivia stole a glance. 'Ugh, right, I see what you mean. How about using some prawns? I'm sure we've got some in the freezer.'

'Brilliant.'

With the fish wreckage consigned to the bird table, Lawrence speared a juicy prawn and remarked, 'Christopher's just become a father too, you know.' He took a gulp of wine. 'I think he's still in shock.'

'In shock?'

Lawrence nodded. 'He thought all that was behind him. He's not exactly in the flush of youth. He must be in his late sixties by now, and I got the impression his wife's a good deal younger.' He speared another prawn and devoured it. 'Anyway, we had enormous fun talking about the old days and, I hope you don't mind, but I've invited them to our little soirée tomorrow.'

'That's fine,' said Olivia, 'as long as you promise not to dress up in drag and prance around the garden, frightening the sheep.'

Justin gave a cursory knock and burst into Madeline's office, clutching a thin file.

'Ah, Mr Waverly-Hawkins at last, have you…?'

'There were ninety-eight premature births during March within a twenty-mile radius of Vicar's Moor Wood. Cross referen…'

'We were concentrating on a ten-mile radius.'

'I considered that to be a rash assumption,' said Justin. 'So, as I was saying, I found ninety-eight women who gave birth prematurely. Eight babies had a growth pattern that followed the same developmental line predicted by Dr Lawson's measurements of the remains. I eliminated two of them…'

'Why?'

'Their mothers were over five foot five inches in height,' he snapped, before pressing on. 'Four of them were sent letters informing them that they'd missed their eight-week review. I've listed their names and addresses here.' He removed a single sheet of paper from the file and thrust it into Madeline's hand.

Madeline stuck her tongue out at Justin's retreating figure. She glanced down at the sheet. 'Rose, get in here quick!'

Rose skidded to a halt in front of Madeline's desk. 'You yelled?'

'Look at this.'

Rose looked. 'Brilliant, just four names, so, what's the problem?

'This name here,' she said, pointing to the third name on the list.

'Dr Olivia Hamilton, yes, so?'

'I know her. She lives in Binton-on-Wiske. She's a friend of Carla Marchese, who just happens to be a good friend of my mother.'

'Gosh, right, well, it's probably not her then,' said Rose.

Madeline leaned back in her chair and rubbed her forehead. 'No, probably not.'

'You don't look convinced,' said Rose.

'There's just something nagging in the back of my brain,' said Madeline. 'I don't know, so bloody frustrating.'

'Try not to think about it,' said Rose, 'that's what my mother always says *Don't think, it will come.*'

'And does it?'

'Annoyingly, yes.'

'Right. Well, while I'm not thinking about that, we need to ascertain where these women were when Lilly Green was abducted, and why they missed their eight-week appointment. More importantly, we need to ensure that the baby in their care is actually theirs, agreed?'

'Agreed.'

'Good. I'll show Avery what we've got and see if she's happy that it's enough to warrant requesting DNA and then we can get started.'

Gathering the files together, Madeline made her way over to Avery's office only to find it locked. 'Does anyone know where Avery is?' she yelled.

Constable Jones responded. 'She's on some weekend jolly. A Superintendent Seminar thingy. Back on Monday.'

'Shit.'

'Is there a problem?' Rose called out from her desk.

'Avery's away so we can't do a bloody thing until Monday.'

'Why not?'

'Because, Rose, I don't want to alert these women to the fact that we're closing in before I've got Avery's go-ahead.'

'Excuse me, ma'am.'

Madeline whirled around. 'Yes, Constable Welsh, isn't it?'

'Walsh, ma'am. Constable Walsh.'

'Right, Walsh,' said Madeline. 'So, what is it?'

'That reporter Guy Richards rang. He thinks he may have some information pertaining to the Lilly Green case, ma'am.'

'What information?'

'He wouldn't say.'

'Oh, for goodness sake!'

Steve pressed on. 'He wondered if you'd be prepared to speak to him.'

'Did he indeed?'

'Yes, he…'

'It was a rhetorical question.'

'Right, yes. Sorry.'

'I don't speak to reporters, not if I can help it.'

'He did seem to think it was important, ma'am.'

'I'm sure he did. They always do.'

Chapter 12
Saturday 20th July

Madeline sat at her desk in the study, absentmindedly stroking Zelda's head, as she continued to look through the Lilly Green files. 'I'm missing something, Zelda, and it's driving me bloody crazy.' She glanced up at the sound of someone knocking on the study door.

Taking a drag on her cigarette, she yelled, 'What?'

Jack pushed open her door and pointed to his watch.

Madeline frowned.

'Olivia and Lawrence are expecting us, come on.'

'What?'

'They're having a garden party, remember? Lawrence wants to show us the photographs he…'

'I'm not going, Dad. I've got too much to do. You go, explain I'm too busy.'

'Doing what exactly? You told me there's nothing more you can do until Avery gets back. Sitting at home brooding isn't going to speed things up.'

'I'm not brooding. I'm reviewing the case files,' said Madeline. 'There's something nagging at me, I just can't put my finger on it. It's driving me loopy.'

'Come on, poppet, you've been at it all day. Put the files away.'

Madeline stubbed her cigarette out. 'Oh, right yeah, just like you would have done when you were working on a case and Mum wanted you to stop, like that you mean?'

'Fair point. I'll offer your apologies. Don't work too late.'

'Oh, good one, Dad, pot, kettle, black.'

'I hope you don't mind,' said Christopher. 'But I've come alone. Mary isn't comfortable leaving Emma with babysitters and so…'

'Of course we don't mind,' said Olivia. 'But you could have brought the baby with you.'

'I did suggest that but…'

'No matter, don't give it another thought,' said Lawrence. 'Now then, what would you like to drink?'

'Have you got any lager?'

'Loads. Jack, ready for another one?'

'Wouldn't say no.'

'And for you, Barbara?'

'Oh, another wine please.'

'Carla?'

'The same please.'

'And last, but by no means least, Olivia?'

'I'll have a wine too.'

'So, two lagers and three wines coming up.'

Carla watched as Lawrence made his way up the garden. She waited until he'd stepped up onto the decking and disappeared through the back door, before turning to Olivia. 'You said he took loads of photographs; be honest, how many?'

'Hundreds.'

'Oh God, really?'

'I'm afraid so. But fear not, I asked him to be selective. He assures me he's only printed some of them.'

'Here we are folks, drinks up,' yelled Lawrence from the decking. 'I've got the albums here too. I thought we could have a look at the photographs, now Christopher's here.'

'How many albums are there, Lawrence?' asked Carla.

'Six.'

Carla whirled round towards Olivia. 'Selective?'

Having completed the mammoth task of admiring over five-hundred photographs of Amelia, the grandparents and Olivia, taken from various angles in front of numerous taverns, walking through bustling markets, sat on various beaches, posing outside quaint churches, gathered around large trestle tables, eating and drinking, with a selection of aunts, uncles and cousins, the women left the men on the decking and retreated to the lawn. 'Jesus, Olivia, my head's spinning.'

'I did try to discourage him, Carla, but those digital cameras make it all too easy to snap away.'

'Jack's just the same,' said Barbara.

A hoot of laughter from the decking resounded around the garden, as Lawrence jumped up and rushed into the cottage.

Olivia exchanged a look with Carla. 'I've no idea,' she said.

Lawrence stepped back out onto the decking sporting a blonde wig, with a fluorescent pink boa flung around his neck. He slapped a battered photo album onto the green metal bistro table. 'Feast your eyes on that,' he said.

'On what,' spluttered Jack, putting his beer bottle down, 'you, or the album?'

Lawrence did a twirl. 'Why, sir, the album of course.'

Jack flicked open the album and burst out laughing. 'Well, I'll be damned.'

Olivia glanced up, as more laughter drifted down from the decking. 'Oh, for goodness sake. He promised he wouldn't.'

Christopher leaned over the album. 'Hah! Oh, I say, will you look at that, there we are in our full and splendid glory.' He took a swig of beer. 'I should have brought my albums, but Mary—oh well.' He took another swig.

'You've got to admit we look striking,' said Lawrence.

Jack peered closely. 'Even with that beard, Christopher, I agree you scrubbed up very nicely indeed,' he boomed.

Barbara waved her arms and hissed, 'Jack, for goodness sake. You'll wake Amelia.'

'Sorry, dear heart,' said Jack, releasing another raucous hoot of laughter.

Barbara and Olivia struggled to their feet.

'Watch out,' whispered Jack loudly. 'Wives on the war-path.'

'Whatever are you up to?' said Barbara.

Jack pushed the photo album across the table. 'Take a look at this, love of my life,' he said. 'It will explain everything.'

Barbara raised her eyes to the heavens. 'Honestly, will you boys never grow up?'

Jack patted Barbara's bottom. 'Never, I hope.'

'Lawrence I…'

'I know, Olivia, sorry, I just couldn't resist,' said Lawrence, with a sheepish grin.

Jack glanced down at the photographs again and gave a gasp.

'What's up?' said Lawrence, 'Fallen for one of our dashing creations?'

Jack gave a weak smile and cleared his throat. 'Perish the thought. No, it's the names scrawled underneath.'

'What about them?'

'Just your name, Lawrence, it's, well, it's unusual.'

'Yvette Young,' sang out Lawrence. 'Yes, of all my creations, she was my favourite.'

Madeline was shaken awake by Jack. She raised her head from the desk and peeled a page of the Vicar's Moor Wood file from the side of her face. 'Dad?'

'You need to hear this.'

'What?'

'It's about that name you told me about, Yvette Young.'

'What about it?'

'Lawrence has just been showing us photographs of himself from the late eighties and early nineties, when he was stationed at Fulford.'

'As well as his holiday snaps, gosh, I'm sorry I missed that.'

'Don't be facetious, Maddy. The point is, the photographs were taken when he used to dress up as a drag queen to entertain the troops.'

'Dad, it's late, get to the point. What's that got to do with Yvette Young?'

'His alter ego, his femme fatale, went by the name Yvette Young.'

'Bloody hell.'

'There's more.'

'More?'

'Yes, this alter ego of his was a blonde.'

'A shoulder-length bob-style blonde?'

Jack nodded.

'And has he still got the wig?'

'He came onto the decking wearing the bloody thing.'

Madeline struck her forehead. 'Fuck!'

Zelda, who'd been sleeping on the rug in front of the unlit fire, opened her eyes wide, sat up, wandered across the study and jumped up onto the desk.

Madeline bent down and retrieved a file from the floor. Extracting a sheet, she handed it to Jack. 'Take a look at this.'

'What is it?'

'The current suspect list for the Lilly Green case.'

Jack scanned the short list. 'Olivia's name's here.'

'I'm aware of that, Dad.'

'Bloody hell, Madeline, you surely can't think she had anything to do with that. She doesn't seem the type.'

'That's rich, coming from you. You've always told me that, given the right circumstances, anyone is capable of anything. And you have to admit, it's a bit of a coincidence, her husband using the same name the perp used.'

Jack ran his hands through his thinning hair. 'Yes, I suppose it is.'

'And something's been niggling away at the back of my brain, Dad; a thought that wings its way into focus and then dissolves again, so frustrating.'

'About Olivia?'

'Yes, something Mum said about her.'

'What did she say?'

'Seriously?'

'Sorry.' Jack squeezed his eyes shut and rubbed his forehead. 'There was that time when Olivia disappeared from the village. It caused a bit of a stir, your mother…'

'What? When?'

'Oh, I can't remember. Ages ago—oh, no hang on, shit,' exclaimed Jack.

'What?'

'I think it was a couple of months ago.'

'In May?'

Jack nodded.

'Has Mum gone to bed?'

'No, she's just sorting out a night cap for…'

Madeline grabbed Jack's hand and dragged him towards the door. 'Come on, I'll join you.'

The cat jumped down from the desk and followed.

Barbara spun round as Madeline burst into the living room, dragging her father behind her. 'Madeline, you look awful.'

'Thanks, Mum.'

'I'm just mixing your father a drink. Do you want one or shall I…?'

'I'll have a whisky, thanks,' said Madeline. 'Mum, when did Olivia go missing from the village?'

Barbara handed Madeline her drink. 'She didn't go missing, she simply drove down to London, to help out a friend of hers.'

'Whatever,' said Madeline, taking a gulp of whisky, 'when was it?'

'Now you're asking. I'm fairly certain it was a Sunday,' said Barbara.

'It's important,' said Madeline.

'Yes, alright dear, just give me a moment—now, when did Carla and I go over to Thirsk—it must have been a Friday, that's Carla's day off; goodness, it was ages ago.'

'Mum!'

'Oh, hold on, it'll be on the calendar in the kitchen.'

Madeline dumped her glass and dashed off, returning seconds later with the kitchen calendar. 'Was it in May sometime?'

'I think so, yes—give it here, I'll find it—and I do wish you wouldn't put your glass down without a coaster.'

'Sorry.'

'Yes, here we are. It was Friday the tenth of May. Carla and I went over to Thirsk to root around our favourite reclamation centre.'

'The owners must rub their hands together when they see...'

'Yes, thank you, Jack.' She inclined her head towards where Madeline's glass sat. 'We got that table there—late Victorian.'

'And?'

'And what, dear?'

'Olivia?'

'Oh yes, well, the strangest thing, we bumped into her. We both thought she was in London, but it seems she'd driven up to Scarborough the previous day and...'

'Mum, when exactly did she leave the village?'

Barbara glanced at the calendar. 'Let me see, if Carla and I were in Thirsk on the Friday, Olivia must have left the Sunday before. Yes, that's it, on the fifth. Why?'

Madeline grabbed her drink and shot back to the study. The cat dutifully followed. Madeline went straight across to the desk and snatched up the Lilly Green file.

'Bloody hell, Zelda, I knew it,' she exclaimed. 'Anne Smith booked into the Poplars on the fifth of May.' She rifled through the rest of the file. 'And yes, here we are. Yvette Young was in Thirsk on Friday the tenth. Coincidence? I don't think so.'

She threw the papers onto the desk and dashed back towards the door. Zelda flicked her tail and flopped back down onto the rug.

Bursting into the living room, Madeline asked, 'You're certain you saw Olivia in Thirsk on Friday the tenth.'

'I'm certain.'

'And when did she get back to the village?'

'I knew you'd ask me that,' said Barbara, 'and I've been trying to think, but I'm sorry, I simply can't remember. All I know is that it must have been before the nineteenth, because that's when Lawrence got home from his assignment.'

Back in the study, Madeline took a swig of her whisky, logged onto her computer and entered 'Dr Olivia Hamilton' into the search engine. She clicked on the first link. A page opened up showing a photograph of Olivia Hamilton. Beneath it was a brief biography. She leaned forward and began to read the entry.

Dr Olivia Hamilton studied for her PhD under Professor Ian Frazer, York University: 1999-2002. She is currently Managing Editor for the Journal of Physiology, for which she has written several papers on Reproduction and Development.

She, along with her colleague, Dr Philip Sutcliffe, are responsible for coordinating peer reviews, as well as organising Symposia on Reproduction and Development. These are held in March, July and November. Anyone interested in presenting a paper or attending these symposia should either contact Dr Hamilton via email; hamilton@jourphysio.org or Dr Sutcliffe; sutcliffe@jourphysio.org

Chapter 13
Monday 22nd July

Madeline arrived at work to find a sheet of paper Sellotaped to her chair, with the words *Guy Richards Yorkshire Herald rang again. Sergeant Bailey.* She ripped the sheet, screwed it into a ball and lopped it into her waste bin.

Rose popped her head round the door. 'I'm told Avery's not expected back until lunch time.'

'Come in, come in. I learnt something very interesting over the weekend,' said Madeline.

Rose stared at Madeline, her eyes growing wider with each new revelation. 'Bloody hell.' She closed her eyes and took a deep breath. 'Do we know when Olivia returned to the village?'

'Not as yet, no. Before the nineteenth of May is as precise as I can be at the moment.'

'Do you really think, I mean, you know, a friend of your mum and everything?'

'It's not looking good for her, is it?'

Rose shook her head.

'Plus, her line of expertise is reproduction and development. Coincidence?'

'It could be,' said Rose.

'Seriously?'

'They do happen you know.'

'I know that, Rose, but—look, I need a fag.'

'I'll get coffee,' said Rose.

In the courtyard at the back of the station, Madeline smoked her cigarette as she went through the case in her head. Rose stood quietly by her side, kicking absentmindedly at some litter, while she sipped the drink that purported to be coffee. Madeline's drink sat on the ground, untouched.

'It's got to be her, Rose,' said Madeline, gesticulating wildly with her cigarette. 'One, her baby was born in March, premature; two, she's aware of the name Yvette Young; three, she goes AWOL on May the fifth; four, she's seen in Thirsk on May the tenth and, five, she's a bloody expert in Reproductive and Development Physiology. One coincidence I could take, two at a push but *five*? I don't think so.'

'It is stacking up, I agree,' said Rose. 'But I find it hard to imagine a woman who's just discovered her dead baby, having the presence of mind to hunt for a wig her husband used to wear years ago.'

'Not just the wig, she also had the presence of mind to make an identity badge, locate a set of scales and pack latex gloves. This demonstrates careful planning. She knew what she was doing, Rose. She knew she'd have to meet the mothers so she knew she'd need a disguise and a way to gain access into their homes. I reckon she had it all worked out before she even left the village,' said Madeline, stubbing out her cigarette and glancing at her watch. 'Avery should be back soon. Pop down to the tech boys and get them to modify the photograph of Olivia Hamilton from that link, to give her blonde hair. Get a few copies.'

Rose handed a copy of the modified picture to Madeline. 'Does it look like the photofit?'

Madeline held the photograph at arms-length and half closed her eyes. 'Hard to say, but…'

'Madeline, she's back.'

Grabbing the file, Madeline shot across towards Avery's office, calling out as she went, 'We'll need a selection of stock photos of other women with blonde hair, Rose.'

Rose waved a folder above her head. 'Already sorted.'

'Ah, Inspector Driscoll, your expression tells me you've made a breakthrough,' said Avery. 'Take a seat.'

Madeline sat.

'Well, come on, don't keep me in suspense.'

Madeline took Avery through their lines of inquiry, explaining how they'd identified four suspects, with Olivia Hamilton at the top of their list.

'And Justin researched these, did he?'

Madeline nodded.

'And why is Dr Hamilton your chief suspect?'

'Because Major Lawrence Hamilton used the name Yvette Young when he performed in drag in the late eighties and early nineties. It's a strong connection with the case. Either that, or it's a very odd coincidence.'

'It's still not enough.'

'Plus, she was away from the village over the relevant time period.'

'She could have a perfectly legitimate reason for her absence. Have you asked her where she was?'

'I haven't spoken with her yet,' said Madeline.

'Why not?'

'I didn't want to alert her to the fact that she was a suspect before you agreed that we could request DNA samples and…'

Avery held out her hand. 'Let me have a look through the file.'

Madeline took a surreptitious look at her watch as Avery scanned the file.

After a moment, Avery nodded. 'Go ahead.'

Madeline tapped Rose on her shoulder. 'Right, first things first. We'll show Mrs Green these photographs and …'

Rose turned towards Madeline, her mobile clasped to her ear, mouthing the word, 'mother' as she continued with the conversation. 'I'm at work.'—'No, I can't, not now.'—'What?'—'I've told you, I, am, at, work.'—'I'm not being…'—'Right, look I've got to go, bye.' Rose shoved her mobile into her jacket pocket.

'Problem?'

Rose bunched her fists and scowled. 'I swear I'll be arrested for mothericide before long. I know I should be patient, but ever since she moved in with me, Jesus—anyway, sorry, the photographs. We should show them to the other women too,' said Rose.

'Yes, and the manager of the Poplars Hotel,' added Madeline. 'How many sets have we got?'

'Half a dozen.'

'Great—Jones, Walsh over here, quick as you can.' She handed them a set each. 'I want you to show these to the women in Bagby and Sowereby. Don't give them any prompts. Ring me with their responses. Rose, with me.'

Two hours later, Madeline and Rose were sat in the car outside the Poplars Hotel.

'Well, that's that, then,' said Rose.

'In what way?'

'In the way that Olivia Hamilton isn't our Yvette Young.'

'Hang on a moment,' said Madeline. 'No one actually said our blonde-haired Olivia Hamilton *wasn't* Yvette Young.'

'But none of them said she was either.'

'True, although according to Jones, Mrs Fox said it was her at first,' said Madeline.

'And then changed her mind.'

'Again, true.'

'And Mr Shaw wavered.'

Rose rolled her eyes. 'He wavered over all the photographs; he just fancies women with blonde hair if you ask me.'

Madeline turned the ignition. 'The important thing is, Mrs Green said it might have been her, so I'm not jumping to any conclusions.'

'You mean apart from jumping to the conclusion that Dr Hamilton is Yvette Young?'

'She does seem to be the most likely suspect.'

'At the moment,' said Rose, waving Justin's list under Madeline's nose. 'There are four names on this list, *four,* not just Dr Hamilton. We've also got Mrs Willow, Ms Hall and Mrs Campbell to check out.'

'OK, OK, so, where do they live?'

'Topcliffe, Skipton-on-Swale and Pickhill.'

They arrived at Honeysuckle Cottage flushed with success, having spoken with the other women and obtained DNA samples.

Rose knocked at the door. There was no answer. 'It looks like our luck's run out.'

'Bugger,' exclaimed Madeline, scrabbling for a cigarette. 'Maybe Mum knows where she is.'

'Hello, darling. What brings you home so early?'

'I don't suppose you know where Dr Hamilton is, do you? She's not at home.'

'Why do you need to know where Olivia is?'

'Mum,' exclaimed Madeline.

'Oh, right, sorry. Yes, I do know where she is as it happens, dear.'

'And that would be where, Mum?'

'She's in York with Lawrence. It's quite exciting. He's got an appointment with some publishers. Apparently he's writing a book about life in…'

'Any idea when they'll be back?'

'Sometime tomorrow,' said Barbara. 'They're spending the night with her old Professor.'

'Shit.'

'Madeline,' exclaimed Barbara.

Rose snorted.

Barbara turned towards Rose. 'Hello. You must be Rose Scott.'

Rose clamped her lips together and nodded.

'I was sorry to hear of your father's passing. Still, your mother seems to be coping well.' Barbara patted Rose's arm.

'How did…?'

'She and I attend the same bridge group,' said Barbara. 'She says you've been a tremendous support. She worries about you though. It's the same with…'

'Mum, Sergeant Scott and I have work to do.'

'Yes, fine, you carry on. Do give my regards to your mother, won't you? Tell her I'll see her next week, as usual.'

Wandering back up Church Lane towards their car, Madeline said, 'I'm sorry, I had no idea that your father…'

'It's not a problem. He'd been ill for some time and, I know this sounds awful, but in the end, it was a relief.'

'So, that's why your mum lives with you now.'

Rose nodded. 'I know I should be more patient, but God, she's hard work.'

'Come on, let's grab a coffee at Browsers before we head back to the station.'

'Have we got time?'

'It's where Carla Marchese works.'

'Ah, right.'

'Hello there, Madeline,' said Carla. 'Not working today?'

'I am actually. This is Sergeant Scott. Is there somewhere we can talk privately?'

'You want to talk to *me*?'

'Yes, Ms Marchese.'

'Um, right, yes of course. Hannah, I'm just popping into the office with these two police officers.'

'Righto.'

'Would you both like a coffee?' said Carla.

'That would be lovely,' said Madeline, 'lattes please.'

'Hannah could you…?'

'I'm doing them now. I'll bring them through.'

'This way,' said Carla. 'It's rather cramped, but we should all fit.'

Once inside the office, Carla leaned across and closed the door. 'So, what's this all about?'

'Ms Marchese, we…'

'Oh, please, call me Carla.'

'Carla, we're conducting enquiries into the identity of the Vicar's Moor baby and the whereabouts of Lilly Green.'

'Yes,' said Carla. 'I was reading about it in the paper. We were all convinced the remains were going to turn out to be those of Lilly Green. Weird, I mean, does that mean we've got some awful baby murderer on the loose, because…'

'I'm afraid I can't comment on our current investigations. We just need to ask you a few questions about the whereabouts of Dr Hamilton during…'

'Sorry, why on earth would you be interested in Olivia?'

'Again, I really cannot comment,' said Madeline, 'if you would just allow me to ask you a few questions.'

Running her hands through her tangled mass of hair, Carla said, 'Fine. Fire away.'

'Can you tell me where Dr Hamilton went when she inexplicably vanished from the village on May the fifth?'

'Oh, absolutely, yes, no problem,' asserted Carla. 'And, if I may say, 'inexplicably vanished' is a bit of an exaggeration.'

'So, her absence was planned, was it?'

'Well, no, not exactly.'

'Was it planned or not? Did you know in advance that she was going to be away from the village on the fifth of May?'

'No, not as such—look, it's quite simple. She had a phone call from an old friend who was having matrimonial difficulties. Olivia went to offer support. That's the sort of person Olivia is, you see, caring and considerate.'

There was a knock on the office door and Hannah peered in. 'I made you one too, Carla, OK?'

'Smashing, thanks. Just pop the tray on the desk.'

'There you go, enjoy,' said Hannah. 'I'd best get back, bit of a rush on…'

'Can you cope?' said Carla.

'Yes, no problem,' said Hannah, backing out of the office.

'Do you happen to know this old friend's name, and where she lives?'

'Sorry, what?'

'The name and address of the friend who rang Dr Hamilton,' said Madeline.

'I don't think she mentioned the address, I know it was somewhere in London. Olivia did tell me her name, she was at University with her. Just give me a moment, it'll come to me.' Carla threw her head back and closed her eyes as she thought for a moment. 'Penny! The friend's name was Penny, married to some dickhead called Mark, no um, M, M, Marcus. That's it, Marcus.'

'Their surname?'

'I don't think she said. No, I'm sure she didn't, sorry.'

'No problem,' said Madeline. 'Just one more thing, when did Dr Hamilton return to the village?'

'She cut it a bit fine if you ask me. I mean, Lawrence was due back on the nineteenth of May and they were off to Spain a couple of days after that. Still, it all worked out alright in the end.'

'So, when did she actually get back?'

'From Spain?'

'No, from London.'

'I told you. Not long before Lawrence got back, sometime around the seventeenth of May.'

'So, after she left the village on the fifth, you didn't see her again until the seventeenth, is that right?'

Carla nodded absentmindedly.

'Are you sure about that?'

'Yes,' exclaimed Carla, 'of course I'm—oh, no, sorry, hang on, I'm wrong. Your mother and I went to Thirsk the week before that—we went to the reclamation centre; we go there often, much to Jack's—anyway, when we'd finished rummaging around, we decided to visit The Bliss Café, where she and I used to go when we bunked off school. It's a lot swankier now, I can tell you, it…'

'I was asking you about Dr Hamilton,' said Madeline.

Carla's jaw clenched. In clipped tones, she replied, 'When we were in the café, your mum spotted Olivia across the road.'

'And when was this?'

'It must have been a Friday.' Carla glanced over her shoulder at the calendar pinned to the wall. 'The tenth of May.'

'And what was she doing in Thirsk?'

'She said she was 'having some time out.''

'And did she have her baby, Amelia, with her?'

'Why do you ask?'

'Did she?'

'As it happens, no, she didn't. She'd left her with Penny and, before you jump to the same conclusion I jumped to, *not* in London, in Scarborough.'

'In Scarborough?'

'Yes, in Scarborough. Olivia drove Penny and her baby up from London to stay with the parents. They live in Scarborough,' said Carla, reaching for her coffee.

'So, could I just clarify,' said Madeline. 'You're saying Olivia originally went to London to look after this friend.' Madeline glanced at her notes.

'Penny, yes,' snapped Carla.

'And she then drove her to Scarborough.'

'Where Penny's parents live, yes.'

'Fitting in a day trip to Thirsk on Friday the tenth of May.'

'Yes, and your point is?'

'I was just wondering, having delivered her friend safely into the arms of the parents, why didn't she simply come back to the village? Why visit Thirsk?'

'Oh, for goodness sake. She didn't want to dump Penny with her parents and then bugger off. Plus, she was exhausted after all the travelling…'

'As was Penny, I would imagine. And yet Olivia was happy to leave Amelia in Scarborough with Penny and then, somehow, she's able to summon up enough energy to visit Thirsk.'

'I told you, her trip into Thirsk was some time out, that's all.'

'I see, well, thank you for your help, Carla.' At the office door, Madeline turned and added, 'Just one more thing, how did Dr Hamilton seem to you when she got back home from her mercy mission?'

'How do you mean?'

'Was she relaxed, or stressed, and how was the baby?'

Carla thought back to the day Olivia returned to the village and her reluctance to meet up. She remembered Olivia's brief visit to the café the day after her return, when they'd talked about the Lilly Green abduction. She then recalled how, the day after that, she and Lawrence had made a hasty exit from the café before they set off for Spain. The question, 'how was the baby?' reverberated through her head. How *had* Amelia been? She'd only seen the top of the baby's head and her tiny feet. She took a long deep breath and released it as a sigh.

'Ms Marchese?'

'What?'

'I was asking about Dr Hamilton.'

'Yes, sorry, I was just thinking. I remember that Olivia was tired, but that's only to be expected—look, surely to God you don't think Olivia had anything to do with the Lilly Green thing. I mean, that's preposterous.'

'And the baby?'

'Again, she was tired—I didn't really see much of either of them, to be honest. I was working, and Lawrence was due back from, from wherever he'd been, and they were due to fly out to Spain. Olivia had washing and packing to do. She was busy.'

'So, did you see the family before they left for Spain?'

'They popped into the café for a coffee, but they didn't stay long. I didn't have time for a real chat; obviously, if I'd known you were going to be so interested, then perhaps...'

'Thank you again, we'll be in touch.'

As Madeline and Rose made their way back to their car, Rose stopped in her tracks. 'Hang on.'

'What?'

'The timeline doesn't match.'

'Explain.'

'Well, Anne Smith...'

'AKA Yvette Young and, if I'm right, AKA Olivia Hamilton.'

'Yes, she stayed at the Poplars Hotel from the fifth to the thirteenth of May, correct?'

'Correct.'

'Carla Marchese has just told us that Olivia Hamilton returned to Binton-on-Wiske on the *seventeenth* of May. If Olivia Hamilton *is* Yvette Young, then we know she checked out of the hotel on the thirteenth of May, the day Lilly Green was abducted, so where was she between the thirteenth and the seventeenth of May?'

'Oh, hell. That's a bloody good point,' exclaimed Madeline, turning and marching back towards the café.

The general hubbub of chatter ceased the moment Madeline and Rose re-entered. 'It's just like in a western,' whispered Rose, 'when the saloon goes deathly quiet after the stranger enters from the mean streets of some god-forsaken town.'

Carla and Hannah were in conversation over at the counter. They looked up as the café fell silent. 'Hello again. Back for your coffee, you didn't touch a drop while we were chatting,' said Carla brightly.

'There was just one more thing,' said Madeline, leaning across the counter.

'Goodness, another 'one more thing',' remarked Carla.

'You said Olivia returned to the village on the seventeenth.'

'Yes, so?'

'Am I to understand that she was with Penny until her return to the village?'

Carla sighed. 'No, she went to York first.'

'Didn't she want to come back home?'

'Of course she did,' exclaimed Carla. 'What a ridiculous thing to say.'

'So, why the trip to York?'

Carla's brow furrowed as her mouth turned grim. 'Inspector Driscoll,' she hissed. 'Olivia is a perfectly lovely woman. I have already explained to you that she didn't want to abandon her friend in Scarborough and...'

'Yes you have,' said Madeline. 'But I'm asking about her trip to York.'

Carla took a deep breath. 'Yes, and *if* you'd let me finish, I was about to explain.' With fists clenched, Carla continued. 'She bumped into her old Professor and his wife. They were thrilled to see her. They persuaded her to spend a few days with them. Satisfied?'

'The Professor's name?'

'Frazer I believe.'

'Thank you again,' said Madeline.

Hannah turned to Carla, as Madeline and Rose left. 'Do they really think Olivia had anything to do with the abduction of Lilly Green?'

Carla gave a dismissive wave of her hand. 'No, of course not, Hannah, no. They need to check everyone's alibi. They're just being thorough.'

'Well, she was helping her friend, wasn't she?'

'Yes, Hannah, she was—now then, the rush seems to have abated, will you be alright out here for a while, I need to finish off some work in the office.'

Hannah nodded.

Carla sat at the office desk and stared into space, recalling the day when Olivia had 'inexplicably vanished' from the village and the more she thought about it, the more she worried. Olivia's failure to turn up that day with no explanation had been completely out of character.

'I simply can't understand it,' she had said that day.

'Maybe she's forgotten,' said Hannah.

'Yes, it's possible. Baby brain and all that.'

'Just give her a ring if you're worried.'

'Yes, I think I will,' said Carla, scrolling through her contacts and hitting the call button. 'It's going straight to voicemail.'

'Probably on her way then.'

'Yes, I'm sure you're right. Babies, not exactly clock-watchers, are they? No doubt Amelia filled her nappy just as Olivia was about to set off, it's just that,' she glanced at her watch, 'she's over an hour late.'

'Carla, you're obviously worried. We're not busy, so why don't you go over to her cottage?'

'Do you mind?'

'Just go.'

She set off at a brisk pace down Church Street and cut through onto the public footpath, opposite the *Duck Inn*, towards Honeysuckle Cottage. She pushed open the side gate and dashed up to the back door. There was no answer. She hurried around to the front. Again, no answer. She peered through the windows and called. It was unnaturally quiet. Trying not to panic, she wondered if Olivia had left via her front gate and they'd missed each other. Cursing, she dashed out onto Church Lane and ground to a halt. Olivia's car wasn't parked on the road. She looked up and down the lane, in the vain hope that it would miraculously appear.

'Are you looking for Olivia, my dear?'

She whirled around. 'Yes, Peter. Have you seen her?'

Carefully closing the graveyard gate behind him, he ambled across the road towards Carla. 'I have, dear, but it was very early. It must have been around three or four this morning. I was struggling with my sermon, ever the way these days, there are only so many ways of saying...'

'Did she say where she was going?'

'What? Where she was going? No, sorry, we didn't speak. She seemed in a frightful hurry. She threw her bag and baby accoutrements into the boot, then set off at what I considered to be an unnecessary, somewhat dangerous speed, especially with a baby on board.'

'Which direction did she go?'

He pointed to the right.

'Towards Thirsk?'

'Yes, why, is there a problem?'

'No, I um, well, I just wondered. Thanks, Peter, and, good luck with your sermon.'

Peter closed the cemetery gate with meticulous care and gave a cheery wave.

Carla waved back. *Where the hell are you, Olivia*, she had thought.

Hannah burst into the office. 'Sorry, Carla but the steamer's playing up again. Can you come?'

'What?'

'The steamer, it's playing up again.'

'On my way,' she said.

At the office door, Carla stopped. *So, technically Olivia* had *vanished from the village*, she thought. *But she'd rung and explained. She'd gone to London. Olivia will be able to give Madeline all the necessary details.* 'It'll be fine,' she said out loud.

'I know,' said Hannah, 'you just need to twiddle with it.'

'What?'

'The steamer, Carla, the steamer.'

Back at the station, Madeline took the DNA samples directly to Donald.

'How long will it take?' she asked.

'How many samples are there?'

'Eight altogether, three Willows, three Campbells and two Halls,' said Madeline. 'And there'll be three more tomorrow.'

'Just two from the Halls?'

'Father not on the scene. Well, to be more accurate, father unknown.'

'I suppose you want the results yesterday?'

'Naturally.'

Donald rubbed his chin. 'I'll do my best,' he said, 'but I'm making no promises; that's a lot of work.'

'If anybody can turn the results around quickly, then you're the man.'

Donald raised his eyebrows. 'You can flatter me all you like, it won't get the work done any faster.'

Madeline turned as she was leaving the lab. 'You can't blame a girl for trying.'

Donald picked up the samples and smiled to himself. 'That I can't,' he said to himself. 'That I can't.'

Constable Jones jumped up from his desk. 'Inspector Driscoll, I meant to speak to you this morning about this, but you sent me off with those photographs and I...'

'You wanted to talk to me about what, Jones?'

'The car.'

Madeline frowned.

'You asked me to check with my brother about…'

Madeline waved her hand. 'Yes, yes I remember. And?'

'I *have* been nagging him, ma'am, but he only gave me this list last night.'

'Just give it here, Jones.'

'There are quite a few cars actually,' said Jones, handing over the list, 'but I've taken the liberty of highlighting the most likely ones.' He pointed to the fifth car on the list. 'I've excluded this green Aston Martin V8, for example; it's owned by an unmarried retired Major.'

'Well done, Constable, I'll take a look.'

Glancing down the list, as she made her way towards Rose's desk her eyes widened. She handed it to Rose. 'Look at this, recognise any names?'

'Bloody hell, Willow and Hamilton.'

'We're closing in,' said Madeline. 'So, what about those statements?'

'Justin's checking the information Carla Marchese supplied us with. I've looked at the rest.'

Madeline drew up a chair as Rose started to read from her notes. 'Mrs Willow, the one who said she couldn't bear the competitive nature of the other mums at the clinic.'

'Ah, yes,' said Madeline, 'Mr Willow said his wife bought scales to do the measurements herself, but she'd since donated them to charity.'

Rose nodded. 'That's right. He said she was becoming obsessive and weighing the baby every day. Mrs Willow took exception to that, but she did agree she'd given the scales away.'

'So, what about her story that she was staying with her sister in Harrogate from the tenth to the thirteenth of May?'

'I haven't been able to get hold of the sister yet. I left a message on her mobile and then rang Mrs Willow to see if she knew where her sister might be.'

'And?'

'She was out but I spoke to Mr Willow and he said, and I quote, 'who bloody knows? My wife's sister lives in fairyland'. He suggested she might have taken herself off to some remote hippy commune.'

'OK, keep trying.' Madeline checked Constable Jones's list. 'The Willows own a 1970s green Volvo 145 estate so, she's a possibility.'

'I didn't see it when we visited. The garage was open but empty.'

Madeline frowned. 'You're right, Rose, and they were both home. We need to check that.'

'I've made a note.'

'Good. Now what about Ms Hall?'

Rose flicked through her notebook. 'Ah, yes, the delightful, gum-chewing, disinterested Ms Hall, mother of a surprisingly delightful baby, totally at a loss as to who the father was, who told us she *couldn't be arsed* to attend the clinic, because she had better things to do.'

'And did she, as she claimed, leave her baby with her mum from the third to the tenth of May, so she could go to the 'Lights Music Festival' in Leeds?'

'I've spoken to three of the four friends she said she went with. They all confirm she was with them. Her Facebook page is full of photographs taken at the festival. Several of the photographs show a young man tagged as Barry Smith. I've spoken to him and he told me he met her at the festival. He also said he gave her a lift back home on Saturday afternoon.'

'The eleventh?'

'Yes.'

'OK, so we can eliminate her from our suspect list,' said Madeline. 'Who's next?'

'Mrs Campbell. She told us she was staying with her parents in Edinburgh while her husband was away.'

'He's the long-distance lorry driver, right?'

Rose nodded. 'I checked with the haulage firm. They confirmed he was working; delivering to France. I've also spoken to Mrs Campbell's parents and they told me their daughter stayed with them during May and the first two weeks of June. They also told me she attended their local postnatal clinic in Edinburgh for the baby's eight-week review.'

'And, did she?'

'Yes. They have her records on file.'

'So, we can eliminate her from our suspect list too,' said Madeline.

Rose closed her notebook. 'Ready to brave Justin's den?'

'After you.'

Madeline knocked on the back of Justin's filing cabinets and poked her head round. 'May we enter?'

Justin tutted and held up a folder. 'I've spoken to all the relevant parties. It's all in there. Penny Travers. York University 1999 to 2002. Friend of Olivia Hamilton (née Spencer). Graduated with a first. Unmarried. No children. Lives in London. Not seen or spoken to Olivia Hamilton since their university days.'

'And the Professor?'

'Professor Frazer last saw Olivia Hamilton in October 2012 at a symposium held at the University of London.'

'So, the good Dr Olivia Hamilton lied to Carla Marchese,' remarked Madeline, glancing at Constable Jones's list. 'And she drives a 1977, green Renault 6TL.'

'Is that it?' said Justin, thrusting the folder towards Madeline. 'I do have other work.'

Chapter 14
Tuesday 23rd July

Early the following morning, Madeline waited outside Honeysuckle Cottage in Binton-on-Wiske for Rose to arrive.

She nodded her head towards the green Renault. 'I can't believe I've never noticed the bloody thing before,' she remarked, as they made their way to the front door.

'It's not exactly parked in a conspicuous spot; up a small lane on the outskirts of the village.'

'Nevertheless,' said Madeline, knocking on the door. 'I should…'

'Goodness, good morning, Madeline, what brings you here?'

'This is Sergeant Scott, Mr Hamilton. I wonder, is your wife home?'

'Olivia, yes she is. Why?'

'We're in the process of checking on the whereabouts of women during the first couple of weeks of May: specifically, around the time of the Lilly Green abduction. Women who gave birth in March of this year,' said Madeline, adding, with a quick nod, 'For elimination purposes, you understand.'

He frowned. 'You too? Right, well, you'd better come in.'

As they followed Lawrence into the living room, Madeline remarked, 'You said, 'you too', Mr Hamilton, has someone already spoken with your wife?'

'Yes, it was that reporter from the *Yorkshire Herald*, the one who wrote the article about the abduction, what was his…?'

'Guy Richards?' said Madeline.

'That's the one.'

'When was this?'

'Last Friday. The day I went fishing with your father and Christopher,' said Lawrence.

'Christopher?'

'Christopher Baker, a chap your dad and I knew years ago,' said Lawrence. 'Anyway, Olivia's feeding Amelia. She'll be down in a moment. Would you both like a coffee?'

'That would be lovely, thank you. No sugar for either of us.'

'Milk?'

'Yes, both of us, thank you.'

Olivia appeared with Amelia just as Lawrence was placing the coffee mugs on the table.

'Madeline's here with her sergeant.'

'Yes, so I see.'

'They're making routine enquiries about the Lilly Green case. They want to ask you a few questions. Would you like a coffee?'

'Yes please, love.'

'Right; back in a tick.'

'Dr Hamilton, would it be alright if we asked you a few questions about your whereabouts from the fifth to the seventeenth of May? There seem to be a few discrepancies.'

'Discrepancies?'

'Yes, don't look so worried,' said Madeline. 'I'm sure there's a perfectly good explanation. People get muddled. We all live such busy lives.'

'Here you are,' said Lawrence, setting Olivia's mug on the table along with the others.

Olivia lifted Amelia from her lap and handed her to Lawrence. 'Thank you, sweetheart. Could you take her for a bit? She's still unsettled. Perhaps you could take her for a walk to get her off to sleep.' She turned to Madeline. 'That would be alright, wouldn't it, or do you need to ask Lawrence questions?'

'I assume you won't be long,' said Madeline.

'About half an hour, I expect.'

160

'Fine.'

'Come on, little one. Let's go for a walk. You'd like that, wouldn't you?'

Amelia looked up, smiled and gave a gurgle.

The moment Lawrence exited the cottage, Madeline said, 'Right then, Dr Hamilton, I'll get straight to the point. My sergeant and I are a little confused. Back in May you vanished from the village. According to Ms Marchese you were in London visiting an old University friend, Penny Travers.' Madeline paused.

Olivia said nothing.

'We've been in touch with Ms Travers…'

Olivia flinched.

'… and she has no recollection of you visiting her in London during May. In fact, she said she hadn't seen you for years. Perhaps you could explain.'

Olivia looked towards the ceiling, blinking back tears. 'It's a little delicate.'

'Oh, don't worry about us, Dr Hamilton. It takes a lot to shock us.'

'The thing is, I didn't visit Penny. Well, you know that. I wasn't even in London.'

'Where were you, Dr Hamilton?'

'Oh dear, this is very awkward and it's going to sound awful and you're going to get the wrong end of the stick and…'

'Dr Hamilton, just tell us where you were.'

'I was with…' Olivia took a deep breath. 'I was with a colleague of mine, as it happens.'

'And does this colleague have a name?'

'Well, yes obviously; it's just I'd rather not say.'

'Dr Hamilton,' said Madeline, emphasising each word carefully, 'where were you between the fifth and the seventeenth of May?'

'I've told you, with a colleague.'

'I need a name and I need a place, otherwise we'll have to complete this interview at the police station.'

Olivia glanced towards the front door and blurted out, 'I was in Pocklington, with Dr Philip Sutcliffe, at his flat, alright?'

'And he'll be able to confirm that, will he?'

'Yes, he'll be able to bloody confirm it.'

Madeline opened her notebook. 'If you could let me have his address and telephone number.'

Olivia rattled off the information. 'Lawrence doesn't need to know, so I'd appreciate it if you didn't share this with him.'

'Is Dr Sutcliffe married too?' asked Madeline.

'What's that got to do with anything?'

'Well, we don't want to put our foot in it when we contact him. If he's married, his wife might answer the phone and…'

'No, he isn't married, not as such. His wife left him last July.'

'And what was the reason for your visit?'

'It's personal.'

'Dr Hamilton,' said Madeline, 'we're investigating the abduction of Lilly Green, as well as the possible murder of a baby. Your personal life is of no importance in such circumstances. So, I'd appreciate it if you could answer my questions.'

'Fine.'

'What was the reason for your sudden departure from the village on May the fifth?'

'Philip will be mortified. He's so embarrassed by it all.'

'Dr Hamilton, the reason?'

'Alright, alright. I had a phone call from Philip. It was the middle of the night. He sounded distraught and I was frightened he was going to do something stupid. He wasn't coping well with his wife leaving him and, well anyway, I told him I'd drive over to his place immediately. He tried to dissuade me, but there wasn't much conviction in his voice.'

'And when was this phone call?' said Madeline.

'I've just told you—sometime in the middle of the night. Although I suppose it could have been in the early hours of the morning. It was quite a long time ago.'

'The date, Dr Hamilton.'

'Oh, right yes, sorry. It was the night of the fourth or, as I've just said, it could have been the early hours of the fifth.'

'And, just to be clear,' said Madeline, 'you're referring to the fourth or fifth of May this year.'

'Yes,' exclaimed Olivia.

'Well, that all sounds very credible, Dr Hamilton.'

Olivia's jaw clenched. 'It sounds *credible* because it's the truth. Now, if that's everything, I…'

'Just a couple of questions. Why did you feel the need to lie to Ms Marchese? And why such a long stay?'

Olivia slumped forward and rubbed her forehead. She closed her eyes.

'Could you answer the questions, please?' said Madeline.

'Sorry, what questions?'

'I asked you why you lied about where you were, and why you stayed away for so long.'

Olivia cleared her throat. 'Binton's a small place. I was worried it might get the village gossiping, you know, given that Lawrence was away; silly, I suppose.'

'And the reason for the long stay?'

'I told you,' said Olivia. 'He was in a terrible state. I thought spending some time with him, going for walks and doing ordinary stuff, might help him regain some perspective.'

'And did it?'

'Thankfully, yes.'

'And you were there until when?'

Olivia glanced towards the front door. 'I got back to Binton on the seventeenth.'

Madeline consulted her notes. 'I understand you were in Thirsk on the tenth.'

'Yes, so?'

'What was the reason for that visit?'

'I went to the Zillah Bell Gallery.'

'Was that one of the 'ordinary things' you did with Dr Sutcliffe and Amelia?'

Olivia narrowed her eyes. 'You know perfectly well I was alone, don't you?'

Madeline again consulted her notes. 'Ah, yes, so you were. My mistake. So, where was Amelia?'

'Where do you think?' hissed Olivia.

'Well, that's just it, Dr Hamilton. According to Ms Marchese, you left Amelia with Penny Travers, but…'

'I left her with Philip, alright? Now, is there anything else?' asked Olivia, again glancing towards the front door. 'Only I think that's Lawrence returning.'

'And why was that?'

'Sorry? Why was what?'

'Why did you leave your baby with Dr Sutcliffe?'

Olivia sighed. 'I needed some time alone, that's all.'

'To do what?'

Spitting her words like bullets, Olivia said, 'To—visit—the—Zillah Bell Gallery.'

'And did you drive over to Thirsk in your Renault?'

'Yes. Look, is that it, only…'

'Here we are, back safe and sound,' said Lawrence, wheeling the pram into the living room.

'Excellent timing, Mr Hamilton' said Madeline. 'We need to speak to you too now, if that's alright.'

'I'll just park Amelia on the decking,' he said, as he slid open the patio door. 'She's fast asleep.'

'You're not going to tell Lawrence about me being with Philip are you?' hissed Olivia.

'I thought you said your reason for being with the man was perfectly innocent,' said Madeline.

'It was,' snapped Olivia. 'But…'

Lawrence returned and plonked himself down on the settee and flung his arm across Olivia's shoulder. 'So, Officers, what do you need to ask me?'

Olivia threw Madeline a panicked look.

'We're currently working on two cases, Mr Hamilton…'

'Lawrence, please.'

'We're currently working on two cases, Lawrence. The abduction of Lilly Green and the discovery of the baby in Vicar's Moor Wood. To help us with these investigations, we're asking parents of babies born in March if they'd allow us to take DNA samples, for elimination purposes.'

'Oh, right, I see, fine. I don't see why not,' said Lawrence. 'Do we need to come down to the station?'

'No, we have the kit here. Sergeant, could you pop out to the car and fetch it?'

'No problem,' said Rose, as she made her way towards the front door.

'She won't be long,' said Madeline.

Olivia fixed Madeline with an icy stare.

Madeline remarked, 'I see from my notes that Amelia was several weeks premature. That must have given you both a fright.'

Lawrence put his arm around Olivia. 'I didn't know about it at first. I wasn't in the country. Poor Olivia had to cope all alone. The village rallied round, of course, especially Carla and your mum.'

'And she's doing alright?'

'Amelia? Yes, she's our little miracle,' said Lawrence.

'Here we are,' said Rose. 'Who's going to be first?'

Rose placed the two DNA samples in separate evidence bags and sealed them.

'Well, that was simple,' said Lawrence.

'I realise you've just managed to get Amelia off to sleep,' said Madeline. 'But we need a sample from her too.'

'From the *baby*? Why, for God's sake?' exclaimed Lawrence.

'To ensure we have a complete record of the family unit,' explained Madeline. 'It's a cheek swab, like the ones you've just provided.' She nodded towards Rose, 'My sergeant is quite the expert. She's managed to obtain several such samples without waking the babies concerned.'

Lawrence glanced at Olivia. 'What do you think?'

Olivia rubbed her temples and again fixed Madeline with an icy stare. 'You think there's a woman out there who buried her baby in the woods before snatching Lilly Green. And, although this beggars belief, you actually think that woman could be me. That's it, isn't it?'

'It's a possibility that cannot be dismissed,' said Madeline. 'Hence the need for the samples.'

A sharp-edged silence crackled through the air.

Olivia's eye's blazed. 'I can assure you that the baby currently sleeping out there is the baby I gave birth to.'

Lawrence grabbed hold of Olivia's hand and stared at Madeline. 'You can't seriously believe, no, surely not.'

'I'm sorry, but if you wouldn't mind.'

'I *do* mind,' said Olivia. 'I mind very much. I don't know how you've got the nerve to come here and…'

Lawrence pulled his wife towards him. 'This is madness. They can't really think Amelia is Lilly.' He turned towards Madeline again, his eyes pleading. 'Do you?'

'That's why we need the samples, Mr Hamilton. I'm sorry, I know…'

'You see, Lawrence, you see!'

'Dr Hamilton you have the right to refuse permission, but I'm sure you understand how such a refusal could be interpreted.'

Eyes still blazing, Olivia marched towards the decking, leaned over the pram and lifted the sleeping baby into her arms. 'Shush, shush little one. Come on.'

'Thank you,' said Madeline.

'Just get on with it.'

Rose successfully swabbed Amelia's mouth without waking her.

'Is that *finally* it?' said Olivia.

'Just one more question,' said Madeline. 'Does the name Yvette Young mean anything to either of you?'

Lawrence glared at Madeline. 'I take it your father's spoken to you.'

'He mentioned something about you performing in drag, when you were in the Army.'

'In that case, you know that was my performance name so, why the question?'

Madeline turned to Olivia. 'And you were aware of these performances, were you?'

'Am I missing something here?' said Olivia, 'What exactly has Lawrence's drag act got to do with anything?'

'If you wouldn't mind answering the question,' said Madeline.

Olivia sighed. 'What question?'

'Were you aware that your husband used the name Yvette Young, when he performed in drag?'

'Yes!' snapped Olivia.

'Thank you,' said Madeline.

Driving back to the station, Madeline said, 'Something's not right. If she was on a mercy mission to Dr Sutcliffe, why doesn't she want her husband to know about it?'

'One obvious reason springs to mind,' said Rose.

'Yes, it's occurred to me too,' said Madeline.

'Do you think that's it then, an affair?'

'Possibly, Rose, but if so, does that preclude her as a suspect?'

'Right, you give Dr Sutcliffe a call. I'll get these samples down to Donald.'

Rose held the receiver to her chest. 'One step ahead of you—it's ringing—ah, good morning, Dr Philip Sutcliffe?'

'Speaking.'

'This is the Northallerton police,' explained Rose. 'My name is Sergeant Rose Scott and I wonder if you could confirm whether Dr Olivia Hamilton stayed with you at any time between the fifth and the seventeenth of May this year.'

The line went quiet.

'Dr Sutcliffe, are you still there?'

'Yes, sorry, goodness. Has something happened to Olivia? Is she alright?'

'She's fine, Dr Sutcliffe, nothing to worry about. So, was she with you between those dates?'

'Who told you she was?'

'Dr Sutcliffe, I appreciate this might be a little delicate, but we're trying to establish the whereabouts of Dr Olivia Hamilton during this time.'

'Why?'

'Suffice it to say she's helping us with our enquiries and so far she's been most forthcoming. So, was she with you, or not?'

'Right, well yes, as it happens, she was with me.'

'Every day?'

'Mostly, yes.'

'And what does that mean?'

'It means she was with me for most of the time.'

'I'm aware of the meaning of the word 'mostly', Dr Sutcliffe, thank you. I need you to be precise.'

'I'll need to check my diary,' said Philip. 'Give me a moment.'

The sound of paper rustling travelled down the line. 'Here we are,' said Philip. 'She arrived on the fifth and left on the fourteenth.'

'And what about on the tenth?'

'The tenth?'

'Yes, was she with you on the tenth?'

'I think so, yes.'

'You're sure?'

More paper rustling. 'Oh, no sorry, that was she day she left Amelia with me, so she could visit some boring, esoteric art gallery in Thirsk,' said Philip. 'Wild horses couldn't drag me round a place like that.'

'Do you mean, The Zillah Bell Gallery?'

'That's the one. So, is that it, only…?'

'And where did she go on the fourteenth?'

'The fourteenth?'

'Yes, the fourteenth.'

Philip sighed. 'To Masham.'

'And why did she go there?'

'She wanted a few days of peace and quiet, before returning home.'

'A few days of peace from what exactly?'

'Well, *I* don't know, do I? Why don't you ask her?'

'And do you happen to know where she stayed in Masham?'

'I do,' said Philip.

'Where?'

'She stayed in a friend's holiday lodge in the woods.'

'I need the address, Dr Sutcliffe.'

'Woodland View, Market Way, Masham.'

'Would anyone else be able to verify these details?'

'Which details? Her time spent with me, her trip to the gallery or her stay in Masham?'

'All of them.'

'Right, well, while she was with me we went for several walks round and about and we visited the Piglets Adventure

Farm Park in York. We also ate lunch out most days at *The Olive Bistro,* in Market Place. It's a child-friendly place, I'm sure they'll remember us.'

'And Thirsk?' asked Rose, as she typed *The Olive Bistro* into her search engine.

'She met Carla Marchese there, I believe, she's a friend from Binton. Ask her.'

'And this Lodge, who owns it?'

'Paul Davies. He's my technician at the University. He dropped the keys off at mine, just before lunch on the fourteenth. So, is that it?'

'Have you got a contact number for Mr Davies.'

'Just a minute.' There was a clunk and the sound of a drawer opening.

'Work or home number?'

'Both.'

Philip rattled them off. 'Right then, unless there's…'

'Could you explain why Dr Hamilton was with you?'

'Not really, no.'

'And why's that?'

'It's personal.'

'Dr Sutcliffe, how would you describe your relationship with Dr Hamilton?'

'I beg your pardon?'

'I asked how…'

'I heard what you said, Sergeant, I simply fail to see what it has to do with you. You asked me if Dr Hamilton was with me and I have answered clearly that she was. I've given you the name of the restaurant where we dined, so you'll be able to verify that I'm telling the truth. As to my relationship with Dr Hamilton, she's a good friend and a colleague.'

'I understand your wife left you last year.'

'What the hell's that got to do with you? Now, I'm very busy, so unless there's anything else.'

'No, that's it, thank you. We'll be in touch if we need to ask you any more questions.'

Rose hung up and immediately rang Paul Davies and *The Olive Bistro*. At the end of the calls she replaced the receiver with exaggerated care. She pushed herself up, took a deep breath and made her way across to Madeline's office.

Madeline glanced up from her desk. 'Ah, Rose, any joy?'

'I've spoken to Dr Sutcliffe,' said Rose.

'Excellent, and?'

'He confirms that Dr Hamilton was with him until the fourteenth.'

'Not the seventeenth?'

'No.'

'So, where did she go on the fourteenth?'

'He said she went to Masham.'

Madeline frowned. 'Whatever for?'

'According to Dr Sutcliffe, she stayed at a holiday lodge for a couple of days peace before returning home. I've spoken to the owner, Paul Davies, and he confirmed that someone did stay there until the seventeenth.'

'Someone?'

'Mr Davies didn't know who used the lodge,' said Rose. 'He dropped the keys off at Dr Sutcliffe's place on the fourteenth. No one was in, so he posted the keys through the letterbox.'

'I take it you've got the address of this lodge.'

Rose nodded.

'Right, send Walsh over there. *If* Dr Hamilton was there with a baby, someone must have seen them.'

Rose turned towards the door.

'Hang on, before you do that, you said Dr Sutcliffe confirmed that Dr Hamilton was with him until the fourteenth. Have you been able to verify that?'

'Not exactly.'

'What's that supposed to mean, Rose?'

'He told me they ate out on most days at *The Olive Bistro*. I've rung, but there was a recorded message explaining they're closed for refurbishment until the first of August.'

'How convenient.'

'I've got the name of the owner from the website; a Mr Tompkins. Do you want me to ring him to arrange a meeting?'

'Yes, we need to see if Sutcliffe's story holds up. For all we know, he could be Dr Hamilton's bloody accomplice,' exclaimed Madeline. 'Did you ask him about the tenth?'

'I did, and he confirmed what Dr Hamilton told us.'

'That she went to, what was it called?'

'The Zillah Bell Gallery,' said Rose. 'And I've checked with them. All visitors have to sign in. Olivia Hamilton *was* there.'

'What about Dr Hamilton's baby?'

'Dr Sutcliffe said he looked after Amelia for the day.'

Madeline sighed. 'Were the gallery able to say what time Dr Hamilton was there?'

Rose nodded. 'She signed in at 12:10.'

Madeline flicked through the Lilly Green file. 'Right, let's see. Mrs Sinclair received a visit from Yvette Young at 11.30am. The next visit was to Mrs Poole at 12:45—where's that map of Thirsk?'

'It was at the back of the…'

'Got it—now, according to Mrs Sinclair, Yvette was only in her house for about twenty minutes. So, that would mean she left Station Road at 11:50. She could easily have driven the short distance to the gallery and signed in at 12:10. Let's assume…'

Rose cleared her throat. 'You're making an assumption?'

'Yes, fine,' muttered Madeline, 'bear with me for the moment. Let's *suppose* she stayed at the gallery for half an hour. The next visit was to Mrs Poole, at 12:45 in St Giles Close, just half a mile away. It's definitely feasible.'

Rose began flicking through her notebook.

'What are you looking for?'

'The time Carla Marchese said she and your mother spotted Dr Hamilton in Thirsk.'

'Well?'

'Shit, she didn't say. She just said they called into The Bliss Café after they'd finished 'rummaging around' the reclamation centre.' She flung her notebook onto Madeline's desk and peered at the map. 'The café's about half a mile from St Giles Close. Where was Yvette's next visit?'

'To Mrs Lee, in St James Green at 2pm.'

'That's a three-minute walk from the café,' said Rose.

Madeline snatched up the phone.

'Browser's café, Carla Marchese speaking, how can I help?'

'This is Inspector Driscoll,' said Madeline. 'I'm sorry to bother you again, but what time on Friday the tenth of May did you see Dr Hamilton in Thirsk?'

'Oh, I can't remember, it was months ago.'

'You said you went to The Bliss Café on Millgate after 'rummaging around the reclamation centre' so, what time would that have been?'

'Oh, for goodness sake.'

'It's important.'

'Fine, just give me a minute.'

Madeline began tracing the route from Mrs Sinclair's in Station Road to the gallery and then onto the café and then to Mrs Poole in St Giles Close. 'Mrs Marchese, are you still there?'

'Yes, yes, I'm thinking—we must have got to Thirsk at about eleven, yes I'm sure that's right. We were in the reclamation centre for a couple of hours, give or take, and so that means we will have been in the café at around one, one-fifteen. We were both gasping for a coffee by then. Anyway, we'd only been there a short while when your mother spotted Olivia.'

'So, what time would that have been?'

'Oh, I don't know, not long after we got there. Is that it? I've got customers waiting.'

'Just one more thing.'

'What?' snapped Carla.

'I'm assuming Olivia joined you in the café.'

'Of course she did.'

'And how long did she stay?'

'Long enough to drink a cup of coffee, now I'm sorry, but I have to go.'

'Thank...' Madeline stared at the phone. 'She's hung up.'

'So, what did she say?'

'She said she arrived at the café between one and a quarter past one and Dr Hamilton joined them not long after that, staying long enough to drink a coffee.'

'OK, so that would mean she left the café sometime between one thirty-five to one forty-five,' said Rose.

'Giving her at least twenty minutes to get to Mrs Lee in St James Green,' said Madeline, tracing the final line on the map. 'Plenty of time.'

Rose took the pencil from Madeline. 'And look, Byland Avenue, where the car was seen, is just here,' said Rose, 'not far from St Giles Close and opposite Mrs Parker's house on Sutton Road.' Rose traced the route. 'She started here, with Mrs Watson at 9:30, then she went onto Mrs Wright at 10:30 before going to Mrs Sinclair at 11:30. So you see, she's done a loop of the area. Very efficient.'

The sound of a double-decker bus trundling past his flat startled Philip Sutcliffe. He set the phone onto its base station and paced the room. He went back to the phone, picked it up, closed his eyes and put it down again. He pushed his hand through his hair, took a deep breath, snatched up the phone and punched in Olivia's number.

'Hello?'

'Oh, hi Lawrence, it's Philip, is...?'

'Well, hello there, old chap, long time, no hear. How the hell are you?'

'Oh, not too bad, thanks, Lawrence. Is Olivia there, by any chance?'

'Yes, hang on, I'll get her.'

Philip clutched the phone to his ear. He heard Lawrence call out. Heard Olivia ask who was it. Heard Lawrence say it was Philip.

'She's just coming. I'll say goodbye, good to hear from you, I'm on baby duty.'

'Philip,' said Olivia brightly. 'Is everything alright?

'Can you talk?'

'What?'

'I said…'

'No, not you, Philip, Lawrence just called out, hang on, —the what, Lawrence?—It should be in her pushchair— got it?—Excellent—yes fine, see you in a bit.—Philip, hi yes, I can talk. Lawrence has taken Amelia out for a walk.'

'Olivia. I've just had a phone call from the police.'

'Ahh, right.'

'What's going on? Does Lawrence know?'

'No, of course not. They, the police, haven't spoken to Lawrence except to ask him for a DNA sample.'

'You what? Why?'

Olivia cleared her throat. 'They've found the remains of a baby in the woods, just down the road from us.'

'Jesus, so, the DNA?'

'The police are taking DNA samples from families whose babies were born in March.'

'Shit, Olivia. Did they take DNA from Amelia too?'

Olivia nodded.

'Olivia,' yelled Philip. 'Are you there?'

'Yes, Philip, yes, I'm here. And yes, the police took DNA from all of us.'

'But that means…'

'I know what it means, Philip, but I could hardly refuse.'

'No, right; so what do we do?'

'There's nothing we can do, is there?'

'No, I suppose not. You'll ring me when you hear?'

'Yes, Philip, I'll ring.'

Rose slammed the phone down and called out to Madeline. 'That was Mr Tompkins. The earliest he can see us is tomorrow morning at eleven. He said he'll take us over to the restaurant so we can examine the books. Is that alright?'

'It'll have to be,' said Madeline, striding over towards Rose. 'Have you heard from Mrs Willow's sister?'

'No, nothing, and I've rung several more times. It goes straight to answer phone.'

'OK. Well, Mrs Willow's our only other suspect. Let's go and have another chat.'

They pulled up outside The Old Vicarage in Topcliffe and, for the second time that day, made their way up to the front door. Rose nodded her head towards the open garage, where a green Volvo was parked.

'Gracious,' said Mrs Willow. 'Back again?'

'Yes, there are just a couple of things we need to check with you. Would that be alright?'

'Yes, fine. Come in, come in,' said Mrs Willow. 'George has taken Poppy for a walk, but he shouldn't be long—tea, coffee?'

'Coffee, please,' said Madeline. 'We both take milk, no sugar.'

'Make yourselves comfortable through there,' said Mrs Willow, indicating a door on the left. 'You know the way. I won't be a moment.'

The room had been tidied since their earlier visit. The baby toys had been returned to a toy box and fresh track marks in the carpet indicated a recent hoovering.

Mrs Willow bustled in. 'Here we are,' she said, placing the tray on the coffee table. 'Help yourself.'

'Thanks,' said Madeline, reaching out for a mug.

Mrs Willow bobbed her head and smiled. 'As you can see, dear Mrs Wood has been in. She can't abide seeing Poppy's toys lying about. I've told her not to bother putting them away because her father will get them straight out again, but I fear I waste my breath. Still, I suppose she can't hoover round them.'

'We haven't been able to get hold of your sister, Mrs Willow. Do you happen to know where she might be?'

'Well, that is odd. She's always got her mobile with her. I can't understand—oh, dear, what's the date today?'

'It's the twenty-third of July, why?'

'I'm so sorry, I totally forgot. Marion will be at her Retreat. She goes every year. It's in North Wales somewhere. Absolutely no communication allowed.'

'Yes, your husband did mention that might be a possibility,' said Rose.

'She'll be back on Friday. You'll be able to speak to her then.'

'So, who's the driver?' said Madeline.

'Sorry?'

'I noticed there was a car in the garage, a green Volvo, it wasn't there when we spoke to you and your husband this morning.'

'Oh, right,' she gave a nervous laugh. 'That's Graham's pride and joy.'

'Graham?'

'George's brother.'

'Does he live here too?'

'Gracious me, no,' said Mrs Willow, picking up her coffee. 'No, he lives down the road in those new flats. They don't have garages.'

'Ah, so not your car then.'

'No, but he does allow us to use it sometimes. We're all insured and everything.'

'Yes, I'm sure you are, Mrs Willow, I was just curious.'

'I see. So, what was it you wanted to check?'

Madeline took a sip of coffee. 'It was about those scales.'

'I told you. I donated them to a charity shop.'

'Can you remember where you bought them?'

Mrs Willow put her coffee cup down. 'Mothercare. That huge store in York.'

'And what about when you bought them, can you remember that?'

'Gracious me, I'm not really sure. Sometime in May, I think. Why?'

'Could it have been in early May,' said Madeline, checking her notebook, 'the sixth or maybe the eighth?'

'Possibly,' said Mrs Willow. 'I normally go to York on a Wednesday, I don't know why, but there we are.'

'Wednesday was the eighth,' said Madeline.

'That's when I would have gone then,' said Mrs Willow. 'I certainly had them when I stayed with Marion.'

'And you got them in York, you say?'

'Yes,' said Mrs Willow, her tone exasperated. 'Is that significant?'

'I assume you went in the Volvo?'

'No, I went by train.'

'You're sure? I'd have thought it would have been much easier for you in the car—you had the baby, you then had to carry the scales plus any other shopping.'

'Yes, you're right, it would have been,' said Mrs Willow, 'but, unfortunately, the car was unavailable.'

'And why was that?'

Mrs Willow sighed. 'Because, Inspector, it was in the garage in York, undergoing repairs.'

Madeline started. 'Which garage?'

'I don't know. You'll have to ask George, he…'

'Do I hear my name being—oh, hello again,' said George, as he wandered into the living room carrying Poppy. 'What brings you two back?'

'They seem to be interested in Graham's car.'

'Oh, why's that?'

'Your wife was just saying the car was in a garage in York undergoing repairs in May.'

'Yes, that's right. And a bloody nuisance it was too,' said George, handing Poppy over to his wife. 'Can you take her, Caroline, I think she needs changing. Yes, my brother drove it into the front gate-post. Smashed the front light and messed up the nearside wing. It was in the garage for a fortnight.'

'Can you remember which fortnight?'

'I most certainly can,' said George. 'As I said, it was a bloody nuisance. Caroline had to struggle to York on the train on the Wednesday before she went over to her sister's, for one thing and then, because the car still wasn't back, Marion had to drive over here to collect Caroline, and she's a nightmare driver, I can tell you.'

'Mr Willow, *which* fortnight?'

George removed his diary from his inside top pocket and flicked through the pages. 'Here we are. It was picked up from our driveway on Friday the third of May and we didn't get it back until the fifteenth of May.'

'And what garage was that?'

'Jones and Son, on the Leeman Road,' said George. 'Look, sorry, why are you interested in Graham's car?'

'Just one more thing,' said Madeline, 'do either of you recognise the name, Yvette Young?'

Caroline and George exchanged a confused look.

'Means nothing to me,' said George.

'Or me,' said Caroline. 'Sorry.'

'That's fine. Thank you for your time,' said Madeline. 'And the coffee. We'll leave you in peace now. Sorry to have bothered you again.'

Caroline stood. 'Is that it then?'

'Yes, that's it.'

'And what about those DNA thingies?' said George.

'You don't need to worry about those,' said Madeline. 'As we explained, we only need them for elimination purposes. They'll be destroyed once the investigation is complete.'

Madeline burst through the double doors into the incident room. 'Constable Jones, a word.'

Jones leapt up. 'ma'am?'

'Your carefully-constructed list, Jones.'

'Yes.'

'Sergeant Scott and I have just spent an embarrassing half an hour with Mrs Willow over in Bagby.'

A look of mild alarm crossed Jones's face.

'It seems, Jones, that the 1970s green Volvo 145 estate, the one you identified as being owned by Mr G Willow, is in fact owned by *Graham* Willow, Mrs Willow's brother-in-law. And, more to the point, between the third of May and the fifteenth of May, that car was in a garage on the Leeman Road in York. Your brother's bloody garage as it happens, undergoing repairs.'

'I, I um, I…'

'You should have checked, Jones.'

Jones examined the carpet. 'Sorry, ma'am.'

Madeline stormed into her office and snatched up the phone.

'Donald Richards speaking.'

'Give me your best estimate for those DNA results.'

'Dispensing with the pleasantries, are we?'

'Yes.'

'Fair enough. Hold on, I'll check.'

Madeline drummed her fingers on the desk.

'They should be ready on Friday.'

'Right. Fine. Thanks.'

Rose poked her head round the door. 'Alright?'

Madeline growled. 'Not especially.'

'Should we revisit Ms Hall's and Mrs Campbell's statements?'

'Why, do you think we've missed something?'

'No.'

'So, what's the point?'

Rose shrugged.

'Even without the DNA results, we seem to have eliminated Hall, Campbell and Willow from our suspect list.'

'But we haven't spoken to Mrs Willow's sister yet,' said Rose.

Madeline sighed. 'Mrs Willow didn't have access to a car, Rose.'

'Oh, but, hang on,' said Rose. 'Her sister has a car.'

Madeline's eyes flashed.

'Give me a minute. I'll check with the DVLA.'

Moments later, Rose returned. 'Sorry, the sister owns a yellow Volkswagen.'

'It was worth a shot.'

'So, that leaves us with Olivia Hamilton,' said Rose. 'The one you suspected all along.'

'Yes, but oh, I don't know. Let's see what our visit to Mr Tompkins turns up,' said Madeline, as she snatched up the phone again. 'What?' she exclaimed.

'Sorry to disturb you, Inspector, but I've had that reporter on the phone yet again and I just wondered…'

'Bailey, I don't speak to reporters.'

'Yes, I know. I've told him repeatedly, ma'am, but he keeps ringing.'

'Keep telling him to bugger off then,' said Madeline, slamming the phone down.

'Problem?'

'Nothing I can't deal with.'

'Is it Guy Richards again?'

'Bloody reporters.'

'He's certainly persistent,' said Rose, 'do you think you ought to…?'

Madeline speared Rose with a hard stare.

'It was just a thought.'

Chapter 15
Wednesday 24th July

The Olive Bistro was surrounded by scaffolding and cloaked in thick blue plastic sheeting that flapped wildly in the breeze. A man of generous proportions stood outside, looking left and then right as he checked his watch.

He gave a deep, gracious bow when, at 11.10am, a police car pulled up directly in front of him. 'Ah, ladies—Henry Tompkins, at your service.'

'Inspector Driscoll,' said Madeline, holding up her badge, 'and this is Sergeant Scott.'

'Ah, the delightful Sergeant,' said Henry, 'we spoke yesterday.'

'Apologies for our lateness, but…'

'Not at all, not at all.'

'Right then, Mr Tompkins…'

'Henry, please.'

'If you could show us your books for the seventh to the sixteenth of May.'

'Certainly. Follow me. Watch your step. The office is at the back.'

They picked their way through the chaos, as Henry prattled on about the work he'd commissioned and how he had high hopes of attracting new clientele. 'That's where the money is, I reckon. Catering for little family groups is all well and good, but it's the business lunches, the corporate do's and…'

'The books, Mr, Henry.'

'Just through here,' said Henry, as he unlocked the office door. 'They're on the back shelf. 'Which month was it you were interested in again?'

'May.'

'Here we are,' he said. 'I'll leave you to it, if that's alright. I need a quick word with the builders.'

Madeline ran her fingers down the names. 'Shit,' she exclaimed, pushing the book towards Rose.

And there it was, in black and white, lunch bookings for Sutcliffe. A table for two, the words 'with baby' added in brackets, on the 6th, 7th, 9th, 12th and 13th of May, as well as evening meals on the 10th and 11th of May.

Rose looked up. 'It doesn't say who the guest was.'

Madeline growled. 'Good try, but I think we both know it was Dr Hamilton.'

Rose cleared her throat and removed an undoctored photograph of Olivia from her jacket pocket. 'I'll just show this to Mr Tompkins.'

Madeline nodded as she watched Rose leave the office. A knot of anxiety twisted in her gut.

The look on Rose's face when she re-entered the office was enough. 'It *was* her then,' said Madeline.

Rose nodded.

'Bugger and damnation to hell and back,' said Madeline, kicking the back of a vacant chair and sending it spinning. 'That's that then. It's not her either.'

'It would seem not.'

'Shit and double shit.' She threw her hand out to steady the chair and collapsed onto it. 'Right, let me think.'

Rose closed the reservations book and replaced it on the back shelf.

'OK, we know she lied to Ms Marchese about her whereabouts. I thought that was because she was our Yvette Young.' Madeline banged her forehead with the heel of her hand. 'We confronted her. She then told us she'd been with Dr Sutcliffe. We checked. He confirmed her story. But I still thought she was lying.'

'She could have been,' said Rose. 'After all, as you said, she'd lied before.'

Madeline nodded. 'But not this time. She *was* with Dr Sutcliffe and, more to the point, she had a baby with her on…' she glanced over towards the table, 'where's the reservation book gone?'

'I put it back, but I wrote the dates down,' said Rose, opening her notebook. 'She had a baby with her at the lunch bookings on the sixth, seventh, ninth, twelfth, and thirteenth of May, as well as…'

'Exactly! She had a baby with her on the ninth of May. That was the day Yvette Young was visiting women in Bagby and Sowerby, for Christ's sake!'

'And the thirteenth of May was the day Lilly Green was abducted,' added Rose in a quiet voice.

'So, she lied to Ms Marchese just to cover up the fact that she was with Dr Sutcliffe.'

Rose nodded. 'And Mr Tompkins has just informed me that Dr Sutcliffe normally dines with his fiancé, Dr Monica Wilson. She's an anthropologist. She works at York University too.'

'And do we happen to know where Dr Monica Wilson was while Dr Hamilton and Dr Sutcliffe were playing happy families?'

'In Japan.'

Madeline leaned back in the chair and thought for a moment. 'She was our last suspect, Rose. We're back to square one. We need to rethink.'

'We do.'

Madeline pierced Rose with an intense stare.

'What?'

'Any thoughts?'

'Um.'

'It's this name, Yvette Young, that's the key. I simply refuse to accept that it's a coincidence,' muttered Madeline. 'So, who, apart from Lawrence Hamilton's wife, would know about it?'

'Well, everyone who saw his act presumably,' said Rose, with a shrug.

Madeline jumped up. 'That's it, Rose, that's it,' she exclaimed. 'I've been so fixated on Olivia Hamilton that I lost sight of the bigger picture. You're right; *all* the army personal would have gathered together to watch those reviews every year. Genius girl, genius!'

'I aim to please,' said Rose. 'So, back to the station, I'll get Justin to search the military records from that time?'

'Yes. absolutely. Concentrating on premature births has been a bloody disaster.'

Chapter 16
Friday 26th July (Morning)

Dr Lawson arrived at his lab at 8am to find Madeline outside. 'Goodness me,' he remarked. 'Somebody's keen.'

'I was wondering if Donald had sent those DNA results through.'

'Well, I assumed you weren't here on a social call,' said Jeremy, unlocking the lab. 'Give me a moment to catch my breath and I'll check the computer.'

Jeremy removed his jacket and slipped on his lab coat. Humming to himself, he wandered over to the computer. 'Just need to click this file and—yes, here we are, looks like you're in luck. Donald sent the report through last night.'

After several more clicks of the mouse, the printer whirred into action. Taking the printout, he sat at his desk and peered at the results. 'Well, well, well, that *is* a surprise,' he murmured. 'I wasn't expecting that.'

'What?'

'There were no matches.'

'I thought that would be the case.'

'Yes, a shock I know, but it seems that the baby buried in Vicar's Moor Wood doesn't—sorry, you, what did you say?'

'I said, I thought you wouldn't find a match,' said Madeline, with a deep sigh. 'So, that's it, then. All our suspects are currently in possession of their own children, and none of them have Lilly Green.'

Clutching the DNA printout, Madeline took the stairs to the first floor two at a time and dashed down the corridor towards her office.

'Inspector Driscoll, I presume. I've left several messages, but as yet I've had no response. So, if one's will does not prevail, one must submit to the alternative. I have therefore come to you.'

'*Mr* Richards, how did you get…?'

'Into these hallowed halls?' He tapped the side of his nose and fell into step beside her. 'I have my ways. Now, I'm aware of your reluctance to speak to reporters and,' he inclined his head towards her and smiled, 'frankly, given the calibre of some of my so-called colleagues, I can't say I blame you. However, I do wish you'd hear me out. You never know, I may be able to help.'

'Look I…'

'Before you dismiss me out of hand, let me just say this to you: two mothers whose babies were born in March, both absent from their homes when Lilly Green was abducted, both aware of the name Yvette, surname, most likely, Young.'

'*Mr* Richards, it may surprise you to know, I'm perfectly aware of the connection between…' she stopped. 'Hold on, did you say *two* women aware of the name Yvette Young?'

Guy smiled again. 'I did.'

'Right. Well, you'd better come to my office.'

'Lead on, lead on.'

Guy reclined in the seat opposite Madeline's desk, staring at her with an intensity that she found disturbing. She held his gaze. His eyes sparked in the sunlight streaming through the window. He was handsome, she decided. Many would disagree. They would comment on his ears, which stuck out rather more than is generally acceptable, or his large nose and his long, unruly straw-blond hair. His eyes though, no one could argue about his eyes; they were the colour of pistachios and they radiated kindness and compassion. She cleared her throat. 'First things first, Mr Richards, how did you hear about the name Yvette Young?'

'Ah, yes, I thought you might ask me that. I understand the police wanted to keep the name under wraps; perfectly understandable,' said Guy, 'and I hope you appreciate that I didn't reveal it in any of my articles.'

'Duly noted; however, you haven't answered my question.'

'The poor woman didn't mean to. She was mortified when…'

'Mr Richards,' exclaimed Madeline, as she checked her watch, 'I am rather busy. *What* woman?'

'Mrs Parker. She told me she'd already spoken to the police and, as I said, she really didn't mean…'

'Fine. So, go ahead, let's have it.'

'I beg your pardon?'

Much to Madeline's annoyance, she felt her face flush. 'I'm talking about the information you seem so keen to share with me, Mr Richards. I'm waiting with anticipation.'

'Oh, I say,' drawled Guy, his eyes twinkling.

Madeline strode over to her door. 'Sergeant Scott,' she shouted. 'In here, quick as you can.'

'You yelled, M'Lady?' she said, as she marched into the office. 'Oh, sorry, didn't realise you had someone with you. You requested my presence, Inspector?'

'Sit down, Scott. Mr Richards here claims to have information about two women who are aware of the name Yvette Young.'

'*Two* women?'

'Yes, quite.'

They skewered Guy with their best interrogatory stare and waited.

He stared back.

'Well?' demanded Madeline at last.

Such fiery eyes, he thought, as he consulted his notes. 'Dr Olivia Hamilton.'

Madeline and Rose nodded.

'*And?*'

'And Mrs Baker.'

'Baker you say?'

'Yes, do you know her?'

Madeline glanced down at her desk and opened a file. She drummed her fingers on the top sheet for a moment, before closing it with exaggerated care. She returned her attention to Guy. 'Dr Olivia Hamilton resides at Honeysuckle Cottage in Binton-on-Wiske, Mr Richards,' she said. 'Sergeant Scott and I have already spoken to her and, well, let's just say we probably won't need to speak to her again.'

Guy nodded. 'So, I take it you haven't spoken to Mrs Baker.'

'Not as yet.'

'Well, you may be interested to know that her husband knew Lawrence Hamilton sometime in the nineties. They used to perform together in the army; Baker as the red-haired Lucy Lupin and Hamilton as the blonde-haired beauty, Yvette.'

'It may surprise you to know, Mr Richards, that we were perfectly aware of Lawrence Hamilton's performances in the nineties.'

'But not of his connection to Mr Baker, I assume,' said Guy.

'I'm not prepared to comment.'

'Interesting,' said Guy, with a mischievous smile.

'So, how did you find out?'

'What, about Mr Baker's connection to Lawrence Hamilton?'

'Yes.'

'From Mr Baker himself.'

'When?'

'When I called at the Bakers' residence last Friday,' said Guy. 'The day I tried to speak to you. The day I left my first message for you to …'

'Yes, alright, you've made your point,' said Madeline.

'Given half the chance, I think the old boy would have donned his gear and given me a private viewing, but Mrs Baker wasn't impressed, and I was summarily dismissed.'

Madeline clicked her pen rhythmically. 'And where, exactly, does Mrs Baker live?' she asked, each word in time with the clicks of her pen.

'The Old Post House, Long Street, Topcliffe,' replied Guy, in equally rhythmic and clipped tones. 'Within easy access of the A168 to Thirsk.'

'And she had her baby in March, you say?'

'Yes.'

Madeline and Rose exchanged a confused look.

'What?'

'OK,' said Madeline, 'cards on the table. We've been interviewing women who gave birth to premature babies in…'

Guy put his hand up.

'What?'

'May I ask, why just premature babies?'

'Not at the moment, no,' replied Madeline. 'The point is, Mrs Baker's name wasn't flagged up during our search and…'

'Well, presumably her baby wasn't premature,' said Guy.

'Yes, thank you for that astute observation, Mr Richards, but I've just about managed to struggle to that conclusion myself.'

'Right.'

'What's Mrs Baker's first name?'

'Mary.'

Madeline jotted the name down. 'Rose, could you do a background check.'

Rose was already making her way towards the office door. 'On it,' she declared.

Circling the name in red ink, Madeline asked, 'Am I to understand you've been researching *all* the women who gave birth to babies in March?'

'Good grief, no,' said Guy.

'So, why your interest in Dr Hamilton and Mrs Baker?'

Guy explained. 'I talked it through with Merlin and…'

'Merlin?'

'My cat.'

Madeline's eyes widened.

'It can be very useful to voice one's thoughts out loud.'

Madeline inclined her head forwards. 'Yes, I do the same with Zelda. My cat.'

'So, you're a cat person too,' said Guy, a smile tugging at the corners of his mouth.

'You were explaining how…'

'Yes, I was. It's quite simple, once I'd obtained the birth announcements I did what I imagined Yvette would have done; that is, eliminate the women who'd given birth to boys. That left me with twenty-six names.'

Madeline started. '*Twenty-six* names?'

Guy nodded. 'Yes, but of course Yvette only visited twelve of those women before she got to Mrs Green.'

'How do you know that, Mr Richards?'

'How do I know what?'

'Don't be obtuse. How do you know Yvette Young only visited twelve women before Mrs Green?'

'I'm an investigative reporter, Inspector Driscoll, I have my sources.'

'I'm sure you do, Mr Richards, but that doesn't answer my question.'

'No, it doesn't,' said Guy. 'Do you want me to continue, or not?'

'Fine, get on with it.'

'At first, I assumed the remaining thirteen women were simply lucky because Yvette had found *the one,* and that meant…'

'Yes, yes, she didn't need to carry on looking,' said Madeline, frantically rifling through the Lilly Green file.

'Have you lost something?'

'What? No,' said Madeline, closing the file. 'Carry on.'

'But then, after the remains were found, I decided to think again. I'd obtained the birth announcements from *The Post* and *The Herald* and it occurred to me that she, Yvette, might have only looked in one paper. I reasoned that it'd probably have been *The Post*, given that she was staying in Thirsk. It's more local than *The Herald*, you see and...'

'You reasoned that, did you?'

'That look suggests you doubt my word,' said Guy.

'Does it?'

'Yes.'

'Someone told you, didn't they?'

Guy nodded.

'Miss Webb, I assume.'

'Miss Webb?'

'The librarian.'

'The librarian, yes, that's right. I'd momentarily forgotten her name.'

Madeline studied him with a penetrating stare.

'Anyway, that being the case, it crossed my mind that she may have put *her own* announcement in *The Herald*,' said Guy, handing Madeline a sheet of paper. 'These are the twenty-six names. As you can see, some appear in both papers. I've highlighted the nine that were in *The Herald* alone. Those were the ones that interested me and so...'

'And so you paid them all a visit?' said Madeline, glancing at the sheet.

Guy nodded. 'Yes, there were six who lived in Northallerton. I was able to eliminate them immediately...'

'How?'

'Because, when I paid them a visit, I noted that every one of them was at least five foot eight, it must be something in the water.' He glanced up at Madeline and smiled.

'There's a cross by Mrs Smith in Topcliffe too,' said Madeline.

'She's of Afro-Caribbean decent and unlikely to want a white baby as a replacement—so, that just left Hamilton and Baker.'

'Right then, Mr Richards.'

'Oh dear. Sounds like I'm about to be dismissed.'

'Well, not dismissed as such,' said Madeline. 'It's just that…'

'Things to do, places to go?'

'Exactly.' Madeline stood and extended her hand. 'Apologies for not returning your calls.'

Guy stood and gave Madeline a dazzling smile.

Another flush rose in her cheeks. *Bloody hell,* she thought.

'Think nothing of it,' Guy was saying. 'Glad to be of help.' At the door he turned. Running his hand through his hair, he asked, 'I wonder, would you be prepared…'

Madeline held her breath.

'…to keep me informed, you know, about what transpires.'

Madeline exhaled. 'Ah, I see, once a reporter always a reporter. I assume you want some sort of exclusive. Well, I'm sorry, but…'

Guy held both arms up in front of his face. 'Steady on,' he cried. 'That wasn't what I meant at all, although, now you mention it, it would be a most admirable gesture on your part, given your obvious distaste for the press and all those associated with it. No, I just hoped you'd let me know if the information I've provided proved useful. No more, no less.' He gave a theatrical bow and turned on his heel, calling out as he made his way across the incident room, 'I bid you farewell.' After a quick social call to the labs he made his way back to his old Mini, convinced that the rather fetching Inspector and her Sergeant would be winging their way to speak to the Bakers within the hour.

Madeline stared at the sheet of paper she'd removed from the Lilly Green file while Guy had been speaking. 'Shit, how the hell did we miss this?' She gripped the edge of her table. 'Rose,' she yelled. 'Get in here.'

'I haven't finished the background…'

'Just get in here.'

'What?'

'Look,' said Madeline, thrusting the sheet into Rose's hands.

'What am I looking at?'

'The seventeen names from the *Thirsk Post.*'

'Right, and?'

'The names Yvette Young copied out.'

'Yes, and she visited twelve before she found Lilly.'

'Yes, yes, I know that, but now look at this sheet,' she said, handing Rose Guy's list. 'These are the names from the *Thirsk Post* and the *Yorkshire Herald.*'

'But Miss Webb explained that Yvette Young only accessed the *Thirsk Post*, she was quite adamant about it.'

'Jesus, Rose, I *know*, but we didn't ask what is now the screamingly bloody obvious question, did we?' exclaimed Madeline.

'Sorry, and that is?'

Madeline dragged her hand through her hair. 'Why *didn't* she look at the *Yorkshire Herald*?'

Rose frowned.

'Look at the nine highlighted names.'

Rose looked.

'Those nine women chose to announce the birth of their babies in the *Herald* only, Rose. Notice any familiar names?'

Keeping her head down, Rose nodded. 'Dr Hamilton and Mrs Baker,' she said in a tremulous voice.

'Why the bloody hell didn't I think to check the *Herald*? I'm an idiot.'

'Well, that makes me an idiot too,' said Rose.

'Quite,' snapped Madeline.

Rose blanched.

Madeline scrabbled around for Constable Jones's list. She ran her eyes down the names. 'Oh, this gets better and better,' she wailed. 'When Guy Richards mentioned the name 'Baker' I thought, no surely not, but it seems...'

'What?'

'Mary's husband is *Christopher* Baker; ring any bells?'

'Christopher...?'

'On Tuesday, Rose, when we were at Honeysuckle Cottage. Lawrence Hamilton told us he'd been out fishing with a bloke called Christopher Baker.'

'Shit, that's right. He said he was an old friend.'

'And, according to Constable Jones's list, Mr Christopher bloody Baker owns a green 1970s Saab 95 V4 estate.'

Madeline and Rose stood stock still for a moment.

'Right, get back to your search on Mary Baker. I'll— fuck, what now?' exclaimed Madeline, as she grabbed the phone. 'Yes!'

'There's no need to snap, my dear.'

'What is it, Jeremy?'

'I thought you might be interested in a little anomaly I spotted on the printout, after you left,' he began. 'But, if you're busy then, well, no matter.'

Madeline clenched her jaw. 'Just had a reporter in my office,' she said, as if that was explanation enough for her rudeness.

'Have you indeed?' he said. 'Let me guess. Was it Guy Richards?'

Madeline took a sharp intake of breath. 'How did you know?'

'I know his father.'

'I fail to see how knowing his father could have alerted you to the fact that the man was just in my office.'

'Dear me,' said Jeremy. 'And there I was thinking you were such a good detective.'

Madeline could hear the smirk in his voice.

'Guy Richards' father is the chief forensic scientist in our lab, my dear,' continued Jeremy, a smile playing at the corner of his mouth.

'Donald Richards is Guy's father?' she exclaimed.

'Got it in one.'

'Well, I, I…'

'He popped down here just a moment ago to say hi to his old man.'

'He never said.'

'According to Donald, Guy, that's Donald's son…'

'Yes, thank you, Jeremy, I think I've fully taken on board the fact that Donald Richards is Guy Richards's father.'

'Yes, well, as I was saying, in Donald's opinion, Guy would be much better suited to police or private investigative work. Apparently, he's very astute.'

Madeline gripped the handset. 'The reason for your call, Jeremy?'

'Oh, yes, the anomaly. It's not directly pertinent to the case, but interesting nevertheless.'

'If it's not going to help with…'

'It's an anomaly that might be worth following up, but it's up to you, my dear.'

Madeline stared down at the name 'Mary Baker' now circled several times in red. 'Actually, Jeremy, I'm pleased you rang.'

'I'd never have guessed.'

Madeline took a deep breath. 'We've got a new suspect and I wonder if you'd be able to look at her baby's medical records.'

'It would be a pleasure.'

'Brilliant.'

'Now, about that anomaly I mentioned...'

'I'm on my way down Jeremy, so talk soon.'

Madeline dashed across to Rose. 'Can you look up Mary Baker's GP?'

Rose nodded. 'No problem,' she said, as she minimised the file she was working on and loaded up the medical records database. 'Here we are. Dr Sinai, Topcliffe Medical Centre.'

'Thanks. I'm just going down to the lab again. I won't be long.'

'I've double-checked the results,' said Jeremy, brandishing the computer printout. 'And I'm right, look here.' He pointed to the Hamiltons' DNA results. 'Notice anything?'

'What exactly am I looking for?'

'We look for common markers in the DNA. Parents and their offspring will have several common sequences but, if you look here, at the DNA of Lawrence Hamilton and Amelia Hamilton, there don't appear to be any, whereas, if you look at Dr Olivia Hamilton's DNA and compare it with Amelia's DNA, there are several, as we would expect.'

Madeline looked from the printout to Jeremy and from Jeremy back to the printout. 'So, Olivia Hamilton is the biological mother of Amelia but Lawrence Hamilton isn't the biological father.'

'Precisely, my dear, precisely,' said Jeremy. 'As I said, it doesn't help with the Lilly Green problem, but an interesting little snippet, don't you think?'

'Yes, it might explain Dr Hamilton's reticence when we spoke to her.'

'Good, good. Now, you said something about a new suspect.'

'Yes. Mary Baker. Her GP is Dr Sinai in…'

'In Topcliffe. The Medical Centre. Yes, yes, I know him well. No problem. I assume it's urgent.'

Madeline nodded.

'I'll ring him now. He'll be able to email me the records, so I should have some answers for you by the end of the day.'

'Perfect. Thank you.'

Madeline dashed up the two flights of stairs to the incident room. 'How's it coming along?'

Rose started. 'Oh, Jesus, you made me jump—I'm nearly done,' she said, pressing print. 'So, what did Jeremy have to say?'

'He's uncovered an interesting fact pertaining to Dr Hamilton's baby.'

'Really? What?'

'Lawrence Hamilton isn't the daddy.'

'So, Dr Hamilton *has* been playing away from home.'

'So it would seem.'

'Dr Sutcliffe?'

Madeline shrugged. 'Don't know, probably.'

'Anyway, take a look at these,' said Rose, retrieving the printouts and handing them to Madeline.

Madeline scanned the top sheet. 'OK, so Mary Baker, née O'Brien, born 1968 in County Antrim, Ireland, had a baby in 1985 who died suddenly at three months old.'

Rose slapped her hand over the sheet. 'Guess what the verdict was.'

'Cot death?'

'Got it in one.'

'Really? Bloody hell.'

'There's more,' continued Rose in a rush. 'She came over to England in February 1986 and secured a job as a waitress at the Fulford barracks. She met Christopher Baker when he joined the RMP four years later. They both left in 1998 and were married the following year. He was fifty-one, she was thirty-one.'

'And we know that Lawrence Hamilton was at Fulford in the late eighties.'

Rose nodded. 'We do. He was there from 1988 to 1991 and again from 2002 to 2006.'

'I don't suppose you came across any reference to their drag performances?'

Rose smiled. 'Actually, I did,' she said. 'Look at the last four printouts.'

Madeline flicked through to the last sheets. 'Good grief.'

'I know, alarming, aren't they? They're extracts from the Christmas editions of the *Fulford Army Gazette*. They show Lawrence Hamilton performing as Yvette Young in 1988 and 1989, and again in 1990 and 1991, when he was joined by Christopher Baker performing as Lucy Lupin. They achieved excellent reviews.'

'And Mary Baker was at Fulford—when did you say?'

'1986 to 1998,' said Rose. 'And somewhere in that lot,' she added, nodding towards the pile of papers in Madeline's hands, 'there should be a copy of the 1986 personnel photograph. I circled Mary O'Brien. There should also be a copy of a photograph showing the audience at the 1990 review. Note the figure standing on the right of the stage.'

'Oh, well done, Rose,' said Madeline. 'Now then, their baby, born on the twelfth of March this year, was that their first?'

'Yes.'

Madeline screwed her eyes shut. 'Mary Baker must be forty-five now. Rather old to be having babies.'

'Maybe it was unplanned, maybe she was concerned she might lose another one.'

'And perhaps she did.'

'Perhaps she did what?'

'Lose another one, Rose.'

'Oh, shit, yes.'

'Oh, by the way, did we get anything from, what's-his-features?'

'From Justin?'

Madeline nodded.

'Only this,' said Rose, waving a scrap of paper. 'I found it on my chair. He must have put it there just now, while I was in your office talking to Guy Richards. It definitely wasn't there this morning.'

'Oh, yes, Guy Richards,' said Madeline. 'Did you know he was Donald Richards's son?'

Rose nodded.

'You did?' exclaimed Madeline. 'Why didn't you say?'

'I, well, I assumed you knew.'

Madeline's face flushed.

'So, you didn't know?'

'I do now,' said Madeline. 'Anyway, what's on the scrap of paper?'

'It's infuriating. He's always one bloody step ahead.'

'What does it say, Rose?'

'It says: *Re. your request on Wednesday 24th July for information on army personnel stationed at Fulford in the 1980s and 1990s. There were hundreds. The only name warranting further investigation is Mary Baker (née O'Brien). She worked as a waitress at Fulford from 1986 to 1998...* need I go on?'

'Let me have a look.' Madeline glanced over towards Justin's den. 'Don't tell me; Guy Richards spoke to him first,' she exclaimed.

'Justin doesn't really *speak* to anyone.'

'No, you're right, he's not exactly Mr Chatty.'

'He is, however, infuriatingly good at his job,' said Rose.

'There's no mention of the Bakers owning a green 1970s Saab 95 V4 estate, which is a surprise. I'd have thought our wonder boy, brain the size of the universe, Justin bloody what's-his-name—Rose, are you alright? You seem...'

'It's Justin 'bloody' Waverly-Hawkins; the 'bloody', however, is optional,' said Justin from behind Madeline.

'Justin, I...'

He removed the scrap of paper from Madeline's hand, turned it over and slapped it down onto the desk. 'Please note; 1970s vehicle details clearly inscribed here,' he said, tapping the paper with his pen. 'I also added the Bakers' address and telephone number.' With a curt nod he pocketed his pen, turned and continued on his way. 'Harry,' he called, 'I've got that information you asked for. How Curtis missed it—anyway, that's another case we can close.'

Rose averted her gaze as Madeline stared at the back of the scrap of paper.

'Right, come on, Rose, we'd better pay them a visit.'

Twenty minutes later they parked their car on the driveway of The Old Post House. Intent on their prime purpose, they failed to notice the old Mini parked opposite the house.

The door was opened just as Madeline was about to ring. 'Uncanny timing, just passing the door, saw your outlines, can I help you?'

'Mr Christopher Baker?'

'I am he.'

Madeline held up her badge. 'Inspector Driscoll,' she said.

'Driscoll,' cried Christopher. 'Are you by chance related to Jack Driscoll?'

'He's my father,' said Madeline.

'Well, I never. He and I were fishing on the river Swale just last week,' he exclaimed. 'Your father and I worked together, oh, way back, in the eighties, before I joined the RMP. Well, fancy that. What can I do for you, Inspector Driscoll?'

'Would it be possible for Sergeant Scott and I to have a word with your wife?'

'My wife?'

'Yes. May we come in?'

Christopher stood aside. 'Yes, yes of course, but why did you want to speak with my wife?'

'We're making general enquiries about the whereabouts of all women during May of this year, Mr Baker; women who gave birth to babies during March.'

Christopher frowned.

'Baby Lilly Green was abducted in May, she was two months old.'

'Yes, yes, so I heard, appalling thing to happen, appalling,' said Christopher. 'We've already spoken to some reporter and...'

'Guy Richards, from the *Yorkshire Herald*,' said Madeline. 'Yes, we're aware of that.'

'Right, well I'll tell you what I told him,' said Christopher. 'My wife wasn't home at the time. She was visiting an old friend of hers in Whitby, while I was walking the Pennine Way.'

'Nevertheless, Mr Baker,' said Madeline. 'We still need to speak with your wife to verify the details and if, as you say, she was in Whitby at the relevant time, we can eliminate her from the mix.'

'I can assure you...'

A voice called out from upstairs. 'Who is it, Christopher?'

'It's the police, they want...'

There was a loud crash followed by the startled screams of a small baby.

Christopher bounded upstairs. 'Mary, are you alright? Mary, Mary!'

Madeline and Rose stepped into the hall and closed the front door. They could hear muffled voices coming from a room at the top of the stairs. After a short delay, Christopher made his way down the stairs with tremendous care, holding a baby in his arms. 'Crisis averted,' he said. 'Mary was just catching up on a bit of housework. She dropped Emma's bath toys into the bath and, of course, that woke the baby from her nap. Anyway, she'll be down in a tick. Would either of you like a coffee or a tea?'

'No, that's fine,' said Madeline. 'Just a few questions and then we'll be off.'

'Sorry about that,' said Mary, as she stepped into the living room. 'My husband said you wanted to ask me some questions.'

'Yes, did he explain why?'

Mary nodded. 'He said you wanted to ask me questions about where I was in May. Although I fail to see why that should interest you.'

'Before we start, we need to check a few details,' said Madeline. 'When exactly was Emma born?'

'What's that got to do with where I was in May?'

'If you could just answer the question, Mrs Baker,' said Madeline.

Mary folded her arms across her chest. 'The twelfth of March.'

'Thank you.'

Christopher held Emma up above his head, causing her to giggle. 'And isn't she beautiful?'

'Don't be getting her all excited, Christopher, she needs more sleep. See if you can get her to lie down again, otherwise she's going to be fractious.'

'She's looks wide awake to me,' said Christopher.

'Nevertheless,' Mary persisted, 'if you could just try.'

'Right you are. I'll leave you in the hands of these police officers.' He bent down to kiss Mary's head and added. 'You'll never believe it, but Inspector Driscoll here is Jack Driscoll's little girl. Amazing, isn't it?'

Madeline smiled. 'Your husband's just been telling us about his recent fishing trip with my father.'

'Has he indeed?'

'Not just with your father,' said Christopher, lifting Emma up above his head again. 'Who's my beautiful baby then?—but with Lawrence Hamilton too. Hadn't seen him in years, not since 1990.' He started to giggle. 'We were quite the pair of drag queens in our day—oh, you should have seen your daddy back then, Emma, my sweet.'

'I do wish you'd stop going on about that,' snapped Mary. 'And I asked you to stop getting Emma over-excited.'

Christopher's face fell. 'Oh, come on, Mary, I've hardly gone on…'

Mary gave him a stony look.

'Right, anyway, come on sweetheart,' he said, rocking Emma in his arms. 'Let's see if I can persuade you to have some more shut-eye; keep your mummy happy.'

Mary invited them to sit down. Madeline sat on the settee, but Rose remained standing. She glanced around the room. Her eyes alighted on a photograph displayed in a prominent position on the sideboard. As Madeline started asking questions, Rose sidled across to take a closer look.

'Your husband said you were visiting a friend in Whitby in May,' said Madeline.

Mary cleared her throat. 'That I was, she and I knew each other at school.'

'And she would be able to confirm that?'

'Obviously.'

Madeline removed her notebook from her top pocket. 'So, her name and address?'

'Laura Fox, The Paddock, Silver Street.'

'And do you have a telephone number?'

'I'll have to check my address book.'

Walking across towards the sideboard, Mary snatched the framed photograph from Rose's hands. 'I'll thank you to leave our things alone,' she said, placing the photograph back as she opened a drawer. 'Here we are.' She rattled off the number. 'Now, is that all?'

'There was just one more thing,' said Madeline.

'Yes?'

'Have you ever come across the name Yvette Young?'

Mary glanced across towards the door, brushed non-existent dust from her skirt and sat back down. 'I don't believe so, no.'

'No? That's odd. I was under the impression that was the name used by your husband's friend, Lawrence Hamilton, in their drag act.'

'Was it?'

Madeline flicked back through her notebook. 'Yes, here we are,' she said with a smile thrown towards Mary. 'Christopher Baker's first stage appearance as Lucy Lupin was with Lawrence Hamilton, who performed as Yvette Young. It was at a Christmas Army Review, in December 1990, at Fulford Barracks.'

'If you say so,' said Mary.

Madeline turned a page of her notebook and flattened it down. 'I also see you started working at the Fulford barracks in 1986. Is that correct?'

Mary nodded.

'Now, that *is* interesting, because Lawrence Hamilton's first performance was in 1988. At a Christmas Review put on for all employees, military and civilian.'

'So?'

'So, I would imagine that's when you first came across the name Yvette Young, wouldn't you?' Madeline closed her note book and locked eyes with Mary.

'I really can't remember.'

'Sergeant, could you show Mrs Baker the photographs from the *Fulford Army* Gazette?'

Rose laid the photographs out on the coffee table.

'If I could draw your attention to this one,' said Madeline, picking up the photograph from 1990. 'Do you see this figure standing to the right of the stage?'

Mary nodded.

'Who would you say that was?'

Mary's jaw clenched. 'Me.'

'And the figures on stage?'

'Christopher and Lawrence,' hissed Mary.

'Performing as?'

'Drag queens, by the looks of it.'

'And here we are, look, in the caption it says they performed as Lucy Lupin and Yvette Young,' said Madeline, handing the photograph to Mary.

Mary examined the caption with exaggerated concentration. 'So it does,' she said, tossing it back onto the coffee table. 'And perfectly ridiculous they looked too.'

Christopher breezed back into the living room with Emma in his arms. 'Who looked ridiculous, darling?'

'I thought I asked you to get Emma to lie down,' snapped Mary

'I tried, my love, but it seems she's got other ideas.' He tickled Emma's feet. 'And we all know who's the boss in this house, don't we?—oh, I say, where did they come from?'

'These are from the *Fulford Army Gazette*, Mr Baker,' said Madeline. 'I was just asking you wife about your performances with Lawrence Hamilton. She couldn't seem to remember the names the pair of you adopted. I thought these might jog her memory.'

Christopher threw a puzzled look towards Mary. 'She couldn't remember?'

'Two grown men prancing about in women's clothes. I'm sick to death of it all, so I am.'

'You enjoyed it back then,' said Christopher.

'That maybe so,' snapped Mary, 'but for the love of God, enough now.'

Madeline cleared her throat. 'Mr Baker, you mentioned you were walking the Pennine Way.'

Christopher shifted his gaze away from Mary's stern face. 'Yes that's right, Inspector.'

'When was that exactly?'

Christopher screwed his eyes shut. 'Give me a moment…'

'I can answer that,' said Mary. 'He left, as he does every year, in the first week of April, and he didn't get back home until the nineteenth of May. He went even though I'd just given birth to our baby.'

'Please, Mary, let's not go over that again.' He turned and smiled at Madeline. 'It's a regular commitment. I don't like to let down old friends. Now, is there anything else?'

'That seems a long time, Mr Baker,' remarked Madeline. 'I thought it took about three weeks.'

'It does, if you do just one way. John and I do the return as well,' he said, as he bounced Emma on his knee.

'I see, and did you drive up to the Peak District for the start of the walk?'

'What, and leave Mary without transport, certainly not,' said Christopher. 'I caught the bus to Northallerton, then the train to Newcastle, where John met me.'

'Is that it, Inspector?' asked Mary.

'Not quite. I take it you wouldn't object if we took samples of your DNA.'

A frown flickered across Mary's face.

'Is that really necessary?' said Christopher.

'It's a simple procedure, Mr Baker, a cheek swab. Nothing invasive,' said Madeline. 'We'll need a sample from you all, including the baby, so we can eliminate your family from the investigation.'

'Oh, right, I see,' said Christopher.

'I've never heard the like. I really don't think...'

'Come on, Mary, the Inspector's just explained, they need to do this to eliminate us from the investigation.' He glanced down at Emma cradled in his arms. 'Imagine if someone had snatched this little one.' He shuddered. 'Imagine how we'd feel. We'd want the police to do everything in their power to get her back, wouldn't we? So, come on, what possible harm can it do?'

Samples safely stored away, Madeline stood. 'Thank you for your cooperation. We'll be in touch to let you know the results. It would be helpful if you didn't leave the area.'

Christopher gave a wry laugh. 'We're not likely to be doing that in the near future. This little one,' he said, nodding towards Emma, 'likes her routine at the moment.'

At the door, Christopher apologised for his wife's rudeness. 'Emma hasn't been sleeping too well recently, teething you see, Mary's at the end of her tether.'

Christopher returned to the living room just as Mary was hanging up the phone. 'Who was that?'

'Weirdly enough,' she said, 'it was Laura.'

'Laura, from Whitby?'

'Yes—she wants me to go and stay with her again.'

'When?'

'Well, that's just it, darling, she wants me to go up there today, as in now.'

'I assume you said you couldn't go.'

'She seemed very distraught, Christopher, and remember she was very accommodating when I foisted myself and Emma on her. You wouldn't mind, would you?'

'Mary, the police have just asked us not to leave the area and now you're…'

'It's Whitby, Christopher, not Columbia. In the unlikely event that the police need to speak to me again, I can be back in an hour or two, for goodness sake!'

'Well, I suppose so. It just seems a bit much, frankly.'

Mary rushed to her husband and gave him a kiss. 'Hold onto Emma for a bit. She'll be able to sleep in the car. I'll go and pack,' she trilled. 'Laura needs looking after this time.'

'She's not ill, is she?' asked Christopher. 'We don't want Emma to catch anything.'

'I'm not stupid, Christopher.'

'So, what's the problem then?'

'Laura asked me not to say.'

Christopher frowned.

'It's nothing sinister, don't worry,' said Mary, giving her husband a dazzling smile, before adding. 'Now, I really should go and pack. Are you OK with Emma for a bit?'

Christopher stared down at Emma with adoration. 'For a life time, Mary, for a lifetime.'

'I won't be long,' she said, as she made her way upstairs.

Christopher called up. 'As a matter of interest, how long will you be gone for?'

'I'm not sure. I'll ring you as soon as I know, OK?'

'I suppose it will have to be,' he muttered.

Putting their seat belts on, Madeline said. 'Try ringing Laura Fox.'

'It's ringing—gone to voicemail—Ms Fox, this is Sergeant Scott, Northallerton police,' said Rose. 'Please call as soon as you get this message, we just need to ask you a few questions, nothing to worry about. Thank you.'

'Mrs Baker was definitely on edge,' said Madeline.

'She was, and did you notice the photograph on the sideboard?'

'No, but I saw her reaction when you picked it up.'

'It was a professional family photograph of the Bakers with their baby, taken on March the twenty-ninth this year, by the Phase 3 photographic studio.'

Reversing out of the drive, Madeline asked, 'And?'

'Mary Baker's dress.' She paused, and announced with a flourish. 'It was floral; poppies on a cream background.'

Madeline almost stalled the car.

'The studio's just outside Sessay,' Rose added. 'Turn right at the bottom of the road and it's about four miles away.'

Guy saw Madeline and Rose drive away and decided to remain watching the house. He retrieved a cheese sandwich from the glove compartment and was just settling back to eat, when a movement from across the road caught his eye. The Bakers' garage door was opening. He could make out the dark shape of a car parked inside and he watched as Mary eased herself into the driver's seat. He heard the engine fire up. Once clear of the garage the car fell silent again. He bit into his sandwich and continued to watch. Mary got out and unlocked the tailgate. The front door opened. Christopher appeared with a black holdall slung across his shoulder and carrying a folded pushchair. He staggered towards the car and loaded both into the back.

Keeping his eye on the house, Guy finished his sandwich and started on his apple. As he took the first bite, the front door opened again. This time Christopher appeared with Emma in a carseat. He carried her over to the car and strapped her in. Mary followed. After a brief exchange with Christopher, she got into the car and backed the green Saab onto the road. She drove off, tooting the horn and waving as she went. Guy chucked his half-eaten apple onto the back seat and followed.

The proprietor of Phase 3 provided Madeline and Rose with a copy of the studio group photograph showing Mary in the floral dress, as well as a copy of a close-up of Mary Baker's face.

Back at the police station, Madeline handed Rose the photographs. 'Take these down to the tech boys. Get them to alter the close-up to give Mrs Baker shoulder-length blonde hair. I also want them to obscure the details of the faces in the group photograph, including the baby's face. Tell them time is of the essence. I'll get these samples down to Donald and let Avery know what's happening.'

Chapter 17
Friday 26th July (Afternoon)

Rose walked into the Poplars Hotel while Madeline waited by the car.

Holding her badge, Rose approached the reception desk. 'Mrs Shaw, I'm Sergeant Scott.'

'Hello again, love. What can I do for you now?'

'Would you mind taking a look at these,' said Rose, handing her the group photograph.

'I can't make out the faces, but the woman's wearing a dress just like the one Anne Smith was wearing.' Norma brought the photograph closer to her face. 'Is this the woman then? The one who snatched Lilly Green? God, is that actually Lilly she's holding?'

Rose gently eased the photograph from Norma's grasp and showed her the close up of Mary Baker.

'My god, that her. It is, isn't it?'

'I'm sorry, I can't comment at the moment. But thank you for your help,' she said, as she made her way back to the car.

'Well?' said Madeline, taking a final drag on her cigarette.

Rose nodded.

The front door was snatched open. 'Have you found Lilly?'

'May we come in, Mrs Green?' said Madeline.

Sally's shoulders dropped, she grabbed the doorjamb. 'Oh, no, no, oh, God.'

'It's alright, Mrs Green, we haven't come with bad news,' said Madeline. 'We just have another photograph we'd like you to look at.'

Sally nodded. Leaning against the wall she shuffled down the hallway and led them into the darkened living room. She lowered herself onto the settee.

'Mrs Green, would it be alright to switch the light on?'

'What?'

'The overhead light, Mrs Green. So you can see the photograph.'

'Oh, right, yes, yes, fine.'

Madeline removed the photograph from her inside jacket pocket and slid it across the coffee table.

Taking a deep breath, Sally picked up the photograph. 'Oh, God, it's her,' she gasped. 'That's the bitch who took Lilly. Have you found her? Have you found Lilly?'

'Are you positive?'

'Absolutely bloody positive,' she said, throwing the photograph down onto the table.

'It's just, well, you did say one of the women in the other photographs we showed…'

'I said the other one *could* have been her.' She picked up Mary's photograph again. 'Whereas this one is definitely her, I'd stake my life on it.'

'Right, that's all we need,' said Madeline.

'Are you going to arrest her and, and bring Lilly home?'

'Mrs Green, finding the woman doesn't necessarily mean we've also found Lilly.'

'She has a baby, yes?'

Madeline nodded.

'Then it'll be Lilly.'

'Our labs are checking the DNA now.'

'I knew it, deep down I knew it.' Sally hugged herself. 'I can still feel the weight of her, you see; I can still feel the warmth of her body next to mine—just bring Lilly home.'

Screeching to a halt outside the Old Post House, siren blaring, lights flashing, Madeline parked the car across the driveway, blocking a potential escape route.

Christopher flung open the door within moments of their arrival. 'What in God's name is going on?' he yelled.

'We need to speak with your wife, urgently.'

'Well, I'm afraid you're out of luck.'

Madeline stopped in her tracks so abruptly that Rose collided with her back. 'Out of luck?' said Madeline. 'What's that supposed to mean?'

Christopher raised himself to his full imposing height. 'I'm not sure how else to put it, Inspector. It's means exactly what it implies. You're out of luck. She isn't here.'

'Where is she?'

'On her way to Laura's in Whitby.' He glared at Madeline. 'Will you kindly turn that infernal thing off?'

Madeline nodded at Rose.

Rose turned the siren off.

'When did your wife leave, Mr Baker?'

'I fail to see what that's…'

Madeline took the final few steps towards Mr Baker. 'When, Mr Baker?'

Christopher glanced at his watch. 'About twenty or thirty minutes ago.'

'Mr Baker, we have reason to believe your wife may be able to help us in our search for Lilly Green.'

'Oh, for goodness sake, don't be ridiculous. How? I told you she wasn't even here when that baby was abducted.'

'Exactly.'

'What do you mean, 'exactly'?'

'Mr Baker, I think it's possible your wife took Lilly Green.'

'Have you completely lost your mind? I'm not sure if you recall but, given you were here such a short while ago, I assume you noticed we have a baby of our own.'

'And where might that baby be now?'

'What a ludicrous question, Inspector. Emma's with my wife.'

'On her way to Whitby?'

'Yes.'

'Did your wife…?' Madeline began. 'Sorry.' She snatched her phone from her pocket and glanced at the screen. It displayed 'unknown'. 'Excuse me,' she said. 'I've got a feeling I need to take this call.'

'Inspector Driscoll?' hissed the caller. 'Guy Richards here, currently at the Moto Wetherby service station on the A1(M), watching Mary Baker fill her car with fuel. Please advise.'

'Which direction is she heading?'

'South.'

'Give me your car registration.'

Guy recited it. 'I know what you're thinking. It's old. But, don't worry, this old mini has never let me down.'

'Keep your distance, but stay in pursuit. I'll have back-up with you shortly.'

'Mr Baker, I don't wish to alarm you, but your wife isn't on her way to Whitby. She's currently heading South on the A1(M).'

Christopher rocked backwards. 'What? But, I, I don't understand. What?'

'The registration number of your car.'

'What?'

'I need the registration number of your car.'

Christopher rattled it off.

Rose scribbled the number down and dashed back towards their car.

'There should be a patrol car in the vicinity. Inform them that Guy Richards is currently in pursuit. Warn them there's a baby on board and to take care. Follow, but do not apprehend.'

Rose nodded.

'Now then, Mr Baker, shall we step inside for a moment?'

Without a word, Christopher entered his house. Once inside, Madeline explained their suspicions.

Christopher remained silent.

'Do you understand?'

Still he said nothing.

'Mr Baker, I'm sorry, but I need to know you've understood,' said Madeline. 'So, I say again; we have reason to believe your baby passed away in May, and was buried in Vicar's Moor Wood by your wife, prior to the abduction, by her, of Lilly Green.'

Christopher collapsed onto the sofa, rocking back and forth. A rattling moaning came from the depths of the man's chest.

'Mr Baker?'

Christopher looked up, his face ashen. Still he said nothing.

Madeline glanced at her watch. 'Look, I'm sorry but we have to leave now. Is there anybody we can ring to come and sit with you?'

Christopher continued to rock back and forth.

'Mr Baker, I...'

The rocking stopped abruptly and Christopher fixed Madeline with an icy stare. 'This is crazy. You've obviously made a mistake. Mary had a phone call from Laura. Some sort of crisis, Mary didn't say what, said it was confidential. And I, unlike you, believe my wife. She said she was going to Whitby, therefore that's where she's going.'

'On the A1(M) heading south?'

'*If* she's on the A1(M) heading south, I'm sure there's a perfectly good reason for that,' said Christopher. He stared into the middle distance. 'Maybe Laura asked Mary to call in somewhere like—well, like York, for example. Yes, that'll be it,' he declared. 'I remember now. Laura's father lives in York. I expect Mary's delivering a message.'

'Wouldn't it be easier for Laura to ring her father herself? York must be what, twenty-five miles in the wrong direction; quite a diversion for your wife.'

'I realise that,' snapped Christopher. 'I can't think. Perhaps it's a message that couldn't be delivered over the phone. I simply don't know, but I can assure you, Inspector, *if* my wife says she's going to Whitby, then that's where she's going.'

'Fair enough, Mr Baker, if you say so, but I'm afraid we really do have to go,' said Madeline, again glancing at her watch. 'Please remain here, we'll be in touch.'

'I'm hardly likely to go anywhere, am I?' said Christopher. 'Mary will be ringing me as soon as she arrives in Whitby.'

'Fine. If your wife should ring you…'

'She will.'

Madeline handed him her card. 'When she does, would you be good enough to let us know.'

'With bloody pleasure.'

Guy first noticed the police car trailing him once he was on the M62. He remained a safe distance behind Mary Baker's car and the police car remained a safe distance behind him, radioing their position to the Northallerton control centre at regular intervals. This information was relayed simultaneously to Madeline and Rose, who were currently driving at speed, lights flashing and siren blaring again, some miles behind. Rose checked the map as each new position came through. 'Shit, I reckon she's heading for Liverpool.'

Madeline put her foot down. 'She intends to take the baby across to Ireland,' she exclaimed. 'Radio the Freeport police security. Explain the situation; tell them to tread gently.'

As they were driving along the A5080, just outside Liverpool, Rose received a call on her mobile. 'Hello, Sergeant Scott here.'

Madeline glanced across at Rose with a quizzical expression. Rose put her thumbs up and mouthed the words, 'Laura Fox.'

As Mary approached the security checkpoint to the docks, she slowed down. The police car following Guy flashed him and he got out of the way. The police car sped up, overtook Mary's car and slewed to a halt across the road. A security officer dashed towards the Saab and banged on the driver's window. 'Mrs Baker?'

Mary nodded.

'Could you step out of the car please?'

Mary exited her car. She glanced over her shoulder and caught sight of Guy, leaning nonchalantly against his Mini. The colour drained from her face.

The officer followed Mary's gaze. He lowered his voice. 'A newspaper reporter, I believe. No doubt stirring up a scandal, as is their custom.' He gave Mary a dazzling smile. 'I'm Inspector Shane O'Connor. Try not to worry, we'll soon have it all sorted.'

'A scandal?'

Inspector O'Connor shrugged. 'All something of nothing, I'm sure. Now, if you could just come with me.'

'Of course, officer, I'll just get Emma. I'm afraid the sudden stop has woken her.'

'Can you manage?'

'Yes, thank you, officer—come on, little one.'

'She's a darling, to be sure,' said O'Connor. 'A credit to you.'

Mary gave Inspector O'Connor a beatific smile as he led her through the Freeport police security entrance. They made their way to a small office containing a single table and a few chairs. The long, thin windows were positioned high up along the back wall and, even though they were open, the room was hot and stuffy. It smelt of dust and sweat. Mary sat on one of the chairs as directed. A young female officer sat beside her. The sound of a phone ringing drifted into the room, followed by shouting and laughter. In the room, the plaintive cries of the baby became more insistent.

Mary dug around in her bag and extracted a baby bottle. She handed it to the female officer. 'She needs feeding,' she said. 'Could you warm this up? Not too hot mind.'

The officer glanced up at Inspector O'Connor, who nodded.

Peace was restored as soon as the baby's mouth made contact with the bottle. Inspector O'Connor looked on at what, to all intents and purposes, was a perfect scene of mother and daughter bonding. It took him back to the time when his daughter had been a babe in arms. Mary looked up at him. The pain radiating from her eyes, as she clung onto the baby and rocked back and forth, tore at his heart. A young constable entered the office and whispered in his ear.

'Mrs Baker, I've been informed that some police officers have arrived. They'd like a quick word. I do hope that's alright,' said O'Connor.

Mary continued feeding the baby.

'Alright, constable, show them in.'

'Hello again, Mrs Baker,' said Madeline.

Mary's eyes narrowed. 'I don't want to talk to you. Leave us alone,' she said, turning her body towards the back wall.

Madeline approached her. 'Mrs Baker, I'm sorry, but I'm going to have to ask you to let me take the baby.'

'You can't, you can't take her,' she sobbed.

Madeline stepped a little closer. 'Mrs Baker, I can see how well you've cared for the baby, but…'

'Keep away,' she screamed. 'What do you think I am, some sort of monster?'

'You're not a monster, of course you're not. So, please, just take a minute to think about Mrs Green.'

Mary removed the now empty bottle from the baby's mouth and placed it on the desk beside her. She sat the baby up and gently rubbed her back. 'Mrs Green is young,' said Mary matter-of-factly. 'I'm forty-five.' She stared at Madeline. Her face pale, her expression bleak.

The wall clock ticked loudly. A ferry horn blasted in the distance. Another phone rang in the outer office and the sounds of people laughing drifted in through the open windows.

Inspector O'Connor cleared his throat. 'Would you be wanting a cup of tea, Mrs Baker?'

She swung her gaze towards O'Connor, and gave him a radiant smile. 'That would be lovely officer, thank you.'

'Sugar?'

'Two spoons, please.'

The female officer stood.

'It's alright, Constable Walker. We'll get one of the lads to brew a cup for a change, shall we?' He opened the office door. 'Evans,' he yelled, 'one cup of tea, two sugars, quick as you can.' He turned back to Mary. 'I remember when my daughter was just a baby; Fiona, that's my wife, drank gallons of tea, goodness knows why. I could understand it if she breast fed, they say you need to keep your fluid levels up but she, like you, bottle fed. Perhaps it's just instinct, I don't know. Mysterious lot, you women,' he said, as he edged closer to Mary.

Constable Evans arrived with the tea.

'Ah, excellent, Evans, if you could hand it to Mrs Baker here,' said O'Connor, leaning down towards the baby. 'Here, let me take her for a moment while you drink your tea.'

And it was done.

Inspector O'Connor took the baby and handed her to Madeline in one swift movement. Mary threw the cup to the floor and lunged towards Madeline. O'Connor and Evans restrained Mary who watched, helpless, as Madeline took her baby away. Mary collapsed to her knees, howling like a trapped animal. O'Connor and Evans exchanged a panicked look, as Rose knelt beside Mary and threw her arms around her.

'Walker,' said Inspector O'Connor, 'get the doc in here.'

'I don't need a bloody doctor,' screamed Mary. 'Emma, Emma, where's that bitch taken my Emma?'

'Mrs Baker, the baby's fine,' said Rose.

'Where is she?'

'We need to get you home. I expect your husband's worried about you. Come along now, up you get,' said Rose.

'I'm not leaving without Emma.'

'The baby's going home as well, Mrs Baker.'

With the help of O'Connor and Evans, Rose managed to get Mary to her feet.

'Get your hands off me.'

'Mrs Baker, you need to come with me now,' said Rose.

'Fine, just get these louts to let go of me.'

Rose nodded towards Inspector O'Connor.

Evans and O'Connor let go.

'Thank you,' said Mary. Straightening her cardigan, she threw an icy look towards Inspector O'Connor.

Still clutching Mary Baker's arm, Rose said. 'Before we go, I need to read you your rights.'

'Is that so?'

'Mrs Mary Baker, I'm arresting you for the abduction of Lilly Green from 50, Front Street, Thirsk, on May the thirteenth this year. You do not have to say anything. But it may harm your defence if you do not mention when questioned something which you later rely on in court. Anything you do say may be given in evidence.'

Mary closed her eyes.

'Mrs Baker, do you understand?'

'Yes,' hissed Mary.

Mary sat on the back seat, directly behind Madeline, with Rose by her side. She stared out of the car window and watched in silence as a young female police officer carried the baby towards another police car.

Madeline wound the window down and Guy leaned in. 'I'll follow you back and then…'

A huge dollop of spittle radiated in an arc from the back of the car and hit him in the face. He automatically pulled back, striking his head on the window surround. Showing remarkable restraint, he acknowledged Mary with a small shrug as he straightened up, removed a large handkerchief from his jacket pocket and wiped his face.

Driving off to follow her fellow officers, Madeline glanced Guy in her rear-view mirror, rubbing his head as he made his way back towards his Mini.

Back at Northallerton police station, Mary was taken to an interview room. Constable Brian Jones was stationed at the door.

Emma was handed over to Julia Hayes, the duty social service worker. 'What's your estimated timescale here?' she asked.

'We should be able to confirm that Emma here is Lilly Green by Monday, if not before,' said Madeline. 'The DNA samples are already with our experts.'

'Right you are. I'll leave the contact details for the foster carers with the desk sergeant,' said Julia. She adjusted the position of Emma in her arms. 'A heavy little thing,' she remarked. 'She's certainly been well cared for.'

'Excellent,' said Madeline. 'Thank you. Right then, come on Rose, we've got a suspect to interview. You go on ahead. I'll fetch the case files from my office.'

'Excuse me,' said Guy.

Madeline swung round. 'Oh, Mr Richards, I forgot all about you.'

'You certainly know how to hurt a man.'

'Look, I'm sorry, but...'

Guy held up his hand. 'It's alright. I take it my services are no longer required.'

'Well no, not really, but well, thank you, you've been a great help.'

Guy ducked his head. 'At your service,' he said, as he moved towards the exit. 'Good luck with the interview.'

'Mr Richards.'

Guy turned. 'Yes?'

Madeline walked towards him. 'I, well I feel I owe you a sincere apology, you know, for not returning your earlier calls. If I had...'

Guy reached out and touched her arm. 'The important thing is you've got her now.'

Madeline nodded. 'And I really should...'

'Get on with the interview.'

Madeline nodded again.

'I'll talk to you again soon—I hope,' said Guy.

A trace of a smile played across Madeline's lips, as she dashed up to her office. She retrieved the Lilly Green and Vicar's Moor Wood files from her desk. She was about to leave when she noticed a blue folder on her chair, with a post-it note stuck to it; *Report on Emma Baker, as requested. See front sheet; interesting reading, my dear. Jeremy.*

Madeline opened the folder. 'Well, well. Now that *is* interesting. Well done, Jeremy.'

In Topcliffe, Christopher Baker was still waiting for his wife to call. He checked his watch again. He couldn't understand why he hadn't heard from her. He'd reasoned that, with a diversion to York, his wife should have reached Whitby by 3pm at the latest. He'd risked ringing her mobile a couple of times, but it'd gone straight to voicemail. It was approaching 6pm. An uneasy feeling settled like a boulder deep within him. He walked over to the sideboard and removed Mary's address book. He picked up the phone and dialled Laura's number.

'Hello.'

Christopher cleared his throat. 'Hello, Laura?'

'Yes, who's that?'

'It's Christopher, Christopher Baker. Sorry to bother you, but could I have a quick word with my wife?'

There was no response.

'Laura, Laura can you hear me? Oh, stupid question, if you can't hear me then you can't hear me asking if you can hear me. Right, I'll hang up and…'

'It's alright,' said Laura. 'I can hear you.'

'Ah, good, excellent,' said Christopher. 'So, can I have a word with Mary?'

'I'm sorry.'

'Whatever for? I just want a quick word with her. After you phoned her this afternoon she set off immediately and that was hours ago.' Christopher felt his stomach heave. 'Hasn't she arrived yet?'

'But I'm not expecting a visit from Mary. I haven't seen her in years, we…'

'What do you mean?' demanded Christopher. 'You saw her just a couple of months ago.'

Again there was no response.

'Laura, are you still there?'

'Yes, Christopher I'm still here,' said Laura. 'Look, I don't know what's going on. This is awkward, but I can assure you I did *not* see Mary a couple of months ago. I've spoken to the police and…'

'The *police*? What police? When?'

'There was a message from a Sergeant Scott, Northallerton police; I rang them an hour or two ago, they were asking me whether Mary had stayed with me in May and I told them, like I've just told you, that I haven't seen Mary in years. They also asked me if I was expecting a visit from her today and I'm not.'

'So, why did you ring her?'

'I didn't ring Mary, Christopher. Look, I'm really sorry, but I've got to go, I hope Mary's alright, I…'

Christopher slammed the phone down. With shaking hands he reached into his pocket and removed Madeline's card. He dialled the number.

'Northallerton police.'

'This is Christopher Baker,' he croaked. 'I need to speak with Inspector Driscoll. It's urgent.'

'You've come through to the main desk, sir. I'm afraid Inspector Driscoll is—oh, no, just a minute, here she is.'

Sergeant Bailey handed the phone to Madeline. 'Mr Christopher Baker for you.'

Madeline covered the mouthpiece. 'Sergeant, has Mrs Baker been given tea?'

Sergeant Bailey nodded.

'Excellent,' she said, as she put the phone to her ear. 'Mr Baker, good of...'

'My wife,' he spluttered, 'have you found my wife? I've just spoken with Laura and she, and she...'

'Your wife's here, at the station. I'm just about to interview her.'

'Where's Emma? Where's my baby?'

'She's safe, Mr Baker.'

'*Where* is she?'

'She's being looked after by a foster family just for...'

'What? A *foster* family? Why? I'm her bloody father. She needs to be with me. I'll come and get her now.'

'Mr Baker, I need to—hello, hello?'

She handed the phone back to Sergeant Bailey. 'It seems Mr Baker's on his way to the station. When he arrives, ask Constable Walsh to show him into interview room B. Tell him to wait with Mr Baker. Explain I'll be with him as soon as I can.'

Mary, a mug of tea cradled in her hands, sat opposite Rose in the main interview room. Constable Brian Jones stood motionless by the door. Mary glanced across at him a few times, but said nothing.

'Ah, good, you've got your tea,' said Madeline, as she entered the room.

Taking a seat next to Rose, she switched on the tape recorder and announced the time and the names of those present.

Mary kept her eyes down and slowly rotated her mug in a continuous clockwise motion.

Madeline slid Jeremy's folder along the table towards Rose. Attached to the top cover was a fresh yellow sticky note. *Mr Baker on his way. Look inside folder, top sheet.*

'Now then, Mrs Baker,' began Madeline. 'Do you understand that you're now under arrest for the abduction of Lilly Green on May the thirteenth, 2013, from 50, Front Street, Thirsk?'

Mary nodded.

'I'm sorry,' said Madeline. 'We need you to speak for the tape.'

A strangled 'yes' escaped Mary's lips.

'I've been told you've turned down your right to have legal representation, is that correct?'

Mary nodded.

'For the tape, Mrs Baker.'

Mary looked up and gave Madeline a cold, hard stare. 'I did.'

'So, just to be clear. You do not have to say anything. But it may harm your defence if you do not mention when questioned something which you later rely on in court. Anything you do say may be given in evidence. Do you understand?'

Mary nodded, sighed and then muttered, 'I understand.'

Madeline opened the Lilly Green file and studied it for a moment. 'My main cause for confusion is your statement that you were visiting your friend, Laura Fox, in Whitby, at the time of the abduction. We've spoken to Ms Fox and she has no recollection of such a visit.'

Mary continued to rotate her mug.

'Perhaps you've muddled the dates,' suggested Madeline. 'My mother told me that for several months, prior to and after my birth, she misplaced her brain; apparently it's quite common.'

Mary gripped the mug for a moment and then, with inordinate care, began to rotate it in an anticlockwise direction.

Madeline pressed on. 'We've shown your photograph to Mrs Green and…'

The rotating stopped.

'…she's identified you as the woman who came to her home posing as Yvette Young.'

The rotating started up again.

Keeping her eyes fixed on Mary, Madeline began to tap the Lilly Green file with her pen.

Mary lifted her head. The eyes staring at Madeline were devoid of emotion.

'Mrs Baker, do you want to revise your statement about where you were between May the fifth and May the thirteenth?'

She shook her head.

'I'm sorry, Mrs Baker, but for the tape.'

Mary sighed. 'I do not.'

'Is there anything, anything at all, that you'd like to say to us?'

She shrugged her shoulders.

'Mrs Baker, did you visit Mrs Green on…?'

'Where's my baby? What have you done with her? I want my baby back. I want my baby back *now*.'

'The baby we took from you is perfectly safe, Mrs Baker.'

'Is she with Christopher? Oh, I should have rung him, he'll be wondering what's happened to me.'

'I've spoken to your husband,' said Madeline.

'Is he here? Can I see him?'

'I believe he's on his way.'

'So, where's Emma?'

'She's safe,' repeated Madeline.

'Where? What have you done with her?' spat Mary.

'Mrs Baker, I…'

'Christopher will take her. Yes, she'll be fine,' said Mary, concentrating once again on rotating her mug. 'She'll be fine. She'll be fine,' she repeated. 'Christopher will look after her. He's good with her.'

'It's such an awful thing and it must have been a terrible shock for you,' said Madeline, flicking through the file, 'especially as it'd happened to you before.'

Mary snapped her head up and glared at Madeline.

Madeline pressed on. 'Yes, here we are. It was in 1985, and goodness me, you were only seventeen. And then for it to happen all over again twenty-eight years later. Well, I simply can't imagine how you must have felt.'

'Think you're so clever, don't you?' spat Mary. 'Think you've got all the answers. You know *nothing.*' She slapped her hand down onto the table.

Rose jumped.

'*One* thing I wanted, just *one* thing and I had it, for one brief moment, I had it, and then, and then, it was gone,' she said, as she swept her hand across the table sending her mug crashing to the floor. 'I made one stupid mistake when I was a kid. I was punished then and now I'm being punished again,' she screamed. 'Dear God in Heaven, there are people out there who've done terrible, unimaginable things and do they get punished? No they don't, no they don't.' She buried her head in her arms and began to sob.

'Constable, fetch Mrs Baker a fresh cup of tea,' said Madeline. Glancing up at the clock, she added, '18:45, Constable Jones has left the room.'

Rose reached across towards Mary, but Madeline shook her head.

After a short while the sobbing subsided and Mary raised her head. She dragged her hand across her mouth and nose. 'I just wanted it all to be as it was. I just wanted Emma to grow up. Is that too much to ask? *Tell me*, is it?' she exclaimed.

'No, it isn't too much to ask,' said Madeline. 'Life hasn't been fair to you. But, Mrs Baker, you need to understand your first baby's death wasn't your fault. Cot deaths can happen to any baby. Nothing you did or didn't do would have changed that outcome. It's a terrible, indiscriminate event. The parents are not to blame. *You* were not to blame.'

Mary gripped the side of the table and swayed from side to side.

'Is that what happened to Emma too, Mrs Baker?'

Mary closed her eyes and began to count, 'One, two, three, four, one, two, three, four,' as she continued to sway.

'Our medical officer has been in touch with your GP,' said Madeline, opening Dr Lawson's blue folder. 'He has Emma's medical records. We know about her respiratory infection, Mrs Baker. We know you had to monitor her breathing.'

Mary opened her eyes. They were filled with pain. 'I was so tired,' she said. 'Christopher was away. I'd hardly slept. I had the monitor with me. I always had it with me, so I did. I just, I just fell asleep.' She squeezed her eyes shut again. 'When I woke up the monitor alarm was buzzing. I rushed upstairs. I, I didn't know how long the alarm had been going, I prayed so hard but—oh, God.' She took several deep breaths before continuing. 'She looked so peaceful lying there in her cot. But when I, when I touched her little head it was as cold as marble.' She let out a deep-throated moan.

'I'm very sorry for your loss, Mrs Baker,' said Madeline. 'And I appreciate how hard this must be for you, but can you tell me exactly when this happened?'

'Well I don't know exactly, do I,' she screamed, 'given that I was bloody asleep.'

'I appreciate that, Mrs Baker,' said Madeline. 'I meant could you tell us when you actually found your baby in her cot?'

Mary struck the side of her head with the heel of her hand. 'It's a moment stuck here in my head. A moment that will never leave me.'

Madeline nodded. 'And that moment was when, Mrs Baker?'

'I found my daughter, Inspector, dead, stone cold dead in her cot at 3am on Sunday the fifth of May. Satisfied?'

'And what did you do after you found your baby?'

Mary shot Madeline a look of pure hatred. 'You know what I did next. I buried my poor innocent and I left her, in an unmarked grave, may God forgive me,' she said, rapidly crossing herself.

'And where was that, Mrs Baker?'

'Where was that? Where was that, Inspector?' she yelled. 'You know where!'

'I'm sorry, Mrs Baker, but I need you to tell me, for the tape.'

Mary leaned towards the tape recorder and said, in a calm, quiet voice, 'I buried her in Vicar's Moor Wood, under a tree, near the lake—it was a beautiful spot,' her voice cracked. 'Peaceful, so it was.'

Madeline glanced at the file. 'Thank you. Now, I know this must be hard for you, but do you think you could take us through what happened after you left the woods?'

Mary took a deep breath and began to speak in a monotone voice. She explained how she'd sat in the car. She told them how, as she'd sat there, a plan began to take shape. 'The Poplars Hotel was the first place I saw. Nondescript, on the outskirts of town and close to the station.' She dragged her hand through her cropped red hair and smiled. 'The York Salon was so helpful. I told them I'd had cancer.' Mary looked heavenwards and closed her eyes. 'A terrible lie but, well, needs must. They suggested a complete change.' She leaned back. Her face contorted into a grimace. 'The moment they put the blonde wig on my head the name came to me. Ironic, so it was.'

Her voice became animated as she told them about the birth announcements. 'I was so excited when I found those names. I thought, she's bound to be there, bound to be.'

Her eyes, full of tears, shone as she continued. 'Twelve babies I saw and not one of them was right. Not one of them was my Emma. I prayed to God. I begged him.'

She folded her arms across her chest and began to rock. 'The moment that woman answered the door and I saw her, I knew. My heart leapt. God had answered my prayer; he'd given Emma back to me. She was perfect.'

'Who was perfect, Mrs Baker?' said Rose.

'Baby Lilly.'

'You do understand she isn't Emma, don't you?' said Madeline.

'Of course I do,' Mary snapped. 'I'm not deranged!'

'And when you saw Lilly Green, what did you do?' said Madeline.

'I took her home, to be with me, where she belonged.'

Madeline closed her eyes and sighed. 'Mrs Baker, I'm now charging you with the unlawful burial of a baby, namely one Emma Baker, aged two months, in Vicar's Moor Wood on Sunday the fifth of May. Do you understand?'

Mary nodded.

'For the tape, Mrs Baker.'

'Yes, I understand.'

'I am also charging you with the abduction of Lilly Green, also aged two months, from 50, Front Street, Thirsk, on the thirteenth of May. Do you understand?'

Again, Mary nodded.

'I'm sorry, but you need to speak, for the tape, Mrs Baker.'

'I understand.'

'Sergeant Scott will take you down to the cells.'

'So be it,' said Mary. 'Could you let my husband know where I am? I wouldn't want him to worry. He'll be expecting me to call him soon. He'll take care of the baby. He's a good man.'

Madeline crossed the corridor to Interview room B. She gave Constable Walsh a brief smile, as she extended her arm towards Christopher. 'Mr Baker, good of you to come in, if…'

'You can forget the flannel. Where's Mary?'

'Mr Baker, please take a seat.'

'I'll continue to stand, thank you.'

'Mr Baker, we've just charged your wife with the abduction of Lilly Green, and…'

'You've done what? Are you insane? Where exactly do you imagine my wife has hidden Lilly Green? In some secret compartment in Emma's pushchair perhaps, or under Emma's cot?'

'No, Mr Baker, I don't believe that,' replied Madeline. 'I'm sorry but, as I explained to you earlier, we had reason to believe that your baby passed away in May and was buried in Vicar's Moor Wood, by your wife, prior to the abduction of Lilly Green. Your wife has just confirmed…'

Christopher slumped down onto the chair. He held his head in his hands, as if it were too heavy for his neck to support. 'No,' he screamed. 'No. I'm not listening to this. You're deluded, completely and utterly deluded.'

'It wasn't your wife's fault, Mr Baker. Your daughter…'

Mr Baker put his hands over his ears and began to hum.

Madeline reached out towards him.

He flailed his arms over his head. 'Don't touch me,' he yelled. 'Mary's been under a lot of strain. She's been so very tired.'

'We appreciate that, Mr Baker, but we've spoken to Ms Fox and…'

'Yes, well so have I as it happens, and she's obviously muddled. She's going through some sort of crisis. She's not thinking clearly. Ask Mary.'

Madeline cleared her throat. 'I realise how difficult this must be for you, but...'

'Oh, do you? Do you really? Well I must say, that *is* a comfort.' He balled his hand into a fist and struck the table. 'I demand to see my wife.'

'I'm afraid that isn't possible, not at the moment.'

Rose entered. She nodded briefly and sat next to Madeline. 'I've asked for coffee to...'

'I don't want bloody coffee. I want to see my wife and I want to see her *now*,' demanded Christopher.

'You'll be able to see her soon, Mr Baker,' said Madeline. 'In the meantime, perhaps you could answer a few questions to assist us with our enquiries.'

'If it will clarify your mind, Inspector, and show you how wrong you are, then I'd be delighted.'

Madeline checked her notebook. 'Shall we start with your whereabouts between the fifth and thirteenth of May?'

'Don't you pay attention, Inspector? I've already told you where I was,' he snapped.

'If you could just remind me, Mr Baker. We need to check.'

Christopher slammed his fist down again. 'Oh, right, I see. You think Mary and I, for reasons best known to ourselves, decided to get shot of Emma and replace her with another baby, is that it? And while I was busy burying our dead baby, Mary was off on her jaunt to find a suitable replacement. You're out of your mind.'

'Just answer the question, Mr Baker.'

'Fine!' he yelled, 'fine. I was walking the Pennine Way with John Morris. We go every year. We stay at B&Bs along the route; the same ones every year.'

Madeline glanced at her notebook again. 'Your wife said you left in the first week of April and didn't return until May the nineteenth, is that correct?'

Christopher wrenched his dairy from the inside pocket of his jacket and threw it across the table. 'See for yourself.'

Madeline turned the thin pages of the diary. She saw that Christopher had noted his position along the route each day; starting on April the tenth and returning on May the nineteenth.

'It's a long time to be away from your wife when she'd just had a baby,' said Madeline.

Christopher shifted in his seat. 'So you said, Inspector. I'm not getting any younger, you know. The walk takes me and John a few days more each year—we probably won't be doing it anymore.'

'So, Emma was only a few weeks old when you left, and nearly two months old when you returned.'

'Yes. And your point is?'

'Babies change a lot in the first few months, don't they?'

'Of course they bloody do, they don't, however, metamorphose into a completely different baby.'

'Have you got your friend's telephone number?'

'It's at the back of the diary.'

Madeline handed Rose the diary. 'Ring John Morris and check on these dates, Sergeant.'

'For the love of God. You've already decided, haven't you? Well, let's just see, shall we? I'd love to see your reaction when you find out you're wrong. I shall await your apology with anticipation.'

Epilogue

Sally Green gulped for air as the tears fell. She laughed. She hugged the baby to her chest. She turned her face upwards and Stephen kissed her. The tears flowed down his face too. He turned towards Madeline and Rose. 'I, I…'

Madeline held up her hand. 'It's alright.'

Sally locked eyes with Madeline. She started to speak, but her voice cracked as more tears fell.

'The department held a collection,' said Madeline, thrusting a parcel into Stephen's hands. 'A welcome home present for Lilly. It's just a teddy bear and well, anyway, there we are.'

Stephen cleared his throat. 'That's very kind. Thank you.'

Sally dragged her gaze away from Lilly's face. Her smile was beatific. 'Thank you,' she gasped, 'thank you.'

Back at the station, Madeline and Rose were greeted by raucous cheering. Acknowledging the tirade of congratulations with smiles and muttered words of thanks, they made their way through the throng towards Rose's desk. With a sigh, Rose collapsed onto her chair.

'I'll just clear my desk, and then I think we deserve a drink,' said Madeline.

'You're on,' said Rose.

Madeline turned away from Rose and was confronted by the expansive chest of Inspector Soames. 'Bloody good show, never doubted you for a second,' he said. 'Sadly, it seems I'm to be second in line for that drink, though.'

'Nonsense, Richard,' said Madeline. 'You're welcome to join us.'

'Ah, but I fear Rose will also be manoeuvred into second place.'

Madeline frowned.

'Rather large bouquet of flowers currently residing on your desk,' he said.

Aware of several pairs of eyes peering at her, she extracted the card from its small envelope. Her blush, as she read the card from Guy, led to an eruption of hooting and catcalling. Replacing the card with slow deliberation, Madeline felt a Cheshire cat grin spread across her face.

Rose waved her arms at her fellow officers. 'OK, enough already,' she said. 'Haven't you all got work to do?'

Sniggering and muttering, like naughty school children, they returned to their desks.

'They mean well,' said Rose, as she joined Madeline.

Madeline nodded. 'I know.' She removed the card again and handed it to Rose. 'What should I do?'

Rose read the card. 'Well, put it like this,' she said. 'If he was asking me to join him for a drink at the Fox and Hounds, you wouldn't see me for dust.'

Madeline lowered her voice. 'He is rather scrumptious, isn't he?' she said, as she picked up her phone. 'Yes?'—'Right, tell her Sergeant Scott will be down in a few minutes to escort her up to my office.'

'Who's that?' said Rose.

'Apparently, Dr Olivia Hamilton wants a word,' said Madeline.

'Here we are,' said Rose, 'Inspector Driscoll's office.'

Madeline rose. 'Dr Hamilton, what can I do for you?'

'Would you like a tea or coffee?' asked Rose.

'Yes, thank you, a coffee would be lovely. Milk, no sugar,' said Olivia, pulling up a chair.

'So?'

'Madeline—I can call you Madeline, can't I?'

'Of course you can.'

Olivia gave a brief nod. 'And please, call me Olivia.'

'What can I do for you, Olivia?' repeated Madeline.

'I'll get straight to the point, Madeline. It's about our DNA samples.'

'Uh, uh.'

'They don't match do they?'

'There did seem to be a slight anomaly.'

'So, you know that Lawrence isn't Amelia's biological father.'

Madeline nodded.

'Here we are,' said Rose, clattering into the office, 'two coffees.'

'Smashing,' said Madeline, flashing her eyes towards the door.

'I'll just put them here,' said Rose, placing them on the corner of Madeline's desk, 'and leave you to it. Reports to write, phone calls to make. It never ends.'

'It's not what you think,' said Olivia, as Rose pulled the door shut. 'It was all a terrible mistake.'

'Olivia, it's nothing to do with me.'

'I suppose you've guessed who the father is.'

'Well, I did wonder about your visit to Pocklington.'

'Philip found out that Amelia was premature. He put two and two together and came to the conclusion that the baby could be his.'

'And is she?'

Olivia nodded and bowed her head. 'Yes. It's not as if I make a habit of that sort of thing. I still don't really understand how it happened. I mean, Philip and I were supposed to be working, finalising the details for a symposium. But he was in such a state when he arrived— oh dear, it's all going to sound so sordid.'

'It's alright, you don't...'

'I need to tell someone, Madeline,' exclaimed Olivia, 'it's been eating away at me since last July; the sixth, to be precise.' She took a sip of coffee. 'If only I'd told Philip not to bother coming up. It's not as if there was that much more to do. I could have managed. Lawrence was away, you see, at a briefing in Aldershot. Carla and Martin, he was the man who we bought the cottage from—anyway, they were helping with unpacking and decorating. If only I'd accepted Carla's invitation; gone with her and your mother to the reclamation centre in Thirsk on the sixth, instead of which, oh God.'

Olivia buried her head in her hands.

Olivia had printed out what she'd hoped was the final list of Symposium delegates. She was about to make a start on assembling the Introduction and Welcome packs when Philip arrived.

'Brilliant,' cried Olivia, 'you've arrived just in time to...' she stopped, as she took in the appearance of the man stood on the step. 'Philip, whatever is it? Come in, come in,' she said, gently ushering him towards the settee. 'Would you like a coffee, or perhaps something stronger?'

'I don't suppose you have whisky, do you?'

Olivia dashed towards the kitchen. 'As it happens, I have. It was a gift from some of Lawrence's team, no idea if it's any good but...'

'It'll be fine,' croaked Philip.

Olivia handed him a generous glassful. He took it and downed it in one. Holding out the glass for a refill, he said, 'Please join me, I can't bear to drink alone.'

After the second glass of whisky, Philip blurted, 'Sylvia's left me.'

'Oh, Philip, that's awful.'

'The bitch.'

'Was it, well was it ... another man?'

'No, that's what so fucking hard to take. It's not that she'd found a younger, more virile man, no, she, she just said she couldn't stand being married to me anymore.'

'Philip, I ...' Olivia said, as she tried desperately to think of something positive to say.

'And don't bother trying to think of something positive to say, there isn't anything.'

'I'm so, so sorry.'

Sobbing like a child, Philip fell into her arms.

Olivia patted his back and muttered soothing words until he'd cried himself out.

'Is there any more whisky left?' he croaked.

Olivia poured him another.

'Thanks. Sorry about that.'

'Nonsense, all perfectly understandable. I just wish there was something I could do.'

'Well, there is, oh, no, sorry, don't…'

'What? Come on, out with it. I meant what I said.'

'Well, I don't suppose I could stay here for the night, could I? It's just, I can't bear the thought of going back to that empty house.'

'Of course you can,' said Olivia.

'I don't want to put you to any trouble. I can sleep on the settee.'

'Don't be ridiculous,' said Olivia. 'I'll make up the spare bed.'

'It's just for the night. I'll have to get back tomorrow, my parents are arriving.' He let out a strangled laugh. 'They're expecting a happy evening of family harmony and joy.'

'I'll do it now,' she said. 'Help yourself to the whisky.'

Olivia was straightening the duvet when Philip walked in. 'I thought you might need some help.'

'Oh, typical man,' she giggled, 'I've just finished.'

'Ah, so I see, sorry. Anyway, I took the liberty of opening this,' he said, revealing a bottle of champagne. 'It was for when we'd finished the symposium stuff, but, well…'

'Waste not, want not?'

'Exactly.' He lowered himself onto the bed, patted the duvet and produced two glasses from his jacket pockets. 'Come and sit here.'

The following morning, Olivia bustled around the kitchen, brewing coffee, frying eggs and mushrooms, grilling bacon, toasting bread and slicing tomatoes ready for the pan. She kept squeezing her eyes shut, trying to block out the memory. As she reached up towards the cupboard for the tomato sauce, a pair of strong arms enveloped her waist. She stiffened momentarily.

'I swear I could smell that bacon the moment I turned into Church Lane.'

Olivia relaxed and fell into the hug. 'Lawrence, you're back early. I, I, I've missed you so much.'

Lawrence kissed the top of her head. 'And I've missed you too.'

Olivia freed herself and turned to face him. She stared into his eyes. 'Oh, Lawrence, I love you with all my heart, you do know that, don't you?'

'Oh my, such a serious face,' said Lawrence. 'Is everything alright?'

'Yes, yes, of course,' she said brightly. 'I just love you and well, I wanted you to know.'

Lawrence tossed his jacket over one of the kitchen chairs. 'Well that's good, because I love you too,' he said. 'You look tired though. I take it the symposium stuff took longer than expected. I noticed Philip's car's still parked outside.'

Philip stumbled into the kitchen, a bath towel wrapped around his waist and rubbing his hair dry with a hand towel. 'You wonderful woman, that bacon smells—ah, hi there, Lawrence,' he said, as he clutched the hand towel to his chest. 'This isn't what it looks like, I can assure you.'

Lawrence's gaze shifted from his wife's tired face to take in the semi-naked figure of Philip.

The sharp crackling noise of eggs frying in the pan filled the kitchen.

Droplets of water slid down Philip's neck and torso. He glanced towards Olivia and, in a voice at a higher pitch than normal, said, 'Fantastic view across the fields from that bath.' He cleared his throat.

A frown played across Lawrence's face. 'Yes, it was one of the things that Olivia fell in love with when we first came here.'

'Philip's wife walked out on him,' blurted Olivia. 'He was in a terrible state when he arrived and…'

'And your charming wife looked after me. Yes, she, well she fed me and allowed me to hunker down in your spare bedroom for the night,' said Philip, his voice still shrill. He cleared his throat again. 'Just couldn't face going back to an empty house.'

'No, right, of course,' said Lawrence.

'I'll put some clothes on,' said Philip. 'And then I'll leave you both in peace.'

Olivia scooped the eggs onto a warmed plate and tossed the sliced tomatoes into the empty pan. Spitting and sizzling sounds filled the room. Keeping her head down, she pushed the tomatoes around the pan. She started to hum.

'Yes, fine, you get dressed,' said Lawrence, 'but you can't leave without breakfast. It looks like Olivia's cooking up a feast here.'

'That's very kind, but I…'

'Nonsense, I insist,' said Lawrence, nodding towards the food. 'There's plenty, isn't there, Olivia?'

'Of course you must stay for breakfast,' said Olivia in a small voice.

Olivia lifted her head and gave Madeline a weak smile. 'It was excruciating. Philip shovelled his breakfast down, shook Lawrence's hand, kissed me on my head, said thanks for being so understanding and left.

'Your coffee's getting cold,' said Madeline.

Olivia swept her hair back with both hands and rubbed her temples. She picked up her cup, took a sip and grimaced.

'Shall I ask Rose to get you a fresh cup?'

'No, no, it's fine. Oh, Madeline, when I found out I was pregnant, I shut my eyes to the possibility that Lawrence might not be the father, well, not the biological father anyway. I just couldn't bear it. Lawrence and I have wanted a baby for so long.'

'We won't be keeping the DNA records, Olivia, not now we've found the culprit. They'll be destroyed.'

'I see, right, good. It's not that Philip wants to make trouble or anything, it's just that he's met a woman, an anthropologist...'

'Monica Wilson.'

Olivia gasped. 'How did you know that?'

'I'm a detective, Olivia.'

'Right, yes, I see. Anyway, he, Philip I mean, he spoke to a friend of his who works in a private lab. They specialise in paternity cases, so I went over and stayed with him. Monica was away, well you probably know that too. I stayed with him until we knew for sure.' Olivia took a deep breath. 'Obviously, I couldn't tell anyone, so I made up that ridiculous story about Penny. One lie led to another, then another and it just got more and more complicated.'

'So, you've known since May that Lawrence isn't Amelia's father.'

Olivia nodded. 'It's awful, I know.'

'But you're going to have to tell Lawrence at some point.'

'I know, Madeline, I know, but not just yet.'

'Well, don't worry. I won't say a word. As I said, it's nothing to do with me.'

Olivia closed her eyes and breathed deeply. 'Thank you. So, what will happen to Mary Baker now?'

'She's out on bail. We're awaiting a trial date.'

'She won't go to prison, surely?' said Olivia. 'She needs professional help.'

'I agree, but it's out of my hands now.'

Even though the sun was beating down, every window of the house was shut, curtains drawn, rooms blind to the outside world. Upstairs, Mary was huddled in the corner of the nursery, her face buried in Emma's yellow cot blanket. Downstairs, Christopher sat at the kitchen table, cradling a cold cup of coffee.

Christopher dragged himself up the stairs. He looked through the door of the nursery. He knew he should go to his wife, take her in his arms and offer some comfort. But he couldn't. He simply didn't recognise the women crouched in the corner. He closed his eyes and turned away. He crept downstairs, took his keys from the ceramic bowl by the front door and left.

Mary heard the car engine. She didn't move.

Christopher backed the car onto Long Street and headed out of the village. He drove the six miles to Vicar's Moor Wood and parked in the small lay-by on the Newsham Road. He trudged along by the side of the lake until he came to the damaged willow tree, where he sat and looked out across the lake. In the distance, he could make out the sound of children laughing and dogs barking.

At the base of the Willow were various tributes left by strangers; cards, small teddy bears and fading flowers. Christopher wondered idly where this bizarre tradition originated. He had no recollection of it happening in Britain in the past when someone had died, or been killed, and he wasn't sure if he found it a comfort or not. On reflection he thought not. It was macabre.

A flash of white off to his right caught his eye. A small white-haired terrier barked, darted towards Christopher and darted away. Christopher made eye contact with the dog and it became silent and still. Man and dog stared at each other.

The terrier's owner was a little way back along the lake path. He approached Christopher slowly. 'Morning,' he said. 'It's Mr Baker, isn't it?'

Christopher frowned as he gave a small nod.

'My name's Ben Graves. I recognise you from photos in the papers.'

The terrier gave a little yelp, rushed up to Christopher and began licking his hand. Tears began to fall down Christopher's face.

'Scamp, here boy,' shouted Ben. 'I'm sorry, mate.'

Christopher managed a smile. 'It's alright. He's a lovely little dog. The papers said it was a dog walker who found the, who found…'

Ben nodded. 'That's right,' he said, as he patted Scamp.

Both men stared out across the lake. Scamp barked. Ben turned his head towards Christopher. 'If you don't mind me saying, you look like you could do with a drink. My local's just back there,' he said, pointing along the lake path. 'Do you fancy joining me?'

Christopher closed his eyes. The thought of returning to his home filled him with dread. He nodded. 'A drink would be good.'

Ben patted Christopher's back. 'I've called a taxi for you.'

Christopher lifted his head from the table and peered around the bar. 'It's alright, my car's parked…' he screwed his eyes shut. 'Hell. Where did I leave the bloody car?'

'I expect you parked in the lay-by on the Newsham Road, but you're in no fit state to drive. It'll be fine there. You can pick it up in the morning.'

The taxi pulled up outside the Old Post House at 11.30pm. Christopher paid and stumbled into the house. It was cold and dark inside. Unable to negotiate the stairs with any degree of confidence, he collapsed onto the settee.

He awoke with a start a few hours later, sat bolt upright and listened. Desolate silence. Rubbing his eyes, he focused on his watch: 3am. He shivered, struggled up and groaned, as a sharp pain shot across his back. Bent double, he made his way into the hallway and, step by laborious step, up the stairs.

A shiver that had nothing to do with the temperature went down his spine. He crept towards the bedroom and peered in. He pushed the door open and walked towards the bed. Empty. A small, tight knot developed in his gut. He crossed over to the bathroom. Empty. He called out. Silence, deathly and complete, rang in his ears.

He walked towards the nursery. The door was ajar, and he could see dappled silhouettes of stars and moons dancing across the walls, cast by the mobile still hanging above the cot. He went in and flicked on the main light. Mary was slumped on the nursing chair, her left arm dangled limp, fingers grazing an empty gin bottle. Her face was drawn and pale. He stumbled towards the chair and reached out to shake her. The body was cold, the eyes wide open and cloudy.

Sitting on the bedside cabinet was an empty glass and three empty pill bottles. He picked them up one by one and examined them: Temazepam, Co-codamol and Migraleve. Taking care, he replaced the bottles exactly as he'd found them. Resting against the small nightlight was a lilac envelope, inscribed with his name. With shaking hands, he removed the single sheet of paper. The words, written in his wife's beautiful script, came into focus. He managed to read the first few words; *I am so, so sorry...* before tears burnt his eyes.

He screwed up the page and stuffed it into his jacket pocket. Head down and eyes closed, he staggered backwards. He swore as he collided with the doorframe. Raising his head, he opened his eyes, and once again, took in the terrible tableaux. Christopher slammed his hand against the main light switch. The reappearance of the dappled silhouettes of stars and moons caused him to sway. He grabbed the doorframe and pushed himself into the hallway. Shaking, he reached for the stair rail. Taking several deep breaths, he took one step down, then another, then another, until he reached the bottom. He stood, still gripping the stair rail, as a shudder shot through his body. He pulled his jacket tight across his chest and stumbled through the rooms turning on every light, snatching back every curtain and flinging open every window.

Madeline and Rose found him sitting on the front step, bathed in light from the open doorway. He'd been there from the moment he'd called them. Without speaking, he stood and entered his home. Madeline and Rose followed.

At the top of the stairs, he pointed towards the open door of the nursery, where star and moon shapes continued to dance across the walls. 'She's in there.'